Clever Girl

A Nellie Bly Novella

Cover by Robert Kauzlaric

ISBN-13: 978-1944540517

www.davidblixt.com

Published by Sordelet Ink
www.sordeletink.com

CLEVER GIRL

A Nellie Bly Novella

DAVID BLIXT

EDITED BY ROBERT KAUZLARIC

SORDELET
ink

CLEVER GIRL

CONTENTS

Author's Note

The events of this story take place six months after the novel *What Girls Are Good For*, in which Elizabeth "Pink" Cochrane becomes a reporter. Taking the pen-name Nellie Bly, she writes stories focusing upon the poor, the dispossessed, the cheated and swindled. Most especially, her stories focus upon working women.

After three years of writing for the *Pittsburg Dispatch*, she moves to New York City and goes undercover at the insane asylum on Blackwell's Island to expose the mistreatment of the women held there. Her story is published in the pages of Joseph Pulitzer's *New York World*, and makes her a star.

Between that story and this falls the novelette *Charity Girl*, in which Bly's mother moves in with her, and Bly begins seeing Dr. Frank Ingram, one of the doctors in the asylum during her stay.

This is what happened next . . .

"A professional lobbyist is a plague spot upon the body politic."

—*Judiciary Committee*
State of New York
May 1, 1888

"Tell a story to catch a story."

—*Nellie Bly*
April 18, 1888

REPORT

OF THE

JUDICIARY COMMITTEE, ON THE INVESTIGATION ORDERED BY THE ASSEMBLY, IN REFERENCE TO CHARGES MADE IN THE *NEW YORK WORLD*, OF APRIL 1, 1888, TOUCHING THE LEGISLATIVE INTEGRITY OF CERTAIN MEMBERS OF THE ASSEMBLY.

TESTIMONY

WEDNESDAY AFTERNOON, APRIL 18, 1888.

PINK COCHRAN, sworn, testified as follows:

Examined by MR. SAXTON:

Q. Will you please tell us what your name is?

A. My name is Cochran.

Q. Your first name?

A. Is it necessary that I should give it?

Q. Yes, I think you had better tell us.

A. My first name is Pink.

Q. Where do you reside?

A. New York, at present.

Q. Can you give us your address in New York City?

A. Yes, sir. 69 West Ninety-Sixth Street.

Q. That is where you reside?

A. Yes, sir.

Q. Are you married?

A. No, sir.

Q. And what is your occupation?

A. Well, some call me a journalist, and some call me a reporter. A newspaper writer.

Q. You are engaged in the journalistic business?

A. Yes, sir.

Q. And on the staff of the *New York World*?

A. Yes, sir.

Q. A reporter for that paper?

A. Yes, sir.

Q. How long have you been in that business?

A. About three years.

Q. And you write articles for that paper over a certain signature, do you not?

A. Yes, sir.

Q. And what is that signature?

A. "Nellie Bly."

Q. And you are the lady, I believe, who made an investigation in regard to our methods in lunatic asylums?

A. I did.

Q. Which was published in the *New Work World* and elsewhere?

A. Yes, sir. That was my first work on the *World*.

Q. Had you been engaged in the newspaper business before that?

A. Yes, sir.
Q. Not for the *New York World*?

A. No, sir. Not in New York.

Q. How long have you lived in New York City?

A. Well, almost a year. A year next month.

ONE

WITH AN *E*

NEW YORK, NY
SATURDAY, OCTOBER 29, 1887

"THE SUPREME DUTY OF CIVILIZATION is to end and abolish any government, any at all, whose security depends upon the denial of justice!"

I felt my heart flutter as my ears absorbed the speaker's words. Justice was on my mind. Or rather, injustice.

"We must reject any system of government that has rewards for the corrupt and punishments for the pure! That bestows coronets upon traitors and ropes upon patriots. That heaps praises upon the vile and ordure upon the righteous!"

Hear, hear! my pulsing blood roared, carried along by a rhythm that rolled and swelled like an inexorable sea. The speaker was intoxicating, with his tall, commanding figure, his expressive features, and his deep, authoritative voice. Yet he could hardly be a decade older than I was! *Is this swooning?*

"I care not with what arms such a government may be sustained. I care not what generals may command them, what wealth may equip them, what implements of destruction may aid them. The history of the world shows they will be defeated, confounded, and overthrown. For they will be warring against a kingdom as invincible as nature, and as old as truth, a kingdom which has prevailed against all the empires ever founded by man. It does not command armies, though no hosts have been able to overthrow it. Defeated it has often been, destroyed it can never be. The ruins of ancient dynasties are the monuments of its irresistible might. The history of nations which once held power, and abused it, is the record of its inexorable decrees. Its authority does not spring from this earth, but its jurisdiction embraces the whole universe. For that kingdom is the kingdom of justice, coextensive and coexistent with the Kingdom of Heaven!"

He paused for applause, and applause he received. My little gloved hands collided again and again. *Would it be too much to whistle or stamp my feet?*

The speaker thrilling my heart was a first-term congressman whose surname I would always remember, because I shared it—though he spelled it differently. William Bourke Cockran, lawyer and lawmaker for the 12th District. *To think I missed having him as my representative by just a few measly blocks! Maybe I should move . . .*

"As the struggle for Irish independence is a struggle for the vindication of justice, its success may be delayed, but cannot be denied. To doubt its ultimate triumph would be to doubt the existence of the God from Whose throne justice flows, in Whose hands justice resides, by Whose might justice will be made triumphant!"

What I enjoyed most was how he spoke in such a conversational way, as if we were at a dinner party and I was the only one he was addressing. So often, political speeches felt halting and strained. It was why I had never cared much for reporting on politics. But this man's powerful delivery transported me. Though he'd lived in New York for years, his native Irish accent gave his speech a musicality that was utterly delicious.

"England cannot do justice in Ireland. She is absolutely incapable of it. She has failed signally and dismally. Ireland must be released from this incubus. She must be delivered from this body of death, called English rule. She would not deserve to exist if she accepted these conditions of degradation. She will never accept them. She will continue to fight until she is granted the right to guide her own footsteps to the freedom, the justice, the unending prosperity known as Home Rule!"

Stirring! Little wonder so many people had braved the worst blizzard of our lives to come down to the New York Academy of Music just to hear him speak on Irish Nationality. He had recently angered his own party of Democrats by defending another congressman, a Republican, who had been in danger of being ejected on a technicality. Cockran's speech was said to have been so stirring that he'd saved the Republican's seat all on his own. Tammany Hall couldn't have been happy with that. *A politician of integrity, principles, and wit? Might as well believe in fairies.*

By his cadence, I could tell he was closing in on the end of his speech. "For in a society where there is democratic tolerance and freedom under law, many kinds of evils will crop up. It happens everywhere. But give them a little time and they breed their own cure. It is the natural way of the world, and the way of the natural world. There is enough for all. The earth is a generous mother. She will provide, in plentiful abundance, food for all her children, if they will but cultivate her soil in peace, and in justice. Thank you."

The two hundred people in the hall positively exploded with appreciation, the roar of our thundering hands echoing all around. Standing at my side and rapturously clapping, Mother was certainly in his thrall. Even my cad of a brother was applauding, though far more laconically, as if his cynical praise was for the performance more than the substance. Having no ideals or morals of his own, Albert was incapable of appreciating them in others. *Maybe he should have gone into politics.*

Strange to say, Albert's presence in the city was our reason for being at this event. He and his wife Jane had arrived on Friday, March 9 for a quick weekend visit, only to be trapped by a blizzard. Worse than a blizzard. They were calling it the Great White Hurricane, with snow in some parts of the state reaching as high as fifty-eight inches—taller than I was!

In Pittsburgh we'd had bad snowfalls, of course. And there, the snow was always covered with a layer of soot from the factories. Still, my first winter in New York was a shocker. Though the snow in the city itself never got higher than two feet, everything stopped. Headlines read:

IN A BLIZZARD'S GRASP
THE WORST STORM THE CITY HAS EVER KNOWN
BUSINESS TRAVEL COMPLETELY SUSPENDED
THE METROPOLIS HELPLESS UNDER SNOW

HARDLY A WHEEL TURNS!
BUSINESS KNOCKED FLAT AS IF BY A PANIC!
PLAYS, TRIALS, FUNERALS, ALL POSTPONED
FIFTY TRAIN LOADS OF PASSENGERS STUCK ON THE MAIN LINES
ELECTRIC LIGHTS OUT!
WHERE THEY ARE, HEAVEN KNOWS

Telegraph lines collapsed. Firemen couldn't get out of their stations, resulting in several houses burning right down to the ground. Former United States Senator Roscoe Conkling collapsed on his way from home to his Wall Street office. They said he'd contracted pneumonia and was at death's door.

I'd initially thought that the worst part of the snow was nobody reading my article about learning to fence, published on the day blizzard started. But I was sorely mistaken. No, the worst part—the very worst—was that the bitter cold and the massive pileup of snow across New York, New Jersey, Connecticut, and Massachusetts meant that railway travel was impossible. Albert was forced to stay.

With my brother's weekend stay in its third—*third!*—week, I was losing my mind. Three days of biting my tongue appeared to be my limit. That first Monday, we'd spent the day like most of the East Coast, watching the snow and wondering if we had enough food and kindling to last. But by mid-week, cooped up with Mother, Albert, and Jane, I had finally snapped. Albert's constant gibes about my intelligence, my money, my profession, my money, my clothes, and my money had broken me.

After dinner on Wednesday, Mother had asked me to clear the dishes. Albert offered to help, then stacked them too high for me to carry. I snapped, "Dammit, Albert, just let me do it!"

Which was all he'd been waiting for.

"Elizabeth!" my mother said sharply from the other room.

"Don't bother, Mother," said Albert smugly. "You know how Pink is."

Me growing angry was always Albert's trump card. And, as always, Mother took Albert's side. It didn't matter that I was now supporting her financially. It didn't matter that I could now send money to my sister Kate, trapped in a failing marriage. It didn't matter that I had respect, notoriety, even fame. Albert was her firstborn, and could do no wrong. Poor Jane tried to be a peacemaker. But as his wife, her loyalties were never in question.

It was my home, and I was the unwelcome one. No wonder Congressman Cockran's invocation against injustice had me thrilling! After the dam broke with Albert, I spent as much time as possible out of my apartment—Senator Conkling's fate seemed preferable to remaining at home one more minute than was absolutely necessary. I still had my story about the fraud calling himself a mesmerist to finish—I had been posing as his student, and had just thought up a nifty, if grim, way to expose his sham. Now that I had an actual desk at the *New York World* offices, I at least had a haven for retreat.

Not that the *World* was without annoyances. As my fame grew, so did the resentment among the male reporters. The man who'd lost his desk to me, Jim Cole, was understandably furious. But somehow, I had also earned the ire of theatre critic Andrew Wheeler, who wrote for various publications under the name Nym Crinkle. My guess was that he didn't appreciate the fact that someone he considered to be an amateur had raised the *World's* circulation far more than he ever had.

Still, the attacks of my newsprint brethren had nowhere near the impact of my actual brother's constant sniping. Rather than face another night of failing to quietly endure Albert's sly remarks, I seized upon a notice in the paper that Congressman Cockran was speaking on Irish Nationalism. Hinting that it might be an interesting story, I hauled my family to the Academy.

Only to be enchanted by—of all things—politics! After the speech, we joined the crowd of people pressing to congratulate the congressman, and I half had it in mind to ask for an interview. When it came my turn to speak to him, I babbled like an idiot. After praising his speech, I said, "My name is Cochrane too, though with a *ch* and an *e*. We added the *e* ourselves. I wonder, might we not be distantly related?"

"Anything is possible, I suppose," trilled the tall, handsome Irishman. "My own father and mother were called Martin and Harriet Cockran, and I was born a Sligoman."

"A what?"

"Sligo is a county, my dear, lying upon the pass into Connaught from Ulster, under the flat frown of Ben Bulben, the mountain of faerie legend, and above Knocknarea, where Queen Maeve was actually buried." I smiled as if I knew what he was talking about. "Whence do your Cochranes with a *ch* and an *e* hail?"

"Pennsylvania," I said. "Apollo. Cochran's Mills, actually. Named for my father."

"He must be so proud."

"He was, I think. He died when I was six. But I think I remember him saying our grandfather came from Ireland."

"What an idiot you are, Pink," said my brother over my shoulder. He shook hands with the congressman and said in a confiding tone, "You must forgive my sister. Facts are not her strong suit. My name is Albert Cochran, no *e*. This is my mother, Mary Jane, and my wife Jane. Our grandfather Cochran came from North Carolina. It was our great-grandfather who came from Ulster. Is Carikel a place?"

"Kerrykeel," said the sleepy-eyed legislator with a chuckle. "Upon Mulroy Bay. About forty miles north of Sligo, in County Donegal, in Ulster territory. My own father's estate was at Claragh, Ballina-carrow, in County Sligo, which he had from his father through the famine. No hint of a Kerrykeel connection, I fear. We would need to check the church records to excavate further than that."

Albert shrugged. "Just as well. Though I'm sure Pink wouldn't mind finding a way to claim you."

I flushed at his clumsy double meaning, my jaw setting and my fists balling. Thankfully, Mother saved me from an outburst and my brother from a slapped face. "You speak so well! You must have heard that before, and often."

"But I never cease to appreciate compliments, madam."

"My late husband was an avowed Democrat," she confided.

"And the wiser man, he! Democracy is a faith, Republicanism is an appetite." A bald man with a long white beard arrived at Cochran's shoulder. "Ah, Charles! There you are! Allow me to introduce another band of Cockrans. Ladies, Albert, this is Mr. Charles Dana."

"We've met," I said acidly, my whole evening spoiled. Dana was the publisher of the *New York Sun*, zealous enemy of the *World*. Worse, since September he'd made several attempts to undermine my reporting and blacken my name.

The phlegmatic Mr. Dana studied me a moment, then drew in a breath of unwelcome recognition. "Miss Bly. How pleasant. What disguise are you wearing tonight? Socialite? Suffragette? Anarchist? How do you plan to drag the congressman's good name through the mud?"

"All I would need to do is question his choice of friends," I retorted. I felt my mother stiffen and Albert's interest sharpening, so I belatedly attempted to defuse the dynamite I had lit. "Mr. Dana, my mother, Mary Jane Cochrane, and my brother and sister-in-law, Albert and Jane Cochran."

"Are they truly yours?" asked Dana, even as he shook Albert's hand. "Or have you hired them for the evening?"

"Charles!" cried Cockran in dismay.

"You'll excuse me, I'm sure," said Dana, unruffled. "This young lady came to me last summer seeking employment. When I turned her away, she found a station at Pulitzer's *World*, where she has made a career of insinuating herself into places on false pretenses."

"Is there such a thing as an honest pretense?" I asked. Cockran laughed, and I grinned. He was not yet an enemy. "What Mr. Dana is omitting is the fact that I made his reporters look bad when they accepted one of my pretenses at face value. This, after he had the audacity to lecture me on how women write their feelings, not the facts."

"Wait," said the congressmen, his brow's coming together in intensity. "You're never Nellie Bly!"

"I sometimes am," I replied, feeling quite clever. "But tonight I'm only here as myself."

"Charles, how did you ever think to turn this one away? She is proof of what I am always saying. In a society where there is democratic tolerance and freedom under law, many kinds of evils will crop up, but give them a little time and they usually breed their own cure. For Blackwell's Island, the cure was Nellie Bly." He gave me a small bow, and I blushingly returned it.

Smiling at Dana, he said, "If only we could cure politics the same way. Send her in, let her root out the troubles, and publish!"

"I could never," I told him.

"And why not?"

"Because in the asylum, no one was truly mad. Whereas in Congress, I understand that everyone is."

Cockran roared with laughter. Even Dana smiled, though he looked liverish. Mother and Jane both covered their mouths to hide their broad smiles.

Albert sighed pityingly. "It's a very old joke, Pink. You didn't even tell it well."

All the way home through the terrible bitter wind, amid the carping of my brother and the soothings of my mother, I was kept warm by a glow of pride tinged with an Irish accent.

That, and the kernel of an idea for a new story.

TESTIMONY

PINK COCHRAN, sworn, testified as follows:
Examined by MR. SAXTON:

Q. Did you come here with a definite purpose in view from New York City to Albany?

A. Yes, sir.

Q. And that purpose was to interview Mr. Phelps, was it, upon the subjects practically that are stated in this communication?

A. My purpose was to find if it was really true that people could be bought by Mr. Phelps.

Q. That was the general purpose of it?

A. Yes, sir.

Q. To interview him with regard to his relations to members of the Legislature here?

A. Yes, sir.

Q. Were you sent up by the *New York World*, the managers of the *New York World*, for that purpose?

A. Well, not exactly. I asked to come, and they said they didn't think I should come, because I would make a failure of it. They said Mr. Phelps had, as far as they knew, been in the business such a long time that he could not be caught, and they advised me not to come.

Q. As a matter of fact, it was with the permission of the paper that you came up here?

A. Well, they said: "Well, you can go, if you are determined."

TWO

BLACK HORSE BRIGADE

MONDAY, MARCH 26, 1888

"I WANT TO GET INVOLVED WITH politics." Sitting behind his massive carved desk, Colonel Cockerill choked on his cigar smoke. Eyes watering, the managing editor of the *New York World* pounded the desk with his fist with each cough, then poured himself some dark liquor from a wide bottom carafe on his desk. Downing it, he got right back on the horse by puffing again. "Dammit, Bly! D'you want to kill me?"

"Not today," I said, smiling impishly.

The forty-three-year-old Ohio native glowered at me, his walrus moustache twitching with a life of its own. "You want to run for office?"

"No!" It was my turn to be incredulous. "Why would I do that? Do you hate me so much that you want me to be a politician?"

Grunting, Cockerill poured himself another shot. "Okey-dokey. My mistake. Happy to hear you have no interest in breaking down that particular door. It would be a helluva stunt to be sure. But the last thing we need is to have a wall of anti-suffragettes outside Mr. Pulitzer's window."

Taking the chair he gestured at, I leaned forward in a show of concern. "How is Mr. Pulitzer?"

"Pretty goddamn awful," replied Pulitzer's right hand. "Light and sound give him terrible headaches. With all the windows here, and the presses always running, he's hardly around anymore." The Colonel did not seem particularly distressed over his employer's plight. Without oversight, he had more control. "He's talking of taking himself somewhere more peaceful until he recovers."

"I'm sorry to hear it," I said dutifully. Truth be told, I had barely met Mr. Pulitzer. He sent me a nice, if brief, note after the Mad-House story, along with a check for a hundred dollars, and another brief note when the book was released.

Colonel Cockerill puffed, then huffed. "So. Politics. What got that gnat stirring? Oh wait—you went to see Cockran last night, didn't you?"

"I did. He was amazing. The way he talks . . . I was carried away."

I frowned. "Did you know he's friends with Charles Dana?"

The Colonel nodded his oversize head. "The one blight on his character, that. But they've been friends for ages. Didn't stop Cockran from representing Mr. Pulitzer as a client."

"He seems a good man. Fair-minded."

"He's that rarity: an honest goddamn lawyer. His clients aren't always worthy. Three years ago, he represented Ferdinand Ward."

"Who?"

Despite his response to my entrance, the Colonel seemed in an uncommonly good mood, which made him expansive. "I keep forgetting how new you are to the city. He's the teenage Wall Streeter who swindled stockholders of seven-goddamn-teen million dollars. Brought down Marine National Bank almost single-handedly. He's the reason President Grant went bankrupt—Grant's son was Ward's partner. The president went to bed thinking himself a millionaire and woke up with four thousand dollars to his name." The Colonel chuckled. "Ward's famous for saying, 'I want to do right, but it seems my fate to do wrong.'"

"And Cockran defended this man?" My estimation of the congressman was suffering.

The Colonel shrugged, unfazed. "Every man deserves a good defense. Besides, I think he did it for the novelty. The issue at hand was admitting evidence of telephone conversations. Cockran fought like the Devil, objecting vehemently that the evidence was inadmissible." The Colonel puffed. "I think he was all in favor of telephone conversations being deemed admissible, and only took the other side to poke every conceivable hole in the precedent."

"But that doesn't make sense!"

"Does to a lawyer. Best way to prove a thing in court is to try to beat it. If you can't find a winning argument against it, you've won."

"So, by losing the case, he won his point?"

"Exactly. As an added bonus, Ward got a term in Sing Sing. I hear he's decorated his cell with an Oriental rug and has his meals sent in. Apparently, he's neighbors with Alderman Jaehne, who confessed, then recanted, to selling the contracts to the city's streetcars, and who is reputed to keep two little dad-gummed dogs with him in his cell. Rumor says they both play poker with the warden."

My brow felt like folded laundry, I was furrowing it so hard. "Maybe I should investigate Sing Sing."

"Ha! Wouldn't that be a coup! Dana would have a fit. However, I can't see you getting yourself locked up there, even if you could pass for a man."

Filing that thought away, I returned to my topic. "So dishonest politicians *do* go to jail?"

"Occasionally," said the Colonel, temporizing with his hand. "Just as often it's the honest ones. Cockran is presently defending Jacob Sharp, who's spent twenty-five years of his life championing a railway station along Broadway. He finally got his plan passed, only to be charged by his rivals with bribing public officials. Half a dozen aldermen went to jail, some fled to Canada, and some saved their necks by testifying against Sharp."

"Wait—this is the Jake Sharp case?" I'd read about it the previous summer as I'd trolleyed myself up and down Newspaper Row looking for a job.

"Exactly. He was convicted, but your friend Cockran got him off on appeal last November. New trial is supposed to start in a few days, though there's some doubt that he'll be up for it. I hear conviction ruined his health."

"I use the train stop on Broadway," I observed.

"We all do. It's who gets to build and run it that the crooks fight over."

I slapped my hands down onto my knees. "This is what I'm talking about. I want to go after corruption, the crooks and cheats who ruin public office. Who is the most corrupt politician in the state?"

The Colonel gazed at me as if seeing a new, hitherto unthought-of possibility in me. "You don't want a politician."

"I don't?"

"No," he said, his lips holding the ring of an *O* to blow smoke. "Politicians come and go. You want to bag the men that own the politicians."

My eyebrows were furrowing so hard you could have planted potatoes. "Who owns the politicians? Tammany Hall?"

"That's the machine that gets them elected. They take the bribes. You want the ones doing the bribing. In short, you want the lobbyists."

Instantly, my train of thought rerouted onto these new tracks. "Do you know who the worst lobbyist is?"

The Colonel puffed several times. "It just so happens, Bly, that I do." Then he shook his head. "But you'll never get him."

"What? Why not?"

"He's been in business longer than you've drawn breath. The law tried once before, and came within a hair of getting him. But he's wily, goddamn wily. Far too foxy to be nabbed by a chicken."

"Foxes make the mistake of thinking the chicken isn't dangerous."

"Because the fox eats the chicken. Not the other way around."

The metaphor wasn't working for me. "He's not actually going to eat me, is he? So why not let him try? He'll find he's bitten off more than he can swallow. What do we have to lose?"

Colonel Cockerill thought about it for a time. He chuckled to himself a couple of times, his face behaving as though he were having a conversation with someone. At last, his eyebrows went up in the universal sign of *why not?* Crossing to the door, he stuck his head out. "Marsh, have Sutherland bring me the file on Foxy Phelps."

CHARLEY SUTHERLAND WAS A LARGE, happy-faced redhead with a booming laugh and a love of practical jokes. The previous year, he had entered the sanctum of rival paper the *Sun* and deposited a black-and-tan puppy on the desk of the city editor, the irreligious "Deacon" Stillman. "Here y'go, Deke! His name is Scamp!"

"We're a cat office," Deacon had replied, only to find himself speaking to Sutherland's back.

Thus, it was said, the *Sun* came to possess the most flatulent dog in New York City. I'd heard the story several times, it being one of a thousand salvos in the war between the *World* and the *Sun*. True or not, the tale had predisposed me to think well of Mr. Sutherland, but I'd not yet exchanged a word with the man himself. As he entered the Colonel's office, blinking and grinning, his expression grew fixed at the sight of me. "You rang, Colonel?"

"I did. We have a story notion, Bly and I. We need to talk about the Third House in Albany."

"That's not my beat," replied Sutherland at once.

"No," agreed the Colonel. "But I've forced you to write enough dad-blasted stories about bills that you're an expert now." Sutherland was too much the gentleman to disagree. "So close the door and talk to us about the goddamn lobbyists."

Sutherland obeyed, taking a chair opposite mine, but looking only at the Colonel. Pressing my lips together, I said, "The Third House?"

"The senate, the assembly, and the lobby," replied the Colonel. "The third branch of the legislature."

"Ah," I said. "Clever. Mr. Sutherland, how does the lobby control the legislature?"

"They have two methods," answered Sutherland, looking somewhere between me and the Colonel. "The first is to buy it. The second is to *appear* to buy it. They much prefer the second way. That way their profits are not decreased."

"How do you appear to buy someone?" I asked.

Sutherland looked up at the ceiling. "The skilled lobbyist has an idea of who will support any given bill, and who will oppose it. So, I approach a lobbyist and tell him I'd like a bill passed through a committee of, say, twelve people. He begins by mentally checking off the names of people he knows are already *for* my bill. Let's say, four of them. He then adds the ones whom he knows, by previous experience, are purchasable. Let's say, three. They're called the Black Horse Brigade, or Black Horse Cavalry. Then he charges me the bribe for all seven, when he's only bribing three. He pockets the rest, along with his fee. That is what the lobbyists call 'velvet.'"

I looked up from my notes, marveling. "They can't even bribe honestly?"

With an appreciative chuckle, Sutherland glanced my way for the first time, though only for a second. "I know. Ridiculous, isn't it?"

"And the worst apple in that rotten barrel is . . . ?" said the Colonel.

"Oh, Phelps, of course."

"Phelps?" I asked.

"Edward R. Phelps, king of the goddamn lobbyists." Colonel Cockerill spoke the name as if it burned his tongue. "Not to be confused with Mr. Edward J. Phelps, America's envoy to England. Remember the *R*. Stands for Rat Bastard."

"Rat Bastard," I agreed, taking quick notes.

The Colonel leaned back, his great walrus moustache bristling. "Charley, what do you have on Phelps?"

"He hails from Hell. I'm not exaggerating. He was born in Spuyten Duyvil, New York, which is Dutch for 'Spewing Devil.' He was raised a Presbyterian, but there's precious little Christian in him. Still, he plays the pious soul. On Sunday, he's always to be found occupying the back pew of St. Paul's in Albany. He has a reputation for donating to missions, but he's famously nearsighted when the collection plate comes around."

"Rat bastard," murmured the Colonel. I found his indignation amusing, as I was certain his only church was the *World*, where he was to be found every Sunday morning, sermonizing and raising the Devil.

Sutherland continued. "Well, I guess too much church turned him toward the law. Not that he's a genuine lawyer! Can't prove it, but I'm certain his degree is fake. Leastways, no one's ever seen it. When asked, he claims to have lost his diploma, and that his alma mater's record office was burned during the war. He once told a judge that the only sheepskin he'd ever had was given to him by his father when one of their sheep died."

"The lying sack of—"

"Colonel," I said.

"Right, right. Go on, Charley."

"Somehow Phelps got in tight with Andrew Johnson during the war, selling the Army shoddy goods. He also did some jiggery-pokery with railroad and oil companies, creating relationships he uses to this day. Started in Albany in '68, making backroom deals lobbying against bills designed to regulate his industrialist friends and their shady dealings. Got good at it. Never been elected to office, but he keeps a library of bills he's had killed, and those he's allowed to pass. He also has photos of every single member of the state senate during the last twenty years. Calls them his memory aids."

"First time I clashed with him," said the Colonel, busying himself with clipping and lighting a fresh cigar, "I was still in St. Louis, reporting on a crooked gas company that was gouging its customers. Phelps managed to derail a bill that would have lowered their prices and slashed their profits. I was never able to prove it, but I was told he was paid a hundred thousand dollars from the gas companies over it."

I whistled. "Is it all about money?"

"Money, and power. He likes being known. He has the cheek, the damned audacity, to hide in plain sight. He's very tight with the *Buffalo Evening News*, as well as the *Weekly Express* up there. He was on board the train that caught fire in '82 when Senator Wagner was killed, and they treated him as a star eyewitness. No mention that he was on the train bribing the senators with a gambling junket."

"So he's popular," I observed.

"Not very, actually," replied Sutherland. "If he walks down the street, members of the assembly duck into stores so they won't be seen with him. He doesn't mind. His assistant is the popular one. Eugene Wood. Phelps doesn't have to attend sessions anymore, and is never seen on the floor. He uses Wood for that. Each to his milieu, I suppose. Besides, there have been enough threats on his life that he doesn't like to show his face much."

"Threats?"

Again, Sutherland answered as if the Colonel, and not I, had spoken. "The story goes that Phelps promised an assemblyman three thousand dollars for his vote several years ago. The assemblyman voted as agreed, and then Phelps hung him up."

"Hung him up?" I asked, leaning into his eyeline.

"That's Brooklynese for 'refused to pay him,'" replied Sutherland, shifting his legs to face the Colonel directly. "Well, our bent assemblyman was not the kind of man to stand that sort of treatment, so he bought a pistol, went to Phelps's office here in New York, locked the door behind him and put the key in his pocket. Catching Phelps by the throat and pointing the revolver at him, he said, 'I want my money or I will kill you.' It was an unhappy position for Phelps, who weakened and drew a check for—wait for it—six thousand dollars. It appears he'd sold the assemblyman twice: once with his consent, once without consulting him. Thinking himself found out, he paid for both times. Ever since, it's said he keeps a little derringer in his waistcoat."

"Has he never been caught?" I asked, exasperated by both the storyteller and his subject.

"The only time he ever came close was in '81, during the Conkling and Platt nonsense."

That name stirred up memories of a recent story. "Conkling? Is that the same—"

"The same idiot who tried to walk to work in the blizzard and is now lying at death's door with pneumonia? The very man," said Sutherland, again shooting me the briefest flash of his grin. "Back then, Roscoe Conkling was in the U. S. Senate with Tom Platt, both representing New York."

"Boss Platt?" Even I knew that name. He controlled the Republican machine in New York State, choosing whom to nominate for what positions in the party.

"That's him. As Grant supporters, he and Conkling were disappointed when Garfield was nominated in his place. They were even more upset that when Garfield won, he wouldn't appoint their people for key positions in government. They were members of the Stalwart faction of the Republican Party, after all, and believed in political patronage. They ended up resigning in protest, thinking that the knuckleheads in the state senate would just hold a special election and reinstate them in a couple months. But they didn't count on the Half-Breed faction bribing senators to vote against them in that special election. Ironic, given that the Half-Breeds esteem merit over patronage. But bribe they did, and liberally. One guess who was at the center of it."

"Phelps."

"Foxy Ph-ph-phelps, yes." I looked at him curiously. "He stutters when he's excited. Anyway, Phelps lived in the same hotel as a state senator named Lo Sessions, and amid all the card games and late-night bull sessions, somehow a ten-thousand-dollar payment came into Phelps's hands, which then turned into cash, which then disappeared into the senator's hands. Then, miraculously, when it came time to hold the special election, Sessions turned the vote against Conkling and Platt, throwing support to the Half-Breeds over the Stalwarts. Thus, the two fools weren't sent back to Washington. Their party was apoplectic, to the point that Phelps supposedly had to dodge a punch in public."

"What happened to Sessions?"

"Well, the Stalwarts were so upset that they did the unthinkable—they turned him in, and by extension Phelps and his accomplices. They were arrested for bribing a member, who took the money right up to the goddamn Speaker's desk during a session."

The Colonel practically bit his cigar in half. "It was a damn close shave, and we almost got him. Phelps's hair turned silver in that one summer. But the not-so-grand jury came back "no bill" for the goddamn lot of them. No indictments for anyone. Sure as shooting, money changed hands there, too."

Out of curiosity I said, "What happened to Conkling and Platt?"

Sutherland waved airily. "Oh, Conkling went on to make an even grander fool of himself. After Garfield was shot, President Arthur offered Conkling an appointment to the Supreme Court. The idiot accepted, then had second thoughts and declined to serve. Can you imagine? Came back here to practice law and half kill himself walking through a cursed whiteout. Platt, on the other hand, has been working like the devil to rebuild the Republican machine and ensure there are no more Half-Breed victories. Hence "Boss" Platt. I know for a fact he's mended fences with Phelps, who is just far too valuable to hold a grudge against. He and Wood get along like peas in a pod. He chose Fremont Cole for Speaker over General Husted, who is considered too honest to be of any use."

I felt the conversation starting to head down a shunt track, and tried to man the switch. "How did the case against them go wrong?"

"Well, the others accused were senators and assemblymen, weren't they? To protect themselves they had to protect Phelps as well. That's where the case fell apart—they formed a bastion of defense for each other. As a result, Phelps feels himself untouchable. Calls himself the king of the lobby. He even had the audacity to sue a fellow called Jones for fifty thousand dollars, which Jones had given as a bribe for senators. When Jones found out that the senators didn't need bribing, he cancelled his promissory note. Phelps, considering himself to be the injured party, brought his suit right up to the state supreme court, to get them to sanction his wrongdoing. Of course, he dropped the whole thing before he had to testify, claiming they settled out of court."

I thought all this over, then said, "Thank you, Mr. Sutherland. I appreciate all your help."

Sutherland looked to the Colonel, who nodded his dismissal. Irked, the veteran reporter departed.

The moment the door was shut, Colonel Cockerill came around to lean against his desk, his toes nearly touching mine. "Phelps has a good thing, and there isn't any-goddamn-thing he won't do, murder included, to hang on to it. He is a briber, a boodler, and a scoundrel. Pulitzer wants him. I want him. I want to eat his heart in the marketplace."

"I'll bring it to you in a box," I promised.

"It could be dangerous. He's an unscrupulous bastard. You sure you can fool him?"

An escape from Albert at home? "Damned yes, I can."

The Colonel stared at me, his beefy moustache twitching again, this time in amusement. "Is that your attempt at cursing?"

"It damn well is."

"Better. Well, if you are determined, you can go. But how? You can't go in as yourself, obviously."

"Obviously."

"To date, you've managed to pretend to be crazy, an unskilled worker, and the mother of an unwanted child. Can you go the opposite way?"

"What do you mean?"

"I mean, can you pretend to be prosperous? Wealthy? Can you imagine yourself as a businessman's wife? That's not a proposal," he added quickly, eyes twinkling.

From his expression, I had the sudden intuition that the Colonel had a new lady in his life. There was not a shred of proof to back up this suspicion, except his general good mood. Nevertheless, it pleased me. If he had a sweetheart, it might stop the infuriating rumors that there was some romantic entanglement between us and that was how I had landed my job.

"I think I can manage it," I assured him. "I'll be a frightened wife asking for the help of this big, strong, handsome—did you say he was handsome?—man."

"He has handsome side-whiskers," said the Colonel with an amused grunt.

"So why is this rich man's wife coming to see Mr. Phelps?" I asked.

"To offer him a goddamn bribe, of course."

TESTIMONY

WEDNESDAY AFTERNOON, APRIL 18, 1888.

EDWARD R. PHELPS, sworn, testified as follows:
Examined by MR. SAXTON:

Q. Where do you live?

A. White Plains, Westchester County.

Q. You spend your time in Albany to some extent during the sessions of the Legislature, do you not?

A. I have all but this year. This year I have not been here much.

Q. Well, you have been here a portion of the time this winter?

A. Yes, sir.

Q. How long have you been here? How much of the time?

A. Well, in the month of January I was only here at the organization. Then I went south in February. I was here twice. I went to the southwest. In March, I was here the forepart of the month, then I went west. Returned to Albany about the twentieth of March.

Q. And have been here since then most of the time?

A. No, sir; I was here about a week or ten days—about a week, and since then I have been away.

Q. And you have been here in former years during sessions of the Legislature, have you?

A. Yes, sir.

Q. For how many years past?

A. Twenty years.

Q. What is your business?

A. Well, I am engaged in railroading. Deal in stocks, grain. Speculator.

Q. What is your business in Albany?

A. When I have been in Albany, I have been looking after bills I have been interested in.

Q. Well, it was legislative business, was it not?

A. Yes, sir.

Q. You have been in Albany, I suppose, principally engaged upon business relating to legislation?

A. Well, yes, sometimes.

Q. Measures before the Legislature? You are commonly known as a lobbyist?

A. Yes, sir.

THREE

ACT THE WIFE

THE COLONEL AND I TALKED it out for another half hour, creating the history for my housewife-in-need persona. In the end, we decided to call Sutherland back—his familiarity with current legislation was invaluable.

"It's the rush time," he informed the Colonel, and, by extension, me. "The final committee reports on bills are due in just over a week, April fifth. This time last year, there were nearly as many bills still in committee as had been reported. Based on the calendar, that gives them just twenty day sessions and twenty-five night sessions to pass over two thousand bills. Meaning, they have to pass over eighty bills a day to get through the list. This is when Phelps works his magic, taking advantage of the rush to kill certain bills . . . and sneak others through."

"Which is easier to do, pass a bill or kill it?" I asked.

"Kill it, undoubtedly. Always easier to say no than yes."

The Colonel nodded at the wisdom of that. "Is there a bill that's already dead in the water, but hasn't been killed officially?"

Sutherland considered. "There's one. Wes Smith's bill, Number 191. It was meant to regulate patent medicine makers, basically forcing all snake oil salesmen to list their ingredients with the State Board of Health in exchange for a certificate, with a hefty fine if there were any changes to the mix."

I looked to the Colonel. "I'm married to a patent medicine maker who stands to lose his livelihood if forced into being honest."

"Phelps will appreciate that," the Colonel agreed. "It's how he views the world. Thinks everyone is as dis-goddamn-honest as he is, so there's no harm in what he's doing." He looked to Sutherland. "You're sure it's dead?"

"As a doorknob. I only remember it because there was a misprint in the docket."

"They misprinted the bill?" asked Cockerill.

"No, the bill lists the right committee. It's just that when they printed the docket of what bills were before which committees, the printer got it wrong. According to the published statement, it's in the Committee on Cities, whereas in reality it's before the Committee on Public Health."

"Perfect," said the Colonel. "Goddamn perfect."

"Does that help?" I asked.

"Charley here says the reason Phelps got off last time was that the lawmakers were all in danger with him. So, we have to craft a situation where they'll all be against him. You'll bribe him to pay off the members of the wrong committee. Your housewife makes such an obvious blunder in front of Phelps, who already knows the bill is dead. You're offering him a bribe for something that will happen whether he takes the money or not. So there's no need to bribe the assemblymen, which means he'll pocket all the cash himself."

"Velvet," I said, catching on. "That way, no assemblymen will have been bribed, so there'll be no need for them to defend him."

"Exactly! In fact, they may cut him dead for not passing along the dad-blamed money he collected as their bribe!" We all laughed, and then Sutherland was again dismissed, this time with the admonishment to keep this under his hat.

"I should be from out of state," I suggested when he was gone.

"Agreed," said the Colonel. "If you were local, he'd wonder why he'd never heard of you. Where do you want to be from?"

The best lies were always close to the truth. "Pittsburgh?"

The Colonel shook his head. "Too far away. Ever been to Philadelphia?"

"I've been *through* Philadelphia."

"Close enough. You're from Philly. More likely to sell your quack remedies in New York State."

I reviewed my knowledge of Philadelphia. It wasn't much, but one fact leapt out. "I'll say he got his start at the Centennial Exposition there."

"Good! What about a name? No more Spanish aliases."

"No, no Nellie Moreno this time. But with all his railroad contacts, he'll have friends in Philadelphia," I fretted. "We don't want him to be able to check up on me. I'll say I'm using my maiden name to protect my husband's business."

"You're good at this. A natural goddamn liar." Puffing, a smile crossed his lip. "You know, the Roman word for president was *consul.*"

"Mrs. Consul," I said, testing it out. "I like the sound of it. After all, I think we're about ready for a woman president around here."

W ITH ALL THE DETAILS SETTLED and a plan in place, I departed the *World.* The snow had stopped falling, but it was still piled high, making valleys of the sidewalks. Turning left, I wasn't watching where I was stepping. One of the snowbanks must have melted a little in the early morning sun, or else a patch of ice had gone uncleared. Regardless, I suddenly found my heel sliding out from under me and my world was upended.

I landed hard—hard enough for other people on the sidewalk to gasp. "Oh, dear!" I heard one woman exclaim.

There was a moment after I landed, before I dared to move, where everything was perfectly still. I lay on the sidewalk, watching my breath rising in pretty little puffs and pretended that if I remained absolutely still, nothing would hurt.

That was, of course, just before the pain set in.

"Allow me," said a tenor-pitched voice, and before I was ready to move, I felt myself lifted to my feet.

"Thank you," I said automatically, easing my arm free from my helper's grip.

"You hurt, miss?"

"I'm fine," I said shortly. I was about to brush him off when, glancing up into his face, I found myself struck dumb by his vividly violet eyes. They were amazing!

His thin lips smiled at what admittedly must have been a comical

expression on my face. "James Stetson Metcalfe," he said by way
of introduction, raising his free hand to touch the brim of his tall
hat. He was certainly handsome. Worse, I could tell that he knew
it, owing to the way he kept his dimpled chin close shaved and his
long straight nose unblunted by a moustache.

I bobbed my head a little—there was no way was I going to attempt
a curtsy after just regaining my feet. "Nellie Bly."

If he recognized the name, he didn't show it. He lifted his strong,
thick eyebrows as he said, "Are you steady? Do you require me to
see you to a cab?"

I wanted to say no, but for some reason my mouth betrayed me.
"That would be very kind."

With a smile and a sigh of long-suffering, Mr. Metcalfe took me
gently by the elbow and guided me around the snowbank, waving
his hand at an approaching hansom cab. Having successfully deposited me in the cab, he asked my destination and relayed it to the
cabbie. With another tip of his hat he said, "Good-bye, Nellie Bly,"
and disappeared from my view. I heard him whistling my eponymous song as he went.

The same instant, the cabbie hitched up and off we went—but not
toward my apartment. None of my own clothes would serve for my
new assignment, so I was headed to Ladies' Mile.

Ladies' Mile was the shopping district between Fourteenth and
Twenty-Third Streets along Sixth Avenue and Broadway. It boasted
all the great shops: Arnold Constable, B. Altman, Lord & Taylor. I
paused by the window of W. & J. Sloane to admire a cherrywood
chair that I thought would look wonderful at the desk in my living room, and then admired some jewelry on display in Gorham
Silver's window.

With all the snow, I'd hoped to be spared large crowds, and my
prayers were partly answered: there were fewer women shopping
than normal. Sadly, this meant I had the attention of all the male
wags who traversed this stretch of New York. High class, middle,
or poor—it didn't matter. They all had the same oh-so-clever thing
to say.

"How can a lady such as yourself not smile in Ladies' Mile?"

"Give us a smile, lady! After all, it's Lady Smile!"

"If you're not smiling, you're clearly no lady!"

"It's too damn cold to smile," I retorted at last, drawing shocked looks and several *tsks* of disapproval. The Colonel would have been proud.

After nearly twenty years of pinching pennies, it was marvelous to at last be able to afford fine clothes. Since Mother's arrival in November, I'd twice brought her to the Mile in pursuit of upgraded wardrobes for us both. *But today I'm not shopping for Elizabeth Cochrane, or even Nellie Bly. I'm buying the costume of Penelope Consul, president of the Patent Medicine Company of Philadelphia.* Swarmed by bored salesladies, I explained that I was attempting to impress my mother-in-law, and required rich but matronly attire.

Trying on outfits was fun at first, but palled quickly. There were too many buttons and hooks to undo between costumes. By the third I was bored, and resolved that the fourth would be my last. So, I ended in purchasing a very conservative black bombazine dress with a silken sheen. *I just have to remember not to sit close to any gas jets or candles, or I'll burst into flames!*

A new outfit required new shoes, and a new hat and coat, so it was evening before I arrived back home. After tipping the boy who carried my packages, I lugged them inside myself, quickly explaining to my unbudging lodgers that I had no time to talk. "I have a new assignment."

"So I see," replied Albert, taking in the boxes. "You're reviewing women's clothing now?"

I opened my mouth to respond, then closed it firmly. Several times, I had found Albert going through my papers, looking for my notes on stories. He never apologized, only laughed and told me I needed to stop imagining things. But I had a sneaking suspicion he meant to repeat his trick from my time in Mexico and hint to everyone that he was the genius behind Nellie Bly, and that his sister was only his façade. It made me sad to do it, but I'd taken to burning all my correspondence. Even my letters from the Q. O., my dear friend Wilson back in Pittsburgh, had gone up in smoke. *Better that than allow Albert any glimpse of my private life.* Those letters would have to exist only in my memory.

Locked in my room—which I was sharing with my mother while Albert and Jane were staying with us—I examined my costume. The dress was fine, but the effect was not. I'd never thought that having a small waist would be a problem, but it was in this instance. Trying on the garment at the store, I'd looked a little too young, almost

like a child playing dress-up. It was time to experiment with some
of the additions I had bought.

I was not normally a fan of wearing a bustle, and tried to get
away with the smallest I could manage. If I was being forced to purchase a new one, I'd decided that it should serve me for more than
this one assignment, so I had invested in a New Canfield Langtry,
the latest invention of the Canfield Rubber Company. It had the
advantage of being smaller than most bustles, resting about half-
way up one's derriere. Advertised as "Light, cool, and adjustable"
and "Extra strong to sustain the heaviest winter clothes," it was just
what I needed.

Next, I tied on the hip pad, and then the bust enhancer, another
pad in the shape of two cups. The girl at Arnold Constable had
initially tried to sell me some bust cream—doubtless one of the
remedies Bill 191 was attempting to put out of commission—but
after seeing my chest in the first two garments I tried on, she'd
pityingly suggested a more drastic treatment: the Princess Bust
Developer. From what she'd described, it was like a metal plunger.
"It worked wonders for my cousin," she'd assured me. I'd shocked
her by declining, though I filed these beauty enhancements away
for future reporting. *So many stories to research! So many frauds
to expose!*

Next came the corset. I was skinny enough that in daily life I
mostly wore a corset as a posture aid. *And, yes, maybe to help me
have a little more curve to my figure . . .* Normally, I wore a Ball's
skating corset. I wasn't wild about the wires, but the elastic midsec-
tion gave me all the freedom of movement I needed.

Mrs. Consul, on the other hand, was interested in limiting her
movement, not enhancing it, so I had given in and purchased a
Doctor and Madame Strong's corset. This was a rival brand to Dr.
Alexander Strong's Tricora corsets, with a bit of name trickery that
the real Dr. Strong would certainly decry, if he actually existed.
The girl at the shop had sworn by the Madame Strong brand. Made
with genuine whalebone, it promised to "relieve the delicate and
vital organs of all injurious pressure." That was good, because I was
going to add pressure with the next step.

Before tightening the laces, I stuffed my middle with a second hip
pad, bolstering my belly with more apparent thickness just where
women didn't like it. And then after hooking the wire bustle frame

to my corset and tightening it all down, I finally donned the bombazine and studied myself in the mirror. Sadly, the pier mirror was in the hall, where both Mother and I could use it. I had no intention of parading myself around where I would be subjected to Albert's gibes and Jane's giggles, so I had to make do with the smaller mirror over my basin.

The effect was certainly more matronly. I also noted that I would have to put my shoes on first, as I could not bend to lace them in this rig. I added a veiled hat with red and green ribbons, and an expensive brooch at the neckline of the dress, then topped it all off with a new heavy, fur-collared winter coat. Donning my gloves, I studied the effect.

Yes. I look like a wife. Whatever that means.

I spent some time trying to imagine myself as a wife. Shoots of gray in the brown. A little weight in the cheeks. A few lines, hopefully laugh lines, not the frown lines Mother had developed at the corners of her mouth. *I suppose that depends on the man I married.*

What kind of man was Mr. Consul? Rich, was all I knew. Also, a charlatan. *Could I marry a man like that?*

Laughing, I chided myself. Who was I to accuse my fictional husband of being a charlatan? I was the one making him up! Though, if I was going to invent a husband, he'd best at least be rich. I had once told Wilson I meant to marry a millionaire.

My laughter died. I'd also said I wanted to fall in love. That was the day I had spoiled everything. I'd kissed him. Wilson, the perfect man: brilliant, infuriating, contrary, kindly, fatherly, and devoted—to his wife. Thank God I had burned his letters before Albert arrived!

Putting Wilson from my mind, I tried to imagine Dr. Ingram's reaction if he were to see me like this. I'd been keeping company with the good doctor for nearly six months, and so far he had done little more than linger when holding my hand in his. Twice, he had brushed his cheek against mine while we hugged goodnight. A true gentleman, and a doctor to boot. *So why isn't he the one I fantasize over? What's the matter with me?*

And what do I do if he proposes?

Whoops! That was something missing from my disguise. I went digging through my jewelry case looking for a ring to wear, but found nothing even remotely appropriate.

Hmm. When Mother had moved into my room, she'd brought her jewelry case with her—a clear statement that deep down she knew Albert's nature. Little did she suppose her daughter would rifle her few jewels!

It didn't take long. She didn't have much by way of jewelry, and most of what she had were pieces I'd recently bought for her. There was a pendant from her first husband, and a couple of earring and necklace sets she'd gotten from my father. Most of the really precious pieces she'd sold after he died, to keep us in clothes and food.

In the corner of one little drawer, I found something wrapped in tissue paper. Unfolding the wrapping, I was stunned. A silver wedding band with a single black diamond. I knew it at once. Her ring from Ford. She'd had to loan Ford the money to buy it, which should have been warning enough. After the divorce, I'd thought she'd thrown it away, or sold it.

But there it was. A symbol of the worst years of our lives. Holding it to the light, I decided it should bring some good into the world. There was even poetry in it. I would use the ring of a scoundrel to expose a scoundrel.

I slipped it on my finger. *A little loose, but it'll do . . .*

"Pink!" called Mother from down the hall. "Dinner is ready!"

I froze like a guilty child. *Dear God, how am I going to get all of this off?*

TESTIMONY

PINK COCHRAN, sworn, testified as follows:

Examined by MR. SAXTON:

Q. I show you a copy of the *New York World*, or a portion of the *New York World* of Sunday, April first, page 19, and refer you to an article there, the principal article upon that page; did you write that article? *[Presents paper to witness]*

A. I did.

Q. And the signature to that is your *nom de plume*, is it?

A. Yes, sir.

Q. "Nellie Bly"?

A. I wrote all of it except the poetry.

Q. You were not responsible, then, for the poetry?

A. No, sir.

Q. Now, this article I see, refers by name to certain gentlemen, members of the Assembly of this State?

A. Yes, sir.

Q. It refers to Mr. Gallagher, of Erie; Mr. Tallmadge, of Kings; Mr. Prime, of Essex; Mr. De Witt, of Ulster; Mr. Hagan, of New York; and Mr. McLaughlin, of Kings. I desire to ask you whether you have any acquaintance with any of those gentlemen yourself?

A. No, sir. I never have seen any of them.

Q. You have never seen any of them to your knowledge?

A. No, sir.

Q. Did you ever have any conversation with any of those gentlemen or hear any conversation which they were holding with any other person?

A. I do not think I ever did.

Q. Then, of course, you do not know anything of your own knowledge, that is, know anything yourself with regard to the integrity of these gentlemen.

A. I did not write that I knew it.

Q. No. I understand.

A. No, sir. I do not.

Q. You do not know anything of your own knowledge?

A. No, sir.

Q. You have no knowledge, then, as to the connection of any of these gentlemen with any measure pending before this Legislature?

A. Nothing. Only what Mr. Phelps told me.

Q. You have no knowledge as to any matter contained in this article, except the statements and declarations of Mr. Phelps in regard to it?

A. That is all.

Q. Now, this article relates what purports to be an interview between yourself and Mr. Phelps?

A. Yes, sir.

Q. There was such an interview, was there?

A. Yes, sir.

FOUR

CONFIDENCE TRICKS

TUESDAY, MARCH 27, 1888

SPEEDING FROM THE HOUSE BEFORE daybreak, I was able to escape without comment from Albert, who was still sleeping. Mother, however, raised her eyebrows at my ensemble. "For a story," I assured her. "I'll be back tomorrow night. I think." Her eyebrows lifted even higher. Only after I was gone did I choke, realizing why.

On train No. 63, leaving at 7:15 for Albany, I plopped down in Seat 3 and waited until I felt that little jolt of relief when the train started to move. Even when the sun rose, the day was gloomy, with clouds scudding across the sky. Having nothing to look at, I fiddled in my seat for something to do. Idly noting that the number of the train was odd, I realized my seat number was odd as well. I counted the number of passengers. Odd. I thought about the date. The twenty-seventh. *Odd numbers! How lucky!*

Eventually exhausting all possible distractions, I slogged through the text of the bill I was off to kill. It was incredibly boring:

STATE OF NEW YORK
No. 191, Int. 298
In Assembly, January 27, 1888
Introduced by Mr. J.W. Smith—Read twice and referred to the Committee on Public Health—*blah blah blah* from said

committee for the consideration of the House and committed
to the Committee of *Who Cares*—Ordered, when printed, to be
recommitted to the Committee on *Asylums for Comatose People*.

An ACT

For the better protection of the public health in relation to the
sale of medicines and medicinal preparations

The People of the State of New York, represented in Senate and
Assembly, do enact as follows:

SECTION 1. It shall be unlawful for any person, firm or
corporation to sell, offer or advertise for sale in this State any
secret or proprietary medicinal preparation or any substance,
fluid or compound for use, or intended to be used, as a medicine
or for medicinal purposes, unless the person, firm or corporation
get on with it shall first file with the State Board of Health a
formula or statement *under pain of being forced to read this
document* showing all the ingredients and compound parts of
said preparation or bust cream, and the exact proportion of each
contained therein, which shall be of *how is this still the first
sentence*, and also the name under which it is intended to be sold.
If said *Bored* of Health shall be satisfied that said bust cream or
its ingredients are not detrimental to public health or calculated
to deceive *the imbeciles who buy it*, they shall issue a certificate,
under the seal of said *Bored*, authorizing the hawking of said bust
cream in this state, setting forth the formula under which the
same is to be hawked, and stating the *lying* name under which the
same is to be hawked, and *why is there an "and" this should be a
new sentence* it shall be unlawful for any other or different article
to be placed in or added to said *how often can they say "said"
without saying anything* to said bust cream, or of a different
article to be placed in or added to said bust cream, or of a different
degree of strength, or to hawk the same under any different name
than as set forth in such certificate, and there shall be paid to said
State *Bored* of Health *I'd like to state that I'm so bored it's risking
my health* for each certificate so stated the sum of $1 for the use
of said *Bored oh thank God that's over.*

SEC. 2 *For crying out loud, there's a Section Two?* It shall be
unlawful to sell, offer or advertise for sale *nope, cannot manage
all this manspeak, must scan for relevant details. Can't sell bust
cream unless it says "Sale authorized by the New York State Board*

of Health." Got it. Violations cost $200, half of which goes to the government. Got it. This doesn't affect licensed pharmacists, who sell legitimate bust cream. Got it. It takes effect immediately, unlike bust cream. Got it. Done and done.

The rest of the journey was spent staring out the window at a world still blanketed in whites and grays. I smiled to myself, recalling how just two years earlier I had boarded a train in a snow-covered city and emerged a few days later in Mexico. I wondered where Joaquin Miller was these days. He'd sent me a copy of his latest work, *Songs of The Mexican Seas*, with an annoying inscription: "To my Nell—Remembering La Viga." It was a reference to a romantic day we'd spent at the famous floating gardens. He'd scrawled that just below the printed dedication: "To Abbie." His wife. From whom he was separated. Who also lived in New York. He'd probably put both our copies in the mail on the same day.

What's the matter with me? I wondered. First Wilson, then Miller—what was it about married men that attracted me? That they were unhappily married? Did that make a difference? Should it? What did it say about me? Nellie Bly, the unhappy home-wrecker.

I thought again of Dr. Ingram. A decent, kind, handsome, unwed, intelligent man who was obviously crazy about me. He was even a doctor! *So why aren't I equally mad about him?* In my head he wasn't Ingram, or Frank, but always Dr. Ingram. What girl in her right mind didn't want to marry a doctor? He'd even met and liked my mother! They could spend the whole evening chewing the rag. Shouldn't that make him ideal? And yet, there I was, resenting Joaquin, whom I had turned down.

I did notice something that morning. Under my matronly disguise, I was experiencing far less mashing. Men tipped their hats to me. But the combination of my garments, the added thickness around my middle, and the bulge of Ford's ring under my glove served to ward off the usual lingering gazes and too-friendly comments. No one told me to smile. As I wore black, they all probably assumed I was mourning. *I should wear black every day.*

Fortunately, I wasn't forced to suffer my own thoughts for too terribly long. Most of the snow had been cleared from the tracks, so my northbound train moved consistently, and what should have taken five hours took only six. I disembarked just after noon, and immediately walked the short distance to a hotel called Stanwix Hall to bestow my two bags and repair any damage to my disguise.

My odd streak did not desert me. I was given Room 15. Entering, I discovered three chairs in the room. Much as I might scoff at them, I had always been one for random superstitions. I looked for patterns in unconnected things, and sometimes made little deals with myself. "If the first word on the next page begins with a vowel, I will have a lucky day." Ridiculous, of course. But it'd been my habit since childhood.

However, I only had one constant superstition: my lucky thumb ring. It was too big for any other finger, as it had belonged to my father. Rubbing my forefinger against it, I began settling in.

By the time I had unpacked, I realized it was already three in the afternoon. *Odd!* It was too late to try Phelps, who would likely be done with his business for the day. I decided to leave it until the following morning, even if it was an even-numbered day.

Besides, for the first time in ages I would have a space of my own. No brother, no sister-in-law. Not even Mother. Just me. Doffing my costume, I drew myself a bath—hot and cold running water in hotels was such a blessing! Even better, I discovered a novel in the same drawer that held the Bible. *The Mayor of Casterbridge*, by someone called Thomas Hardy. In the first chapter, a drunken husband sells his wife and daughter to a passing sailor. Needless to say, I was speared at once, and took dinner in my room so I could keep reading.

The next morning, it was time for me to weave my own fiction. I had breakfast in the hotel restaurant, then returned to my room to perfect my costume. As I dressed, I heard a particularly exuberant peal of bells from more than one church. *Curious*, I thought. Remembering what the Colonel had said about Phelps liking to be seen in church, I wondered if excessive shows of piety were commonplace in the state capital.

At half past eleven, convincingly matroned, I emerged into the chill air. Snow had given way to rain, and the promise of April was in the air. The remnants of snow on the ground were reduced to sad, pockmarked piles of slush. I was grateful that I'd thought to bring an umbrella.

Hailing a two-wheeled hansom cab—*Number five!*—I instructed the driver, "Take me to the Kenmore Hotel."

"Not enjoying the Stanwix, ma'am?" asked my chatty cabbie as he helped me in.

Ma'am? "What? No, it's very nice."

"Ah!" cried the Negro knowingly. "Then you're off to see an assemblyman."

Startled, I had to laugh. "Is it that common?"

Back in his perch, he opened the trap door in the roof to grin cheerfully down at me as he got the horse moving again. "Let's just say there's more business done in the Kenmore than in the halls of the senate. You've never been to Albany before?" I admitted I had not. "Well, these days, if the Capitol is the heart of the city, the Kenmore is the liver—all the dirty stuff passes through it. A shame, given its history."

"Tell me," I said, huddling in the corner of the hansom to keep the rain from blowing in my face.

"Well, the man who built it was the most prominent Negro the city ever had. Mr. Adam Blake Junior. His father came here a slave and lived to befriend the governor, as well as Alexander Hamilton. The Black Beau Brummell, they say. His adopted son was educated right alongside the children of his former master, old Stephen Van Rensselaer III. Well, Adam Junior took to business like a duck to water. Started his twenties as a waiter in a restaurant and ended them owning three restaurants of his very own. He bought the Congress Hall Hotel and fixed it up smart. It was the place to be—so much so that the government chose that spot for the site of their new capitol building. He sold it for a song, and opened the Kenmore. It has everything: elevators, telephones in every room, hot and cold water. The most elegant structure on the finest street in Albany. Such a shame," he added.

"What?"

"He died maybe three years after it opened. His wife did fine work keeping it going, but she sold it last year. The new owners—well, they're fine people, to be sure. But the Kenmore was always a good training ground for the Negro looking to better himself. They even had one fellow go on to become a judge! But no more."

I heard the sadness in his voice, and wondered what it would be like to have a haven like that as a training ground for women, and then to lose it. "I'm so sorry to hear that."

The cabbie shrugged. "Nothing stands forever, ma'am. A thing isn't beautiful because it lasts. But still, there it is, a monument to all a man can do if he's given a chance."

I saw the Kenmore up ahead, a wide and gorgeous six-story red brick marvel that occupied the corner of Pearl and Columbia Streets. It was certainly impressive, and I understood why men of means would want to be seen living in such a place. A new structure was being built just beside it. By the signage, I understood it was to be one of those Young Men's Christian Association buildings. I wondered if the city had plans for a Young Women's one as well, and if it would be so grand, and so prominently placed.

Stop it, I thought to myself as the cab's twin wheels skidded to a halt on the snowy street. *You're not here as a crusader for women's rights! You're a swindler, here to keep your swindler husband from losing his business.*

Thanking my cabbie with a large tip—I was pretending to be a wealthy woman, and the *World* was paying the tab—I marched swiftly into the gorgeous entryway of the Kenmore. The lobby of the lobbyist.

Instantly, I was approached by a half-grown boy in a bellboy's uniform. His brass buttons shone bright. "Can I help you, ma'am?"

Ma'am! "I want to see Mr. Phelps, please."

"Of course, ma'am." Buttons politely escorted me through the lobby of the hotel to the elevator. As we passed by, a number of men seated in the lobby's chaise lounges glanced at me curiously. Playing my part, I smiled nervously at them. I expected them to grin knowingly, but their eyes seemed ringed with suspicion. Albany was a different place indeed.

As Buttons started the elevator on its upward flight, he inquired, "Do you want to send your card up?"

I'd been fretting about the card, the modern passport to polite society. I carried one with Nellie Bly on it, and another with Elizabeth Cochrane. *I really should have some printed with a series of aliases.* Button's question made me wonder if it was possible to get in without presenting a card. After all, I was supposed to be arriving incognito. I immediately decided to simply storm his castle. "No, no card."

Reaching the top floor, I followed Buttons along softly carpeted halls framed by periodic pointed arches. He stopped at a door that bore a little china plate with the number 98. I heard voices within, and grew more nervous—which could only assist my deception. So long as I didn't lose my head.

At the bellboy's second knock, a gruff voice called, "Enter!" I hung back as Buttons entered. Apparently, we were interrupting an uproarious story, for I heard a voice saying, "—so the judge blows the foam off his beer and says to me 'Argumentum ad hominem, sir!' To which my father replies, 'I was very fond of hominy when I was a child, but now I rather prefer it in the liquid state. May I buy you another?'" This was followed by an explosion of laughter.

From my angle I could only spy one man through the half-open door, a lean, gray-haired fellow busily writing at a desk in the center of the room. If I suspected for a moment that this was Phelps, I was instantly corrected. "Mr. Seaver," said Buttons, "I have a lady here to see Mr. Phelps."

"He's in the other room," said this Mr. Seaver without lifting his head. Out of my line of sight, several men chuckled knowingly.

Stepping around the door, Buttons knocked on the connecting door separating Room 98 from Room 99. A moment later I heard him say, "A lady to see you, Mr. Phelps."

"A lady?" said a smooth voice, not at all disagreeable.

"Yes, sir."

"Is she downstairs?"

"Nossir. Right here."

"Very well," came the bemused answer. "Show her to the other door."

Closing the door to Room 98, Buttons led me to Room 99—*Odd!* I thought—and knocked. Instantly, it opened. "Yes? May I help you?"

I had been fully prepared to meet a fat, leering vampire, doomed to suck the blood of his nearest relations. Instead, I discovered a smiling, congenial, bespectacled man of perhaps fifty-five years. He was hardly taller than I was. "Are you Mr. Phelps?"

"Yes, madam," he replied, smiling slightly. "Do come in." Thanking Buttons, Phelps closed the door behind me and held out a chair for me. "Please be seated, Mrs. . . ."

"Consul. Mrs. Penelope Consul." Sitting down, I looked about. This room clearly served as an office, with rows and rows of books upon shelves behind the glass doors of several mahogany lawyer's bookcases. The only piece of furniture which looked out of place was a wardrobe which stood against the center wall. *Perhaps that's where he keeps his cloven hooves and tail.*

Phelps sat in a chair close by me, a reassuring smile on his face. Like his hair, his ample side-whiskers were silver-gray, but his upper lip and chin were clean-shaven. Dressed in plain, tasteful clothes, he was neither robust nor delicate, weighing probably one hundred sixty pounds. Recalling what the Colonel had said about Phelps liking to be seen in church, I decided he would appear right at home there. Not a gaudy monster of politics, but a polite parson. I was reminded not to judge books by their covers, but by their contents.

Adjusting his spectacles on his nose, he looked me over critically. "Well, Mrs. Consul, how may I be of service?"

Armed with assumed innocence and genuine ignorance as to how such affairs are conducted, I licked my lips and plunged in. "Mr. Phelps, I came to consult you on a matter of importance." With a glance toward the partially open connecting door, I added, "I—I hope no one can overhear us?"

"Oh, no, you are perfectly safe to speak here." To reassure me, he drew his chair even closer.

Trying to express reluctant urgency, I said, "I have come to see you about a bill."

His face lit up like a child's over a strawberry soda on an August day, and he rubbed his hands together. "What bill is it?"

"A bill about patent medicines," I answered. "That's our business—well, my husband's. He is ill just now, you see."

"And Mr. Consul's own medicine won't answer?" asked Phelps with a kindly laugh.

I flashed him a smile as a burlesque dancer flashes her garter—a brief glimpse, then gone. "No, alas. I should tell you, Consul is my maiden name. It's why I didn't send up a card. If I were to tell you my husband's name, you would know right off the product we're attempting to protect."

Laying one finger aside his nose, he said, "I understand."

With unfeigned gratitude, I pressed on with my tale. "What happened was this. He sent me to New York from Philadelphia to place some advertisements. When I arrived, a friend who also has a patent medicine told me of this bill. It would ruin us to have to comply with its strictures—New York is our biggest market. At my friend's suggestion I came up to see if anything could be done."

Nodding, Phelps lowered his voice. "Have you the bill with you?"

"Yes," I replied, producing a copy of the misprinted docket from my bag. "My friend gave it to me when he told me about it."

"May I see it?"

"Certainly." I handed it over. As he scanned it, I leaned forward with piteous anxiousness. "Do you think you can kill it?"

"Oh, yes!" said Phelps heartily. "Never fear, I'll have it killed. Pardon me." Stepping into the other room, he returned a moment later with a large ledger in his hand. I noticed that he closed the connecting door firmly behind him this time. Once again, he sat down across from me and, resting the ledger on his knee, ran his finger down an alphabetical list, then turned to a page filled with data on all the bills. Coming to the right one, he became quite pleased. His shoulders relaxed and his face positively glowed as he closed the book and fixed his wolfish smile upon the poor little lamb who had come to be fleeced.

But he was cagey, Phelps was, as much fox as wolf. "What made you come to me?"

"Well, when my friend told me about the bill, I did not want to place the advertisements and so lose all my money. If that bill passes, you know it will ruin our business."

"That is certainly true. If passed, it will definitely hinder the selling of patent medicines. Which I presume is the intent—one that we will thwart, never you fear. But who sent you to me?"

"My friend," I answered evasively. "He said I might consult Mr. Phelps of Albany."

"And who is he?"

I pressed my lips together. "I would not like to give his name without his authority. As I said, he has a similar stake in this matter."

After a pause in which I hardly dared breathe, Phelps shrugged one shoulder. "You see, I only wanted to know because we have had lots of people up here paying to have that bill killed. Do you know Pierce of Buffalo? I thought it might be he who sent you. He is also trying to get it killed. So far, to no avail."

"No, I don't know anyone named Pierce. I never even heard of the bill until two days ago," I said with complete honesty. "I concluded not to go home, so I telegraphed my husband, and he instructed me to come up here."

"Where are you from?" inquired Phelps.

He's testing me. "Philadelphia."

"Ah, the City of Brotherly Love. The Cradle of Liberty. Workshop of the World. I know it well."

Blenching a little, I pressed quickly on before he started pressing me over people and places I wouldn't know. "We make our patent medicine there, but as I said, it sells all over New York State. Do you truly think you can kill the bill?"

"Oh, yes, absolutely! I assure you of that. Now you keep up your n-n-nerve." He shook his head. "Forgive me. Stutter. Ever since I was a boy."

"How trying it must be," I said sympathetically.

"You're kind," he said, patting my knee. Then, cocking his head to one side, he added coolly, "It will take m-m-money, you know."

It was shocking that he would be so brazen. For a moment I felt a thrill, immediately chilled by the idea that he was laying a trap of some kind. *Does he suspect me? Or is he really so arrogant as to state out loud to a complete stranger that he needs a bribe?*

I blinked several times. He continued to smile. I clutched at my umbrella. Head still cocked to his right like a spaniel's, he raised his eyebrows. Clearing my throat, I tried to convey a naïve eagerness, and a complete inability to bargain. "I came to New York with three thousand dollars to spend on advertising. I am willing to pay anything up to that if you assure me it will be stopped."

"Oh, I can assure you that." Pleased as punch, Phelps leaned back, his head returning to center. If he had owned suspicions, somehow the amount seemed to have soothed them. It was the sum the Colonel had suggested.

"I thought when I came up that I would go to see Mr. Smith, who introduced the bill. I thought maybe he would be open to retracting it, in return for a—a consideration. But I didn't know where to find him, so I came directly to you."

"A good thing you did," said Phelps warmly. "You see, Smith is a dissipated and unprincipled fellow. He would have taken your m-m-money and given you no returns. You came to just the right mmman to help you." He dragged out the *m* in *man* to resist the stutter. "And, of course, you don't need to fear losing all three thousand. It won't cost quite so much. Just my expenses, and those of a few assemblymen."

"Members of the Committee on Cities, you mean?"

Phelps walked over to a ledge between two windows, which contained stacks of papers and file folders. Riffling through some papers, he emerged with eight pages containing the names and committee assignments of assemblymen and senators. *Here's the next test.* Due to the printer's error, the bill in question was listed as being before the Committee on Cities, when it was really before the Committee on Public Health. There was no crossover of membership between the two committees. If Phelps was genuinely going to lobby on my behalf, he would steer me to the actual committee I needed to influence.

Pointing to a stack of names in the middle of the second page, he said, "You see, these are the names of the eleven men that can kill or save the bill."

I read over the list:

> Mr. Crosby, of New York;
> Gallagher, of Erie;
> Burns, of Westchester;
> Tallmadge, of Kings;
> Prime, of Essex;
> Mr. De Witt, of Ulster;
> Hagan, of New York;
> Blumenthal, of New York;
> McLaughlin, of Kings;
> Sullivan, of Monroe;
> Cromwell, of Richmond.

Above their names resided the heading AFFAIRS OF CITIES. *Perfect. He's going to try to swindle me.* "Can you get all their votes?"

"Well, we don't need them all, do we?" he said, taking a lead pencil from his coat pocket. "Now, let me see . . ." He placed the paper upon a side table and moved his hand down the list, pricking off certain names. "Mr. Crosby is a rich man and can't be bought. But we can get De Witt (prick), Gallagher (prick), Hagan (prick), Tallmadge (prick), McLaughlin (prick), and Prime (prick). The rest are no good."

Great goodness! If only I can leave the room with that list! Pondering how to achieve that feat, I temporized. "But if the rest are opposed?"

"The majority gains, you see," said Phelps sweetly. Talking of his business had evidently relieved his stutter. "There are six out of eleven I can get."

"How much will it take for them?"

"Hm." Phelps seemed to consider. "I think you can get the lot for a thousand dollars. Plus my expenses, of course."

A thousand dollars. A thousand dollars to kill a bill that was already dead, to bribe six assemblymen who would never see a cent of my money. It would all go to line Phelps's pockets. I wanted to laugh. Unfortunately, my face was ever a traitor to my soul. As soon as I felt myself begin to smile, I buried my face in my hands. With nothing else to do, I pretended to cry.

Phelps leaned forward in sudden consternation. "My dear lady, what's the matter? Is it too much? I thought you said you could manage it."

I shook my head. "It isn't that! I'm willing to pay whatever it may cost to have the bill killed. But it frightens me! I must never be known as connected with this. I wouldn't have it known for anything."

Phelps offered a reassuring chortle as I employed my handkerchief. "Is that all? Why, that's nothing. You'll see. Trust me. This is my business. Why, I stay here all through the legislative season just to watch bills for railroad presidents, insurance companies, that kind of palaver. I'm kept here just to do precisely this. Why, there is a lawyer of the name of Batch in New York who is also assisting me in getting people who want to fight the same bill you are here about. I've had my agents send out hundreds of copies of it. Adding your funds to theirs, it should be no trouble at all."

What a bald-faced liar! Tempting as it was to confront him there and then, I resisted. I needed to escape, with that paper. "You are sure, then, for about three thousand dollars—which I would rather spend this way than lose it in advertising—you can buy these men to kill the bill?"

"Yes," replied Phelps with confidence, "I can have them murder it entirely for that amount, or near it, and dispose of the corpse as well. Now, where can I see you again to make final arrangements?" Which I took to mean payment.

"Any place you name."

"Well, can you come back from Philadelphia on Friday? I'll be in

New York."

"Can you manage it as soon as that?" I asked, wide-eyed.

"Certainly. I'll have everything in place by then. Nothing simpler."

True enough, since the bill is already dead in the water. "Then, yes, I can come back Friday."

"Good, good. Well, telegraph me to meet you at your hotel in New York. Where do you stop?"

My mind raced. "Sometimes at the Sturtevant, and also at the Gilsey. But I dread exposure in this affair. I don't—forgive me—I don't want to be seen in public with you, or to have anyone connect you to me. Could you not appoint a place that would attract less attention? Have you no place I could see you?"

"You might come to my office," he offered.

The one place, of all places, I wanted to go. Making sure I betrayed none of my satisfaction, I said, "Oh, you have an office in New York also?"

"Yes, in the Boris Building. Do you know where that is?" I shook my head. "Well, when you exit the Cortlandt Street Ferry you cross to Broadway, and it is about two blocks below. Number 115, Room 97. Wait, I'll write it out for you." And, to my delight, he took the copy of the bill I had brought and wrote on the margin "E.R. Phelps, 115 Broadway, Room 97, Boris Building."

"How very kind of you," I said, taking the bill and placing it in my bag.

"Now you come down on Friday, meet me there between twelve and one—lunchtime, there'll be fewer people around to see you. If I'm not in when you arrive, wait for me. I'll be there as soon as possible—I live out of the city, you understand. Come prepared to make final arrangements. As soon as those are made, I'll give them the go-ahead to kill the bill."

"Then I can place my advertisements on Friday?"

"Don't place them until you see me." I supposed he wanted to be certain I didn't spend all my money before he was paid. "After you see me you can safely place them. The bill will then be dead, or just as good, it will be harmless. You'll see."

"Thank you," I said. The interview was clearly over, but I didn't rise. I was still trying to think of how to take that marked list of assemblymen who could be bought.

Phelps, however, was ready to be rid of me. Taking my hand, he guided me to my feet. "Why stay in Albany any longer? Why not take the one thirty train for New York?"

A glance at a clock on the mantle showed it was five after one. "I haven't had my luncheon yet."

"They carry an eating car," he insisted, stepping an inch closer to the door in order to pressure me out. "Take that train. It will get you in at five o'clock."

"That will allow me to go on to Philadelphia," I said, appearing to give in.

"That's right. You can reassure your husband. And if you stay any longer, there's every chance you'll be seen," he pressed, using my own lever against me. "If you don't want to raise comment, you'd best go now."

Now that money was promised, I was beginning to suspect that he feared I would discover the truth about the bill if I stayed in Albany any longer. Or that another boodler would snap me up and fleece me of his expected fee. "You're absolutely right." I gathered up my bag and umbrella, breezily plucking up the marked list as well. "I'll take this home to show my husband."

"Give it to me!" Phelps practically lunged for it, snatching it from my grasp. He quickly moderated his tone, forcing a smile. "You see, your husband may know some of these men and may tell them. It wouldn't look well for me to cross off those that can be bought."

"Oh," I said, with unfeigned disappointment.

He seemed to take pity on me. "Look, I'll cross out all the names. Then there's no harm in taking it."

I thanked him even as my heart sank. Here was my only clue to those who Mr. Phelps alleged could be bought. If he crossed out all the names, I wouldn't be able to tell one from the other. And even if I remembered them, I would have no proof! Shutting my eyes, I thought several nasty things about cunning men and odd numbers.

Opening them again, I watched him destroy my clue. He placed the sheet on a book on his desk and pricked little check marks next to the remaining names—excepting Mr. Crosby's—then handed it back to me. Not daring to look at it, I thanked him as I placed it in my purse.

Mr. Phelps guided me out the door into the hallway. "Now remember, come to my office on Friday at noon to settle our business."

"I'll be there," I promised, and thanked him again as I called for the elevator. I saw Phelps return to his comrades in Room 98.

Buttons arrived to open the gate for me. With both door and gate shut behind me, he held the lever for the ground floor. As we descended, I removed the marked list to see if there remained any trace of my proof.

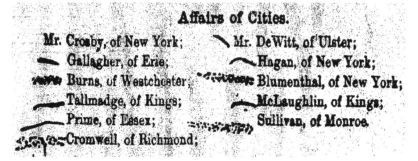

Affairs of Cities.

Mr. Crosby, of New York; Mr. DeWitt, of Ulster; Gallagher, of Erie; Hagan, of New York; Burns, of Westchester; Blumenthal, of New York; Tallmadge, of Kings; McLaughlin, of Kings; Prime, of Essex; Sullivan, of Monroe. Cromwell, of Richmond;

I couldn't believe my eyes. When he first made his marks, he had placed the paper upon the side table. But later, when attempting to disguise his marks, he had placed it upon a book. Scanning the list, I realized at once that the book had not owned a smooth cover, but one of marbled leather. As a result, the lead pencil had made irregular spotted lines next to the second batch of names, while the original six had clean, unbroken lines. The two sets of lines were as distinct as if they had been marked in different-colored ink!

I emerged into the street thanking the rain, book binders, and odd numbers. Then I hailed a hansom. "Stanwix Hall, and quick!"

TESTIMONY

WEDNESDAY AFTERNOON, APRIL 18, 1888.

PINK COCHRAN, sworn, testified as follows:

Examined by MR. SAXTON:

Q. Now, did you make any memorandum of this conversation with him?

A. Yes, sir. Just as soon as I got away from him I did, but not in his presence.

Q. Where did you go to make the memorandum?

A. First I went down to Stanwix Hall, where I was stopping.

Q. Down to Stanwix Hall?

A. Yes, sir. The second interview, I went to the *World* office.

Q. The first interview, did you go immediately from his room to Stanwix Hall?

A. Yes, sir. He wanted me to go home, but I did not.

Q. Did you go to your room there?

A. Yes, sir.

Q. And there you made a memorandum, did you?

A. Yes, sir.

Q. Did you write out any portion of this article there?

A. Oh, no.

Q. Just made a memorandum?

A. Just made notes so that I could get it exactly correct.

Q. Have you got those notes with you?

A. No, I haven't.

Q. Can you tell where they are?

A. Yes. Or I can tell where they were. I tore them up after I wrote my article, as I do all my notes.

Q. You did not preserve them?

A. No, sir, I never do.

FIVE

RIDING THE TRAIN HOME THE following morning, I reflected on my interview as I looked over my notes. What horrified me more than anything was how commonplace it had all seemed to him. It was as if I had been in one of the department stores on Ladies' Mile, where the price for each item was displayed on a little card. Only in this store, it was elected officials available for purchase!

Disembarking, I found New York a different city from two days before. The rain had beaten away most of the snow, leaving only gray patches of slosh here and there. *Oh, good! Now Albert has no more excuse to stay.* My deep desire was to arrive home to find him gone.

But that fervent wish took second place to my fevered excitement to share my triumph with the Colonel. Sending a boy to deliver my luggage home, I sprinted for the *World* offices, eager to burst into the Colonel's office, list held high in triumph.

When I arrived, however, the Colonel was absent. "Out to lunch with Mr. Pulitzer," Marsh informed me, not to be helpful, but rather to imply the Colonel had far more important matters than me to occupy his time.

Frustrated, I went to my desk and settled in to type my notes from the Phelps interview. After that I would check my mail—Nellie Bly got dozens of letters each day, and there was no knowing which one would lead to a story.

Since starting at the *World*, I had felt a palpable sense of exclusion from the other newspapermen, far worse than I ever had at the *Pittsburg Dispatch*. There, I had become almost "one of the boys." Here, I was like the freak at a circus: something to be stared at but never approached. I knew I was resented for walking off the street and getting my own byline when dozens of experienced reporters didn't merit credit. That made sense to me—except that other reporters had come in and jumped the line, gotten their own bylines, and they were considered gods. No, the real reason for their resentment was that I was a woman, the only visible female reporter at the *World*, one with her own desk right there among the pillars and smoke of the newsroom. Sutherland's reluctance to help me, or even look at me, was just one example of how they'd responded to my violation of their little boys' club.

I retaliated by isolating myself, ignoring everyone and everything around me. Occasionally, I would venture over to the curtained cubicle that contained McDougall, the artist who had been drawing images for my stories since Blackwell's. I liked his work, especially his drawings of me: simple, but plucky, with a tiny waist that only slightly exaggerated my own. I didn't sense any animosity form McDougall, but we were hardly friends. At the *World*, there was the Colonel, and then there was everyone else, ranging from begrudging rivals to full-fledged enemies.

Which was why I was surprised to find a hand waving in front of my eyes to get my attention. Removing wads of cotton from my ears, I said, "Yes?"

"Ah! So that's the secret!" chirped the sardonic humorist Edgar 'Bill' Nye. "We all wondered, you see, how you tolerated the language around here."

"It's not the language that requires these," I replied, holding up the little balls of cotton. "I have brothers. It's the noise. I can hardly hear myself think."

"Well, I thought it was time I introduced myself, Miss Bly. I'm Bill Nye."

"That sounds like a vaudeville routine."

"Can't help that," replied the humorist, flapping his hands in a parody of frustration. "One of us is going to have to change her name."

I raised my brows in polite amusement. "And it's supposed to be me?"

"Hey, I came by mine legitimately. You stole yours from Stephen Foster, and the poor man really deserves to get it back. It would make up for the ignominious nature of his death."

"I'm not sure anything can do that," I retorted. "Additionally, I didn't steal the name. It landed on me like a brick. Besides, I don't think it's important where the name comes from. What matters is what you do with it. Maybe one day people will say, 'Wasn't there a song named after that newspaper woman Nellie Bly?'"

Nye erupted with laughter, drawing even more attention to our little conference. "Well, we have to do something."

"Why?"

He handed me three letters all addressed to Nellie Bly. "Our mail is getting mixed up."

That made me offer a genuine laugh of my own, and Nye pounced at once. "Well, you really can smile! Thank you."

"For smiling?"

"My reputation as a humorist was at stake." He pointed to Jim Cole, the assistant at the foreign news beat—and the man whose desk I had usurped. "I bet Cole I could make you laugh. Y'see, the boys are thoroughly frightened of you. None of us have seen you looking anything but grim and determined."

"I do not look grim!" I protested at once.

"I never said you did," replied Cole, coming quickly to join us. "I said 'intense.'"

"That's better," I answered, mollified.

"By the bye," said Nye, "I'm under instructions from old Razzy Wilson to say hello." He waved a hand. "Hello!"

Wilson. I hadn't heard from him since just after the Mad-House story broke. Putting on a brave front, I said, "How is the dear Q. O.?"

"Oh, splendid, splendid. Thriving at the *Commercial Gazette*—which means he's complaining all the time. He certainly didn't enjoy the letter to the editor in January asking for confirmation that he was, in fact, a woman. Seems he knows far too much about makeup to possibly be a man."

My eyes went wide with amazement. My jaw hung slack. Then I started to laugh quite uncontrollably. "Wilson!" I cried—literally cried, with tears running from my eyes. "Wilson, a woman!"

Nye and Cole exchanged glances, but neither understood. Racked with a spasming stomach and giggle hiccups, I explained. "Three years ago, another Quiet Observer piece received a quite different letter to the editor. One written by me, letting him know how far off his understanding of women was. It's how I got noticed by the *Dispatch*," I added.

"Is that how you got started?" asked Nye, perching himself on the edge of my desk.

"Yes. Anger gives me eloquence. They already had a girl columnist, so they asked if I might like reporting."

"Golly, I'm a fool," said Cole dryly. "I got a degree in history, became fluent in French, and spent four years working my way up from the bottom rung. I should have just put on a dress."

"You'd be arrested." Annoyed, I turned to Nye. "How did you get started? Did you always want to be in newspapers?"

"Me? Hardly. I was in school when the war ended, and I thought it was my patriotic duty to ensure nothing like that happened again. Someone said that laws are what hold us together, so I studied law. Honestly, though, I made a pathetic lawyer. Back in Laramie, I tried everything I could do with a law degree. First justice of the peace, then school administrator, city council member, and postmaster. But I was always sending in my stupid little pieces to the newspapers in Denver and Cheyenne. Finally started my own."

"The *Boomerang*," I supplied.

"You've heard of it?"

"Mr. Nye. Everyone's heard of it."

He reddened, a pleased smile crinkling the corners of his mouth. "Being postmaster helped, I confess. Still, like the barking squirrel, it got me noticed. The rest, they say, is a mystery."

"By the way," Cole interjected, fixing Nye with a sly stare, "don't believe Nye here about his name. He stole it, too."

"From my pappy!" protested Nye.

"Nye, yes. But a Bill you ain't, Edgar."

"Edgar?" I asked, grinning.

"The legitimate," replied Nye, rubbing the back of his neck and grinning. "As opposed to Edmund the bastard."

"Edward," I corrected, thinking of Phelps.

Not caring about our cross talk, Cole said, "Ask him where he got 'Bill.'"

All I had to do was raise my eyebrows and Nye's embarrassment heightened. I expected him to explain. Instead he started reciting poetry:

> Yet the cards they were stocked
> In a way that I grieve,
> And my feelings were shocked
> At the state of Nye's sleeve,
> Which was stuffed full of aces and bowers,
> And the same with intent to deceive.

In answer to my blank stare, the humorist said, "Bill Nye, cheater at cards, the villain in Bret Harte's 'The Heathen Chinee.' Don't get frosty, now! He wrote it as satire of anti-Chinese prejudice, and I think it broke Harte's heart when his readers used it to reinforce their own wicked hearts against Orientals."

Cole shrugged. "Just goes to show you that cleverness is lost on some people. You can be as sarcastic as you please, and it sails right over their heads." He looked at me while he said it, as if we were sharing a joke.

"Well, I'd best be moseying on my way," said Nye. "I've cards to mark and sleeves to fill. Miss Bly, it has been a genuine pleasure. With your permission, I may take a page from your book and keep wads of cotton in my desk as well." Tipping me his hat—no man took off his hat in the newsroom, even for a woman—he nodded at Cole and both men started toward their desks.

I had a sudden inspiration. "Nye, wait! You can repay me by doing me a favor."

"Anything," he said gallantly. "Who do you want killed?"

"Do you know anyone in Philadelphia?"

"Several people."

"If I give you a telegram, could you have them send it from Philadelphia to the address I give you? It would have to be done today, though."

"I'll do it right now," said Nye.

I was already scribbling out the text of my telegram:

PHILADELPHIA, MARCH 28.
E.R. PHELPS, ROOM 96 KENMORE, ALBANY, N.Y.
HAVE MADE SATISFACTORY ARRANGEMENTS WITH HUSBAND.
WILL SEE YOU AS AGREED.
                                    MRS. CONSUL

Carrying it away, Nye went straight to the telephone. *There! That should ease any doubts my lobbyist friend may have.*

Heartened by the friendly workplace exchange, the fact that the Colonel did not reappear that afternoon did not disappoint me as it might have. Eager as I was to show him the fruits of my labors—the list of marked names—he would be all the more appreciative after I gave a check to Phelps. His cashing in of a bribe would certainly be all the proof we'd ever need.

I was startled around four o'clock by the reappearance of Cole at my desk. He waved his hand and again I unstoppered my ears, smiling up at him.

"Bly, I'm knocking off. Why not join me? Come out to the Albion. It's where all of us reporters go to unwind our watches at the end of the day."

Next door to the *World* were the offices of the *Army and Navy Journal*, a weekly founded by the Church brothers. To raise money, they rented out the downstairs front rooms of their building as a public dining room called the Albion. I had walked by, but never been inside.

Thrilled to be invited, I hedged. "I'm pretty tired."

"Some coffee will help. Or do you drink tea? Come along! It's not only me. Metcalfe is meeting me there, Sutherland and Crinkle too. We'll see who else we can lasso."

My eagerness battled my common sense. Sense lost. "Thank you, Jim. I should like to go." Gathering up my things, including my precious piece of paper, I walked with Cole to the elevator.

Outside, we turned to the right and immediately entered the Albion, a large, dark-paneled room. Between the dim lighting and the clouds of cigar smoke it was nearly impossible to see. But Cole plunged ahead, my arm in his trailing grip. I followed as he made his way through the crowd three-deep around the stone fireplace, dodging elbows and knees. "Excuse me. Sorry. Pardon me."

As my eyes adjusted, I saw tables with long oak trestle benches in place of chairs. The place was very crowded, full of suits and moustaches and cigars and beer steins.

Only when we reached our table at the back could I really see the room. My heart had been sinking in suspicion. Now I was certain. Cole had deliberately brought me to a place sacred to men. I was the only woman in the place. Masculine faces turned toward me with astonishment, dismay, outrage. The air was rife with hostility.

I considered stalking from the place in a show of maidenly disgust. But that was just what he wanted.

Keeping up his pretense of obliviousness, Cole greeted three seated men holding a table. "Howdy, Crinkle, Sutherland, Metcalfe!" The first man had a full head of dark hair, neatly slicked and coifed, and a giant bushy moustache that bent his face into a perpetual frown. The second, Sutherland, I knew. The third, I saw with a flush, was my thin-lipped, dimple-chinned savior with twinkling violet eyes.

Attempting to add to my discomfort, Cole made grand introductions. "Sutherland, you know Miss Bly, of course."

"Of course," said Sutherland with barely contained glee.

"How could you not? Nellie Bly, allow me to present James Stetson Metcalfe, theatre critic for *Life*. And have you met the *World's* own theatre man, Andrew Wheeler, better known as Nym Crinkle?"

While Wheeler openly laughed at the situation in a most nasty way, Metcalfe was frowning in consternation.

I felt dreadfully on the spot, and wished I knew how to punch like a boxer so I could break Cole's nose. Or Sutherland's, the prankster who likely put Cole up to this. That would stop his smirking.

Very well. I'm the new farting dog story. Nothing to do but brave it out. "I do know Mr. Wheeler. Charley, thanks again for all your help the other day. How do you do, Mr. Metcalfe? I think we met once before?" I asked, hating Cole for his prank and myself for falling for it.

Laughter fading, Wheeler and Sutherland both frowned when I did not burst into tears and race from the hall. I assumed they were in on Cole's jest. Whereas Metcalfe clearly was not. In answer to my greeting, the balding theatre critic rose, but not to address me. I wondered if he even remembered me. "Cole, you're an ass. What do you think you're doing?"

"He's inviting a fellow reporter out for a drink," replied Wheeler dryly. "It's what's *done*, old boy. It's the *thing*."

"Shut up, Crinkle." Only then did Mr. Metcalfe turn to me. One of his brows, his left, seemed perpetually arched. At this moment it conveyed more apology than irony. "I'm so sorry, Miss. This was an unsightly trick. Do you need an escort out?"

"Out?" I asked, making sure my voice carried. "Whyever would I want to go out? I just got here."

Wheeler sneered, Sutherland seemed frozen, and for the first time Cole looked uncertain. "Perhaps we *should* go somewhere else," he suggested.

"Oh, I wouldn't think of it!" I chirped gaily. Feigning an obliviousness equal to his, I signaled a waiter. "Tea, please. With cream."

Judging from the faces around me, that was the most unusual thing yet. But the waiter obeyed.

"By George!" shouted a baggy-eyed older man with a billowing beard and a reverse widow's peak. Rising from a nearby table, he declaimed, "This is going too far! Soon there won't be a single place in the whole town where a man can escape from these hussies!"

I heard outcries of support for him from all around the room. Metcalfe alone protested the application of the term *hussy* to me.

Like I told Nye, anger gave me eloquence. I wasn't always sure it was an admirable trait, but it served me well. "Sir, you are the second most detestable specimen of manhood I have encountered this week. Since I did not slap *him*, I will refrain from slapping *you*. But let it be known that it is not the woman who is creating a public scene."

Wheeler clucked his tongue is disdain. Cole, his smile now as frozen as Sutherland's, swallowed audibly. Metcalfe seemed ready to burst into heroics.

The outraged bearded curmudgeon sputtered twice before exclaiming, "Madam, do you know who I am?"

"No more than you know who I am," I retorted.

The man positively swelled, throwing out his chest and lifting his chin pugnaciously. "I am Colonel William Conant Church, publisher of the *Army and Navy Journal*, co-founder of the Metropolitan Museum of Art, co-founder and former president of the National Rifle Association, founding member of the Military Order of the Loyal Legion of the United States, and, most importantly, owner of this building. As for who *you* are, I neither know nor care beyond the fact that you are an intruder—a damned suffragette, imposing her presence where she does not belong!"

"You were a goddamn brevet lieutenant colonel, Billy, which makes you less of a colonel than I ever was," came a voice from the door.

My heart flooded with relief at the sight of Colonel Cockerill pushing his way through the crowd, Bill Nye at his shoulder. He continued to speak loudly, for all to hear. "As for who the young lady is, if you read any paper other than your own and the blasted *Sun*, you would know her at once. She's the reporter who turned Blackwell's upside down last year, and she's about to do the same to Albany. More than that, she's a goddamn reporter, with as much right to enter a restaurant for reporters as anyone, and more than most of the fatheads drawing pay from either one of us."

It was too perfect. Reaching into my bag, I placed my card on the table between me and Colonel Church. "Pleasure to meet you, Colonel. Nellie Bly."

"That's right," said Cockerill appreciatively. "Best watch out, Church, or you'll be the victim of her next exposé."

Unable to tolerate my interloping presence any longer, Church threw bills down upon the table, gathered up his topcoat and hat, and stormed for the door.

Which left Colonel Cockerill staring between me, Cole, Sutherland, Metcalfe, and Wheeler. The Colonel's eyes narrowed dangerously.

Leaning around him, Nye chirped, "Bly."

"Nye."

The Colonel's eyes settled on Cole, rightly picking out the cause of this scene. "Let's all have a seat." He glanced around to nearby tables for objectors, saw other *World* reporters, and said, "Anyone who works for me, join us. I'm buying."

A slow scraping of benches brought in Anders from the city desk, Jerrold of shipping news, Bernstein from the police beat, and the artist McDougall. Metcalfe pulled out the bench for me to sit, with Wheeler unwillingly on my other side. Thinking I should greet them, I realized I didn't know any of their first names! Around the *World*, people only employed surnames or nicknames.

The waiter returned with my order. Spying it, the Colonel grinned. "Tea?"

"Tea," I said. "It's what all the good hussies drink." That got several chuckles and a bark of a laugh from the Colonel.

"I've always wanted to be a hussy," replied Nye puckishly. "Tea for me. With cream," he added in a parody of me. Nye was a famous beer drinker.

The Colonel snorted. "Tea for me, too. Sugar." He stared around at the other *World* workers, each of whom sheepishly ordered tea as well. Wheeler rolled his eyes to convey his disgust.

Above the solidarity, above even the sense of triumph, I was enjoying Cole's agonized embarrassment. He was the last to order, and he asked for coffee.

The Colonel turned his intense stare upon me, and I wondered if this was how he had looked when he'd shot a man in his office back in St. Louis. "Now, Bly, if you goddamn please, what in the world are you doing here?"

Cole shot me a panicked glance. Though I was furious with him, I now felt like laughing, or crying, or both at once. In trying to prove I didn't belong, Cole had achieved the opposite. I had been defended as a member of the *World*.

Victorious, it would be ungracious to turn him in. Besides, I never liked tattlers. "This was a kind of a dare, Colonel. I thought how interesting it would be to write a story on how men act when they think no woman is watching. Silly, I suppose."

The Colonel was no fool. Still, he nodded as if he believed my tale. "Typical Bly. Well, welcome to the Albion."

A silence followed. I had to imagine that, were I not present, the men would break into ribaldry and, perhaps, belch? Or perhaps they might have launched into a high-minded debate over Shakespearean sonnets? Whichever was true, my presence was a clear deterrent. Just as the snow had ground the great city to a halt, so my company had thrown a blanket of ice water on the usual conversation.

So, I chose to fill the void. "Does anyone mind if we talk business for a minute?" Miniscule shakes of the head and half-shrugs. Looking to the Colonel, I said, "I got him."

Puffing his cigar to life, his eyes lit up at once. "Spill."

I told him about the interview, and the marked paper. Sutherland perked up as I mentioned the names, and I told him, "It's exactly as you predicted. He listed off a bunch of assemblymen he said he could buy."

"Do you remember them?" demanded Sutherland.

I started reaching into my bag, but Cockerill put his hand over mine. "Not here. That list is a treasure. Guard it with your life."

Chastened, I put it away. Fortunately, I'd written my notes up twice already, once by hand and once on the typewriter, so the names were floating around in my head. "Let me see. He said Tallmadge."

"Never. Straight as the day is long. He only got into politics to reform charities, including the local insane asylum."

"Good for him. Gallagher?"

"Him, I'd believe. He's been on the Buffalo Board of Trade practically since birth."

"DeWitt?"

"No idea."

"Prime?"

"Spencer Gilcrest Prime. He might need the money—he runs a little shop. And he sports a fatter moustache than you, Colonel."

"Impossible," said the Colonel, stroking his lip warmer fondly.

I pressed on. "Hagan?"

"Definitely a member of the Black Horse Brigade. He owns a saloon and speculates in real estate."

"And someone else I can't recall."

"I'll wager it was McLaughlin."

"Yes!"

Sutherland nodded, pleased. "He's the Headless Horseman of the Black Horse Brigade. He owes any success he has to the fact that he's related to Boss McLaughlin, head of the Brooklyn Ring. They got the Brooklyn Bridge built, rife with graft, which was why the first caisson caught on fire."

"The good with the bad," said Anders. "That bridge is a feat."

The Colonel nodded. "That's the difference between functional corruption and the looters. Functional corruption lasts forever. Charley, of that list, what are the parties?"

"Four Republicans, two Democrats. At least one innocent man."

The Colonel shook his head. "We can't comment on their guilt or innocence. We just report what Phelps said."

"And get sued for libel," observed Anders, staring at me.

"*We* didn't say it," retorted the Colonel. "We're just reporting what Phelps said. *And* put into writing. That document is a smoking gun, not against them, but that he made the damning statement."

"He also mentioned a Mr. Pierce?" I said. "That a Mr. Pierce was already working to have the bill killed?"

Sutherland burst out laughing, along with several others. "You mean Congressman Pierce? Of course he's working to have the bill killed! Have you never heard of Dr. Pierce's Golden Medical Discovery?"

"Or Dr. Pierce's Pleasant Purgative Pellets?" added Jerrold from shipping, making his only contribution to the conversation.

"That's him?" I demanded, wide-eyed. Mother used the Purgative Pellets.

The Colonel cut through the laughter. "Bly, what's next?"

"I'm meeting Phelps tomorrow for the payment." I turned to Nye. "Mr. Nye, did you get that telegram off?"

"Indeed I did, Miss Sly." He winked at me.

I laughed. "Thank you, Mr. Fry."

The Colonel rubbed his hands together in grim excitement. "Excellent goddamn work, Bly. And what a consarned fool he is, to let you leave with that list. The perils of a pretty face. Hm. Okey-doke. When you meet, don't pay him."

I blinked. "*Don't* pay him? I thought we wanted to catch him depositing a bribe."

"We have enough now. Or rather, we will. It'll be e-goddamn-nough that he wants to get paid. Tell him to meet you at your hotel to pick up the check. Sutherland, you wait in the lobby of—what hotel did you say?"

My mind raced to recall my lies. "I told him sometimes the Sturtevant, sometimes the Gilsey."

"No good. Too easy to lose somebody there. Tell him you're staying at—at the St. James. There's one entrance, Charley can see anybody coming in. That way we have a witness of him attempting to pick up the check."

Sutherland did not look pleased, but he nodded agreement. McDougall said, "Do you want me there to draw him?"

The Colonel shook his head. "I mean, yes, I want art. But no need to see him. Think the fat-cat lobbyist sitting on a pile of cash. Just make his sideburns dad-blasted enormous and it'll be right."

"They *are* special," I agreed.

"Bly, after your interview, come directly to the *World* and write it all up. Give that note to McDougall to prepare it for print." He grinned. "Saturday, we'll send an early copy of the story to Phelps."

I was startled. "Why?"

"So he can comment."

"Will he?"

Sutherland answered that. "Knowing Phelps, he won't be able to resist. We've been after him a long time." The reporter sounded upset.

"This is going to be the scoop of the year," said Cole, a little too enthusiastically. Jerrold and Bernstein made half-hearted toasts to me with their tea.

Bill Nye, at least, seemed genuinely happy for me. "Can't wait to read how your meeting goes, Miss Vie," he said, patting my arm.

"I'll give you a firsthand account, Mr. Dry." *Look at me, trading quips with Bill Nye!*

Rolling his eyes, Wheeler took out his watch and opened it. "Excuse me," he said, rising. "I have a curtain time. Metcalfe. Colonel."

"Crinkle," said the Colonel.

With a withering glance at me, Wheeler moved away, putting on his coat as he headed for the door. *What in Heaven's name did I ever do to him?*

Checking his own watch, Metcalfe shook his head. It was hours before curtain time for any show. Nye filled the silence by asking Metcalfe if he was also seeing a show.

"Yes. It's Margaret Mather's last week at Niblo's before she moves to an exclusive contract at the Standard. Cole and I are off to see her in a revival of Tobin's *The Honey Moon.*"

"Oh, I like her," I said with real warmth. "I saw her Lady Macbeth last month."

"I like her too," replied Metcalfe, grinning. "Though most critics don't. They think she's too indecorous."

"Maybe that's what I like about her," I said, aiming for a wicked glint in my eye.

"Why?" asked Nye innocently. "Does she remind you of anyone you know?"

We all laughed, even the curmudgeons. Cockerill laughed especially hard for some reason. Metcalfe asked him, "What show are you seeing tonight, Colonel?"

Cockerill reddened a little, but said bravely, "*The Main Line.*"

"Back to the Grand Opera House?" smiled Metcalfe. "It *is* quite attractive."

I got the sense that Metcalfe was ribbing him. I also got the sense that the men were restraining their comments in my presence. Clearly my assumption was correct—the Colonel had a sweetheart, or was at least giving some young lady his attention. By Metcalfe's remarks, I further deduced that she was an actress. *Phew! Good luck to him!*

I decided to relieve everyone's minds and depart. Instantly, Cole said, "James and I will walk with you. Stretch our legs before the show."

I had a sense of what was coming, and after our farewells to the Colonel and the rest of the *World* staff, I was proved correct. Just as we reached the street and I was opening my umbrella, Cole touched my sleeve and leaned beneath it. "You're a good sport, Bly. It would've been my job if you peached. Thanks for having a sense of humor."

"A sense of decency," corrected Metcalfe, shoving Cole lightly out into the rain. "A sense of humor is reserved for pranks that are funny." Turning to me, the theatre reviewer arched that incredible left eyebrow at me, this time in wry amusement. "What say we punish Cole and I take you to see Mather instead?"

Surprised, and wondering if he was serious, I made a show of temporizing. "Tempting . . . but I have a big day tomorrow."

"Right! Trapping your lobbyist. Let me tell you, there are going to be a lot of red faces in Albany." His sinister brow twitched even higher over his violet eyes. "At the *World*, too."

It was a warning I did not need. I had seen the others. Sutherland had looked frustrated enough to chew through his own arm. "We'll see. I have to get the story first."

Cole said, "C'mon, Metcalfe! I'm getting soaked."

"No less than you deserve," snapped Metcalfe over his shoulder. Returning his gaze to me, his eyes narrowed. "Here's an idea. Why don't we celebrate your success tomorrow evening? I have two tickets for an amateur production of *The Pirates of Penzance*. Care to join me?"

I froze. *Is this another trap?* He didn't seem that kind of man. But neither was he Ingram, perfectly upright and honest. There was something of the devil in Metcalfe. And I found myself liking it—and him.

"I'd be delighted," I said.

A half hour later I arrived home, hoping to find Albert and Jane long vanished and my room my own again. But those hopes were dashed even before I had the key in the lock, as I heard my brother's voice. I couldn't make out his words through the door, but whatever he was saying, his tone was wry and sarcastic. *Nice to know he's like that out of my presence as well.*

I was barely in the door before Mother was upon me. She was dressed to go out, but not to dinner. She was wearing church clothes. Albert and Jane were as well. "Thank Heaven, there you are," said Mother. "Don't worry, I unpacked for you—goodness, Pink, what a dress that bombazine is. Please don't wear it tonight. I think the gray flannel will be best. Go on, you just have time to change."

"Change for what?" I asked. "Who are we meeting? I can't go out, I have important work in the morning."

Mother's face hardened, and she looked disappointed and hurt at once. Which left it to Albert to fill in the blanks. "Really, Pink, it's bad enough you skipped Ash Wednesday service. But you can't avoid the vigil for Maundy Thursday."

I closed my eyes. I had entirely forgotten that it was Holy Week. That was why the church bells in Albany had been pealing at full force. And we wouldn't even be going to the Methodist church four blocks from us. No, we would be heading almost four miles south along Seventh Avenue in evening traffic. As soon as Mother had arrived in the city, she had fallen in love with the John Street Methodist Church, and it had become her Sunday morning routine. The fact that I stayed home as often as I went was a source of deep disappointment to her—never mind the occasional Sunday when she chose to stay home with me.

But Mother was clearly looking forward to the Maundy Thursday services. So, instead of relaxing at home and mentally preparing for my next meeting with Phelps, I dutifully dressed in the gray flannel skirt and coat so I could attend a night of symbolic foot washing and Tenebrae.

Things got even better. As we left my apartment, Mother said, "Albert and Jane are staying through Easter. Isn't that marvelous?" She said this last with such an intensely earnest look, eye to eye, that I knew I was receiving a preemptive admonishment.

Disregarding Mother's implied warning, I literally groaned. And why not? After all, I was heading to have my sins washed away.

I should have accepted Metcalfe's invitation after all. I could have been at *The Honey Moon*!

TESTIMONY

EDWARD R. PHELPS, sworn, testified as follows:

Examined by MR. SAXTON:

Q. Did you say that you could get those gentlemen whose names I have mentioned, or any of them, for one thousand dollars?

A. No, sir.

Q. Or that in substance?

A. No, sir.

Q. Did you use any such expression as that, or anything similar to that, with reference to those gentlemen, in that interview?

A. No, sir; there was nothing of the kind talked about.

Q. Or at the interview you had with her in New York. You had an interview with her in New York City, did you?

A. Yes, sir.

Q. Where was that?

A. That was at 115 Broadway.

Q. That is where your office is?

A. Yes, sir.

Q. Did you use any such language as that in that interview?

A. No, sir.

Q. Or anything like it?

A. No, sir.

Q. Did you mention the names of those gentlemen, or any of them, during that interview in New York City?

A. No, sir. There was no occasion to.

Q. I did not ask you that. I simply ask you if you did. You say you did not?

A. Yes, sir.

SIX

PAYOFF

FRIDAY, MARCH 30, 1888

AFTER BREAKFAST THE NEXT MORNING, I had to break the news to Mother that I could not attend Good Friday services with her. She made her disappointment manifestly clear. *What, no credit in the bank from going last night?* "I have to work," I explained.

"Don't worry, Mother," said Albert, her white knight. "Jane and I will take you."

The silver lining was that they were gone before I had to don my Mrs. Consul costume. I put a little extra thought into it. A woman staying in hotels might wear the same dress to multiple meetings, but she would at least try to break it up. With that in mind, I borrowed Mother's long sealskin dolman. It had been my Christmas gift to her, as it had reminded her of a fashionable version of the coverings worn by the natives we'd seen in Mexico. Costing nearly two hundred fifty dollars, it was by far the most expensive item of clothing in my home. *Exactly the kind of thing Mrs. Consul would wear on a rainy New York day.*

After puttering about the house for a time, practicing my story, I emerged from my apartment at eleven thirty and had the doorman summon a hansom cab for me.

"The Boris Building," I told the driver. "115 Broadway. No rush." I was already going to be early, and it was only a ten-minute cab ride.

We pulled up before a five-story brick office building. I told the driver to wait for me—I wanted my escape ready—and I took the elevator to the topmost floor. Down the hall to my left was a smoked glass door with a gilded 97. Just below the number was the name EDWARD R. PHELPS. No honorific or any other signifier.

Before I could even knock, the door swung wide, and there was the lobbyist, smiling sweetly at me. "Mrs. Consul! Punctual and perfect, of course. Please, do come in." As he closed the door behind me, I noticed that through its darkened glass pane, one could see the elevator clearly. This explained his prompt appearance.

He was using a cane today, stumping along with it in obvious discomfort as he led me to his left into a dark-paneled room with large windows. A young man sat behind the office's lone desk. There was enough physical resemblance that I hardly needed Phelps's introduction of, "My son, John Phelps. Johnny, Mrs. Consul."

"A pleasure to meet you," I said, timidly shaking his hand before withdrawing mine.

"Pleasure's all mine," said son Johnny. He was handsome in a moustache-twirling sort of way. Taller than his father, he looked fit, as if he played a sport on the weekends. He wore a little hatchet pin on his lapel, the kind little boys wore as a reward for not lying— a reference to George Washington and the cherry tree. I wondered if he wore it as a joke.

Pulling out a hard-backed lawyer's chair for me, Phelps senior winced. "Are you well?" I asked.

"Forgive me. A touch of rheumatism."

"I'm so sorry," I said, seating myself.

He flexed his fingers around his cane. "When I was four, I fell out of a neighbor's tree. They say that's what caused it."

"Was it a cherry tree?" In answer to his curious expression, I nodded at Johnny's lapel pin. Both Phelpses laughed, and the father said, "Yes, of course. And I cut it down so that no other boy would be as tempted as I was."

"Well, perhaps I should send you some of my husband's patent medicine. He swears it will relieve joint pain."

"I would be so grateful," replied Phelps dutifully. The matter raised, he wasted no time. "I suppose you know about the bill?"

"Oh, no," I moaned in seeming despair. "Can't it be killed?"

"On the contrary," said Phelps, smiling so broadly his side whiskers trembled, "it has been killed already."

"No! So soon?" I marveled. "I never . . . how clever you are!"

"Well," said Phelps, opening his hands in an expansive gesture, "I saw that you were anxious to kill the bill, and I told you I would get it done. Well, it's done. That bill will never bother your husband's business again. Johnny?"

With a bob of obedience and a smile for me, Phelps junior plucked up his silk hat. "I'll just go and see about Sunday."

As his heir departed, the king of the lobby crossed to his desk and seated himself in his throne.

"Are you attending Easter service?" I asked.

"What? Oh, Sunday. Yes, of course. But it's also my birthday, you see. April Fools' Day. Quite good, no?"

"But you're clearly no fool," I said in a tone of admiring wonder. "How did you ever manage it?"

Phelps employed a confidential tone. "Why, you see, I went to work on it right away. First off, I had it transferred from the committee that originally had it. As I told you, Mr. Crosby could not be bought. I knew he and some others were determined to pass it, so I went to the ones I told you I could buy and explained to them that I wanted the bill killed. Fortunately for us, they were equally anxious to get rid of it. At my suggestion, they had it reported back to the Committee on Public Health. I knew I could get them easier."

"Oh, how very clever!" I breathed rapturously to this utter rigmarole. He had, of course, done none of this, as it was already before the Committee on Public Health, and already dead even before we spoke. "They did not refuse?"

"No-no. They simply asked what it was worth. I told them one thousand dollars. They promised to do it."

"I'm amazed," I said.

"You see, my dear, that's my business. I'm the head of the lobby."

"Oh, indeed! What a good thing I went to you." Wide-eyed, I inclined my head toward him. In a breathless tone I said, "How can you ever do all the work?"

His chest swelled beneath his waistcoat. "Oh, I'm hardly a one-man band. I keep a lot of runners who watch everything that happens. They report to me, and keep records in my rooms of every bill and every incident connected with it. You noticed when you gave me the bill in the Kenmore I went into another room and got a large book? Well, by that book I at once saw all about the bill and knew just what to say to you."

"What did you say to the committee about the bill?" I asked, curiously.

"I just told them the bill had to be killed, and I told them it was worth a grand—a thousand dollars. I had to give my check for it right off," he added, indicating he was out of pocket on my behalf.

His smile, combined with the heavy implication of my debt to him, caused me to throw up a quick defense, mentioning my fictional husband. "Frank—I mean, Mr. Consul—could not understand how you could buy the whole committee for a thousand dollars. It seems like such a small sum."

"Oh, it wouldn't have worked for anyone who walked in off the street. But, you see, this is my business. I spend all my time at it. I pay these men heavily on other bills, so that makes some bills more moderate."

"Can you have any bill killed?"

He placed his hands flat upon his desk, and in that moment he did look almost regal in his criminality. "I have control of the assembly and can pass or kill any bill that so pleases me. Next week, I am going to pass some bills and I'll get ten thousand dollars for it."

"So much!"

"Pooh! I often get that and more to pass or kill a bill."

I should have probed further, gotten some hint of the bills he was planning on having passed. But I was struck dumb, and genuinely did not know what to say to such brazen effrontery.

Phelps removed a copy of the *Albany Evening Journal* from his briefcase and handed it across to me. The semiweekly was folded to display a list of recent legislative decisions. "You can take this to show your husband that the bill was killed. You will also see an account of it in today's *World*."

Perhaps, I thought, tucking the paper into my bag. *But Sunday's* World *will say so with far more detail.*

Phelps produced a cigar and began the work of lighting it. "Now, Mrs. Consul, I would truly appreciate it if you could tell me who sent you to me. Not that I want to pry into your affairs, you see. But it may be one of my agents, and I want to pay him."

It was on the tip of my tongue to say "Colonel Cockerill," but we still had to close the trap. I could invent a name, but that might make him suspicious. *Best stay on the same track as in Albany.* "I wouldn't be comfortable giving his name without his consent. But I will ask him," I added quickly.

He shrugged, then returned to the subject of money. "I have to pay the money for killing the bill to the committee this week, and as I got it done so quickly, I thought I would deal honestly with you and only charge you two hundred fifty dollars for my expenses. That will make a total of twelve hundred fifty dollars. Could you write a check here for that amount?"

"I—oh, dear, I'm dreadfully frightened," I exclaimed.

He made the show of a man demonstrably bracing himself to be patient with a woman. His smile became tighter, and his telltale stutter returned as he said, "F-f-frightened of me?"

"No, of course not. It's just that my husband told me not to do anything that would connect me with this affair, you see? For that reason, I don't want to give a check made out to you."

He relaxed slightly. I wasn't haggling the price, just the form of payment. "Nothing simpler! Write out a check payable to J. F. Chesbrough. He is a relative of m-m-mine, it's just the same as giving it to me. Or you could make it out in my son's name?"

"No, I'm sorry, I'd prefer not to make it out to anyone named Phelps. You understand." He closed his eyes and nodded sagely. "But this Mr. Chesbrough sounds fine. Send your son up to the St. James Hotel, where I am stopping, and I will give it to him there."

Phelps puffed and blew an impressive ring of smoke into the air over his head. An unholy halo. "That will do. I'll write the name for you," and suiting the action to the word he took from his desk a small white envelope and wrote out "J.F. Chesbrough." In the corner he scribbled the amount, just to be certain, then handed it to me. "My son will go up with you and get the ch-ch-check. Johnny! Johnny!"

So that's why son Johnny is here. The lobby kid does the actual fleecing of the lamb. This could mean trouble. If Johnny were to stick by me to make certain I didn't skip out on the bill, I would have to figure out a way to give him a check. Or to lose him. "Oh, then I might just as well get the money and hand it to him."

"As you please," said Phelps. Taking the envelope from me, he tore the ends and back off of it.

I need to save that name! Quickly, I said, "Give me that. On second thought, I'll write the check and give it to your son."

He handed it back. The name was still clear, but the numbers were partially torn away. I tucked it away with the newspaper just as Johnny made his reappearance.

Sucking and exhaling on his cigar several times, the lobby king frowned at me. I worried my hemming and hawing might have given me away. After a moment he said, "I received your telegram, by the bye."

"Did you?"

"Yes. I must say, it eased my m-m-mind considerably."

"Were you uneasy?"

"I felt qu-qu-queer about you at first," said Phelps speculatively. "You see, it is not the most natural thing in the world for a woman to come to me for such work. First, I thought it was a trap to catch me." He said the word *trap* so clearly that I knew he had almost stuttered on it.

My jaw hanging open, I looked first at him and then at his son. "Trap? Do people try to do that? Should I be concerned?"

"No-no. We can protect you. But, yes, some do-gooders do attempt on occasion to b-b-burst the boiler of government. When I saw how innocent you were, and how honest, I knew you couldn't be one of those. I must say I was surprised, though."

"Well, you see, I didn't know what to do." I didn't have to act in order to seem flustered and embarrassed. "I was so ignorant of it all."

Leaning against the front of the desk, son Johnny glanced me over, and let me see him doing so. My cheeks began to burn. Clearly, he wanted to help cure my ignorance.

"Madam is going up to the St. James," the lobbyist told his son. "You are to go with her. She will give you a check there for some w-w-work I have been doing for her."

I had to find a way to escape them, while still luring them to the hotel for Sutherland to see. "Can't you come instead, Mr. Phelps? I hate to have your son connected with this. Besides, I am better acquainted with you."

"Father, you go," said Johnny, seeing I was not a hen ripe for plucking. "You might as well. You would leave the office in a half hour, anyway."

"Wait," I said suddenly. "I have a cab at the door. I can't be seen riding with either of you. Not if people are watching."

Hoisted on his own petard, Phelps tried to convince me there was no danger. I stayed firm.

"Look, Father," said Johnny, obviously trying to keep his afternoon to himself, "why not take the train and meet her there? You'll probably arrive at the same time."

"He can wait for me in the parlor," I said. "I'll get the money, and when I go in the parlor I will hand it to him. No one will see me there." No one would, because I wouldn't be there.

"Where will you get the m-m-money?" asked Phelps impudently.

"Father, that's nothing to you, so she gets it," said Johnny, and had he not been the offspring of this vile human I would have kissed him in heartfelt thanks.

Grudgingly, Phelps conceded. "In a half hour, in the parlor of the St. James Hotel?"

"Yes," I replied.

I gathered my things and son Johnny walked me to the elevator. "I was extremely nervous over this," I explained to him, my voice full of apology.

"You'll get over that by the time you have another bill to kill," he said encouragingly.

I laughed. "I think you're right."

On the street, I gave the driver instructions to take a roundabout way to Newspaper Row and to pass the St. James on his way. Unlike my Albany cabbie, he didn't offer a hint of curiosity, which made me wonder what strange instructions he must get in a day. But he knew his business, and after ten minutes I felt confident that I was not being followed.

I had him pull up in front of the Albion, and I was tempted to run inside and shout my triumph in Colonel Church's bearded face.

But I had a story to publish. I bolted through the *World*'s doors, took the elevator to the newsroom, and—stuffing my ears with cotton—began writing down the whole interview from memory. At two o'clock, the Colonel appeared. Rather than tell him the whole story, I handed him pages while I circled back to start writing the whole piece from the start. Within seconds he was grinning broadly, though he was already taking a blue pencil to my work. Mentions of his rheumatism and his birthday were struck, as was any mention of the stutter. Nothing was to be kept that would make Phelps look sympathetic.

Dropping the pages down, the Colonel held out his open palm. "Do you have that list?" I passed it over, and he squinted at it intensely. "Huh. You're right, you can see the difference. But it's too goddamn faint. We'll have to make them darker for print. McDougall!" The artist emerged from his curtained workspace and sauntered over to receive the paper and his instructions. In return, he showed me his drawing of Phelps seated atop a pile of money bags, a crown upon his head. "Perfect."

I was closing in on the end of the first draft of the piece when Sutherland appeared, grinning from ear to ear. He went directly to the Colonel's office, which was annoying, as he was working on *my* story. I followed him, arriving just in time to hear him launch into his tale from the St. James Hotel.

"Phelps arrived a few minutes before two, and leaned against a pillar as he waited, looking up and down Broadway for Miss Bly. His son came up—he's grown a moustache since last I saw him—and chatted up his father. Young Phelps then went through the hotel to the ladies' parlor. When he came back empty-handed, they talked again, then headed to the corner of Broadway and Twenty-Sixth. They were going to see me there, so I stepped into Delmonico's. Phelps junior tried the hotel again, and was gone for ten minutes. They decided to try for the Broadway entrance to the hotel, and sonny went in again." Sutherland's grin stretched from ear to ear. "The Delmonico's staff was getting annoyed with me lingering in their window, so I stepped outside and went up to the Hoffman, then doubled back and bumped into Phelps as if by accident."

"You did *what?*" I said, shocked.

"Did you give us away?" asked the Colonel. He did not seem nearly as upset as I was.

"I spooked him for sure. I shook him by the hand and asked after his health—he was leaning hard on his stick. He said his rheumatism was up, but he couldn't help enjoying such a beautiful day after all that snow. I went into the hotel, saying I had a late lunch there, and I bumped into Junior on his way out. From the hotel I saw them travel up to the corner of Broadway and Twenty-fifth. Junior came in one last time, then at ten after three they gave up the ghost and headed off down Broadway."

"Why did you talk to him?" I demanded. "Now he'll suspect!"

"Let him," said Sutherland. "There's nothing he can do now."

"That's right, Bly," agreed the Colonel. "You've got him. In fact, I'll send him an early copy of the story and invite him to respond. Let him dig himself in deeper. He won't be able to help himself." Cockerill's brow darkened. "Bly, there's no conceivable way he can trace you, is there?"

I thought for a moment. "No. I never gave him anything, not even a card. And if he didn't follow me here from the Boris Building, I don't see how he can connect me with my home, or even the *World* . . ." I trailed off, looking at Sutherland.

"Damn," said Sutherland. "He could have the *World* watched. My fault. Sorry, Bly."

"We'll sneak you out tonight," declared the Colonel. "And I want you to have a bodyguard."

"You're joking," I said, even as the blood drained from my face. I had a sudden recollection of being surrounded by Mexican policemen threatening physical harm to my person.

"I'm not. I told you, he's not playing for small change. He stands to lose a business that's making him a fortune. I don't know that there's anything he wouldn't do to protect it."

"I'm going to a show with Metcalfe tonight," I said.

"Really?" asked Sutherland.

"Why not?" I shot back.

He quickly shook his head. The Colonel looked slightly mollified. "I'll talk to him, make sure he gets you home safe. But don't come here again until the story is in print. No need for un-goddamn-necessary risks. Come Monday, I'll figure something out."

EXACTLY AS PLANNED, METCALFE ARRIVED to scuttle me out the back of the *World* offices, though he was forced to wait as the Colonel, Sutherland, and I pored over the story. But at seven o'clock the Colonel announced he had someplace to be, so I allowed Metcalfe to surreptitiously escort me to the New Opera House for the Opera Club's production of Gilbert and Sullivan's *The Pirates of Penzance.*

As it turned out, it was not yet a full production, but an open rehearsal, allowing the reviewers and backers a preview of the show, which would not open for another two weeks. Yet it was fully staged, with costumes and scenery, though some of the drops were for the wrong play—the rocky mountain of the song had yet to be painted.

I felt a fresh twinge of guilt for disappointing Mother on Good Friday, but this was exactly the fun relief I needed, laughing and singing along under my breath with the songs that one could hardly help knowing, so ubiquitous were they.

At one point in the first act, Metcalfe leaned close to my ear. "See her," he whispered, pointing to one pretty chorus girl who was notable more for her enthusiasm than her talent.

"Yes," I whispered back, reminded of my disastrous stint as a chorus girl at the start of the month. In fact, the pretty girl looked familiar, and I could have sworn she had been an Amazon alongside me. What was her name? Eleanor? Lenore?

"Leonora Barner," said Metcalfe, unknowingly resolving my dilemma. "Remember her."

"Why?" I asked.

Grinning, Metcalfe pressed his fingers to his lips. I was frustrated until intermission, when I spied none other than Colonel Cockerill rushing backstage. He was carrying flowers. *He couldn't wait until after the show?* I had no choice but to laugh. *Good for her! I* thought. *At least she won't have to dip into her paltry five-dollars-per-week salary to dine tonight. Little wonder the Colonel's been in such high spirits all week!*

The show resumed, and I was just as amused by the Colonel's rapturous face in the front row as I was by the antics of the Major-General and his daughters attempting to reform the Pirate King and his crew. Cockerill had eyes only for Leonora.

Metcalfe and I departed the theatre as soon as the show was over, with him waving off hails from several acquaintances. Outside, we agreed to take a hansom down ten blocks to Delmonico's—the same place Sutherland had taken refuge while watching Phelps.

Though nothing like the weather of two weeks prior, it was a brisk evening, yet I was perfectly warm, still wrapped in Mother's sealskin dolman. To avoid a quarrel with her, I hadn't gone home to change, so as we emerged from the theatre I apologized to Metcalfe once more for my matronly costume. "I promise, this is not my habitual dress!"

"I understand," he assured me wryly. "In fact, I quite like the idea of escorting Nellie Bly in one of her many disguises. If I were going to write a review of the show, I would be sure to include it."

"You're not going to review it?" I asked. "Didn't you like it?"

"I very much did," replied Metcalfe, tossing his cigarette out the side of the cab. "Though I think it was mostly the company."

I laughed, pleased, but continued to question him. "Do they not deserve your acclaim then?"

"The performers, certainly. But the producers do not. I don't like pirates."

I cocked my head like a spaniel. "You went to see a show about pirates, and you don't like pirates?"

Metcalfe laughed. "I don't mind the seafaring type. But I hate a scoundrel." Seeing my confused expression, he said, "It was an unlicensed production."

"Oh?" I said, no better enlightened.

"Ever wonder why you see so much Gilbert and Sullivan here in the States? It's because American copyright law does not extend to foreigners. They're hailed as geniuses, but those geniuses don't make one red cent from their plays here in America unless they produce the damn things themselves. Excuse me," he added perfunctorily.

I waved away his profanity—around the Colonel, it was a disease one could not avoid catching. I was interested in what he was saying. "You mean no one pays them royalties for their shows?"

"No one in America, at any rate," said Metcalfe grimly. "Explains the popularity of their shows. That, and they're da—*darn* clever. But I try to only review licensed productions. Hurts the actors, I know, but I can't help it. I don't like cheats."

I felt a sudden warm kinship with Mr. James Metcalfe. "Neither do I."

"So I gather!" he said, smiling. "You got your lobbyist?"

"Not just *any* lobbyist," I said. "'The king of the lobby,' he calls himself."

"Oh, does he now?" said Metcalfe, laughing darkly. To my surprise and delight, he began to sing a tune borrowed from the show we'd just seen, with lyrics all his own:

When I sally forth to augment my pay,
I help my friends in an illegal way.
I sink a few more bills, it's true,
Than a well-bred lawyer ought to do;
But many a cad on a first-class train,
If he wants to continue his devious reign,
Must manage somehow to push through
The dirty work that only I can do!

Grinning so hard my face hurt, I joined him on the chorus:

For I'm the Lobby King!
I'm in the Capitol Ring!
Oh! What an uproarious,
Jolly and glorious,
Biz for a Lobby King!

When we were done laughing, I wiped a tear from my eye. "Would you mind terribly if I steal that?"

"Not in the slightest. If you'll allow me to steal this." And he kissed me on the cheek.

I ducked my chin, grinning, and did not protest beyond a chiding "Thief."

"Takes one to know one," replied a pleased Metcalfe, just as the hansom pulled up in front of the restaurant.

TESTIMONY

EDWARD R. PHELPS, sworn, testified as follows:
Examined by MR. MAGNER:

Q. You say you have been up here twenty years?

A. Yes, sir.

Q. Attending the sessions of the Legislature during that time?

A. I was sometimes.

Q. During all that time have you furnished bills for persons who inquired for them?

A. Who wanted them.

Q. And in an accommodating spirit?

A. Yes, sir.

Q. Never charge anything for them?

A. No, sir.

Q. Did you neglect your own business during this time?

A. My own business?

Q. Your own business in New York? This grain business?

A. No, sir.

Q. You do not carry it on up here?

A. You can buy all the grain you want here by telegraph.

Q. You were further away from the market?

A. Probably a minute.

Q. Do you not inconvenience yourself by being up here?

A. Not at all.

Q. Were you employed by any person up here?

A. Not at all.

Q. Were you in the habit of furnishing such information as Miss Bly called for without any charge?

A. Yes, sir.

Q. Have you done it heretofore for charge?

A. No, sir.

Q. Never received any consideration for doing it?

A. Sometimes I have and sometimes I haven't.

Q. Have you ever this year?

A. No, sir.

Q. From whom have you received consideration heretofore?

A. I don't recollect.

SEVEN

FOX HUNT

SUNDAY, APRIL 1, 1888

I SPENT EASTER MORNING WITH MY family. There was no escaping any of it, from early services through a large luncheon. Then came the nauseating farewells between Albert and Mother. She cried a little to see him go. When it was finally time for me to accompany Albert and Jane to the train station, I considered it my reward: the promise of a little resurrection of my own.

While waiting at the station, I couldn't help picking up a copy of the *World*. It was a special edition, and I was gleeful to discover from the newsboy that the paper had been forced to do a reprint because they had all sold out.

"What story have they broken?" I asked disingenuously.

"That girl, Nellie Bly, she got one of the crooks in government. Trapped him neat. A blow from the little guy, yeah?" I grinned, and he grinned back as he pocketed my money.

McDougall's drawing of the crowned Phelps leaning back atop his loot was placed prominently. I read my piece, looking for errors. Finding none, I perused Sutherland's follow-up. It was very wry. And clever! *Why didn't I think to refer to Phelps and his son as being in caucus, or adjourning for the day?*

Over my shoulder, Albert said, "I read it at breakfast."

I waited. It was inconceivable that I was about to be complimented by my elder brother. Yet, somehow, that infuriating hope still rose in me.

"What a clever little liar you are, Pink." With a chuckle, he walked off to rejoin Jane and see to their luggage. They had been forced to buy an extra bag for all the treats and clothes Mother had bought for them.

With *my* money, gotten from being a clever little liar.

When their train left the station, I raced for Newspaper Row and up to the *World*'s newsroom. Just a few years earlier, the *World* had started putting out evening editions, since there was always something new to print at the end of the day. Sunday was the sole exception, however, so I expected to find only a small staff on hand, working to prepare Monday's early edition.

Not so! Things were hopping far more than usual for a Sunday afternoon. It appeared to be all hands on deck. And rather than making a triumphant procession through the newsroom, I encountered a distinct chill—much colder than the blizzard we'd just endured. The rest of the paper had seen the story I had broken, and their resentment was thick in the air.

The sole exception was Bill Nye, who came over to shake me by the hand. "Well done, Miss Vie."

"Thank you, Mr. Wry. But why are you here? Surely the Colonel didn't call you in for this?"

"No. Escaping the requisite family dinner for a spell. And I'm starting up a joke contest through the paper. Need to set the rules. What better day than today?"

"Easter?"

He wrinkled his brow. "April first. The day upon which we are reminded of what we are on the other three hundred and sixty-four."

I laughed at the Twain quote. "It's also Phelps's birthday."

"Ooh! Many happy returns, your highness!" Waving, he sauntered off toward the elevators.

Cheered by Nye's buffoonery, I reached my desk to find a note instructing me to go to Cockerill's office. Refusing to wear a frilly bonnet in the newsroom—regardless of the custom of staying hatted—I shed my coat and Easter headpiece and sped to the frosted glass door. There, I encountered Marsh, who declined to even look at me. So I knocked on the door and stuck my head in.

"Ah! Bly! There you are. About damn time. You'll recognize my guest."

Sitting across from the Colonel was none other than Bourke Cockran! "Congressman!" I blurted, in utter shock.

The Irish-born New Yorker rose to take my hand. "Miss Cochrane-with-an-*e*. What did I say to Charles just a week ago? The ills of the world breed their own cure. And you, it seems, are the cure to many ills. Well done."

"Thank you." As he guided me to a seat, I shot a look of wide-eyed wonderment at the Colonel.

"I asked the congressman here to comment on the story from a legal perspective. After all, he is by now a goddamn expert on bribery."

"Would you mind terribly finding another way of phrasing that?" asked Cockran lightheartedly. "The words *congressman* and *bribery* close together are never appealing."

"You're the one who knows all about appealing," retorted Cockerill.

"Actually, I believe Miss Cochrane has us both beat on that front."

The Colonel frowned for a moment, thrown by my real name. To him, I would only ever be "Bly." Shaking off his confusion, he pressed on. "Bly, ask your friend here what's happening with the Sharp case. He won't give me a straight answer."

The congressman sighed expressively, his smile never wavering. "It's not that I won't. It's that I can't. Tomorrow, we're asking for a delay, due to his health."

"Is that boodler truly ill?" asked the Colonel.

"That he is a boodler is a matter for a court to decide. That he is ill is a matter of fact."

"He was convicted."

"That conviction was overturned."

"Thanks to fancy lawyering, not because of his innocence."

"'Beyond a reasonable doubt' has a lovely ring to it, don't you think, Colonel?"

"And you're still seeking a change of venue?"

"How can a man receive a fair trial when his name has become synonymous with graft, thanks to a deliberate system of perversion, falsification, and misrepresentation on the part of the press to mold the minds of the citizens of this county, from whom the jury must be drawn."

Cockerill grinned. "You're trying out arguments, aren't you?"

The congressman laughed. "We have a hearing tomorrow afternoon. I'm off to see Sharp tonight."

"Off the record, how is he, really?"

"Off the record, and between friends, he is deathly ill. I'm only seeking seven days' delay in the court, because I doubt if the case will not, by that time, have been removed from the courts by death."

At last the Colonel appeared satisfied. "All right. What about Phelps? Care to weigh in? Anonymously, of course—but with a lengthy quote. What do you think of his confession to Bly here?"

"The confession is full, complete, and convincing. Well done," he added, for my benefit, before returning to his answer. "A confession alone, however, is not sufficient to convict. There must be some corroborating proof that the crime being charged has actually been committed."

"Says who?" demanded the Colonel.

"Says the Court of Appeals," replied the congressman coolly. "In the *People v. Jaehne*, the court held that a confession itself was *some* proof that a crime had been committed, and sufficient proof that the defendant had *committed* the crime, but that corroborating evidence was required to confirm the confession. To quote Chief Justice Nelson: 'Slight corroboration is sufficient.'"

"What do we have by way of goddamn corroboration?"

"You have three points. First, the transfer of the bill from one committee to another, along with Phelps's admission that he bribed certain assemblymen to make it happen."

"But the bill was never in the one committee," I objected. "He only *said* it was transferred."

"I see. Watch out, then. They're going to hang their hat on that. But the list of names with the check marks remains your strongest card. Second, you have the various memoranda which Phelps gave to Miss Cochrane, including the clipping containing his office address and the cutting from the check with the name Cheeseborough or whatever upon it. Third, his appearance at the St. James Hotel to get the money, which can be proved by independent evidence."

"In your expert opinion, Cockran, how does it stack up?" asked the Colonel.

The congressman spread his hands. "I am thoroughly convinced that there is sufficient evidence to go to a jury and convict Phelps."

"Thanks, Congressman. Can you jot that down for us?"

"Willingly. Not for attribution."

"Of course. And how about an exclusive on Sharp?"

"Never. You may quote me on that."

"Had to try," grinned the Colonel.

The congressman took his leave, bypassing Marsh, who hovered in the open door like a hummingbird, a paper in his hand.

"Well, Marsh, what's the dad-blamed matter?"

"Phelps, Colonel. He sent his reply."

The Colonel made a half-strangled crowing sound as he leapt up to pluck the paper from Marsh's grip. Dying to read it, I placed myself indecorously over the Colonel's shoulder and scanned, growing angrier with every line:

To the Editor of The World:

I have read with some amusement from time to time the remarkable stories got up by your smart female confidence correspondent, Nellie Bly, who must be admitted to be the champion story-teller of the age. I have no objection to the attention she has now paid to me, but I do object to her resorting to groundless statements that affect other people in her efforts to concoct a sensational romance such as you seem to suppose your readers relish.

The fact is that I had a visit at my hotel in Albany last Wednesday from the fair Nellie, who came to tell me gravely that she wanted my services to kill a bill relating to quack medicines, then in the Assembly. Naturally I asked the dear girl what she knew about legislation, how she became interested in quack medicines and who sent her to me. On the first question she professed an interesting verdancy, to the second she pleaded a husband (which, for her sake, I hope will not long be a false pretense), and to the third she objected to say what valued friend had mentioned my name to her as what you call the "King of the Lobby," but professed to be eager to pay me $4,000 or $5,000 to kill the bill. While I did not know your bogus lunatic, I was well aware that she was an imposter, and I at once set her down in my mind as one of two things—a blackmailer or a newspaper decoy. My usual course would have been to tell her *that I had no business transactions with women and that her husband must call on me if he wished to obtain my services. As it was I resolved to lead my fair visitor on as far as she would go. All my actions were with that object and I intended when it came to the crisis to give her a lesson that would teach her better sense hereafter.*

Now, some portion of what Nellie says about our conversation is true. I met her at her own game and certainly indulged in some tall lying to astonish her. But it is utterly, positively a whole-cloth lie to say that I mentioned the name of a single Assemblyman or even hinted at "buying" anybody. Not a legislator was named while Nellie was in my room, and as a matter of fact I never talked with any Assemblyman on the Patent Medicine bill, never heard it mentioned by a member, and with two of the members named by Nellie I have no acquaintance whatever. The marks put on the committee list produced by Nellie must have been the work of her own fair hands. The story that a portion of them were made by me on a smooth surface and the others on the rough cover of a book is "too thin." No one who wanted to cover up his tracks would be guilty of such folly outside of the lunatic asylum where Nellie played her tricks. Besides, the dear girl in her story says that I "placed the sheet on a book" on my desk and "made crosses against the remaining names." Fibbers should be more careful not to confound straight lines with crosses, or Nellie ought to have made her tally-sheet correspond with her text. Besides, nobody who knows me would for a moment believe that I would talk to any living soul, in jest or in earnest, about "buying" votes. I have had some experience and am not quite a fool.

The plain truth is that while poking fun at the sweet girl, I gave her a list of the committee having the quack medicine bill in charge and advised her to go and see all the gentlemen on the committee. At which dear Nellie started and said, "Oh! I'm afraid of the men, I'd rather do business with you." If I had been a young man, probably I should have considered the look that accompanied the words quite fascinating.

I did give Nellie my address in New York. She had to hurry away from Albany, she said, and wanted me to call at her hotel in New York. I was not to be caught (but was trying to do the

catching), and so allured Nell to my own office. I instructed my
son to be on hand. He heard every word of conversation that
occurred in my office, and I took him with me to the St. James
Hotel, intending, as soon as Nellie gave me a check, to expose
her and threaten her with arrest unless she made a clean breast
of her fraud.

The piece of paper with the name of an old friend of mine,
J. F. Chesbrough, on it, must have been picked up by Nellie in
my office, and the "—50" on it seems to indicate that it was a
memorandum of some business transaction.

I may say, in confirmation of my statement, that immediately
after Miss Nellie took herself and her satchel and her sweet
smile out of my apartment at the Kenmore Hotel, I stepped into
the adjoining room, related the whole story of the remarkable
visit to Mr. Crenell of Rochester and another gentleman, who
were waiting for me, and told them I had made an appointment
with the mysterious female quack actress at my office in New
York and intended to catch her in a trap while she was supposing she was catching me.

I have been twenty years in business. I make no disguise of
my occupation and have nothing against being called a "lobbyist." I do business as legislative against for persons who can
better afford to pay me than to waste time in Albany. But I
never in my life paid nor offered a dollar to any Senator or
Assemblyman to influence him in legislation, and despite the
thoughtless and uncharitable assertions of some newspapers, I
have never known a Legislature in which there were not a sufficient number of honorable, upright men to uphold a meritorious
measure and to kill any attempt at injustice or blackmailing.

EDWARD R. PHELPS
115 Broadway, New York

Champion storyteller. The attention she has now paid to me. Sensational romance. Interesting verdancy. Fascinating look. Phelps
alternated between calling me a liar and—there was no other word
for it—a hussy. A loose woman. A whore.

That was when I determined to demolish him by any means possible.

The Colonel was chortling with ecstasy over the letter, clearly oblivious to the bevy of unsubtle insults readily apparent to any woman. "Oh! Oh! This is too goddamn good! I could kiss whoever wrote it for him. He's given us our follow-up story tomorrow morning!"

"You're not going to publish it!" I cried.

"Damn right we are! Why?"

I pressed my lips together. If the Colonel didn't see it, I couldn't explain why Phelps's language mattered. I simply said, "He doesn't deserve the space."

"Of course he does! That's why I sent him an early copy—so he would comment. Now we can rip his version to shreds in print. I never imagined he would be such a fool! He was trying to catch you? Ha! I notice he didn't warn the police or the government. That's what an honest man would do." He leveled a finger at me. "There's a lesson in there, Bly. No one is as self-destructive as a man who feels untouchable when he's attacked."

"All right. Give me the letter, and I'll write the response." Steaming, I was already stringing words together in my head.

The Colonel actually pulled it out of my reach. "Oh, no! You're not saying another word about this in public."

"What?!?"

"This is going to end in a court of one kind or another. Anything you say can be used to poke holes in the reporting. No, you stand by your story. From this moment on, the rest of the *World* will handle all questions on this."

"But—!"

"But nothing! Look, if Mr. Pulitzer fears anything in God's creation, it's a libel lawsuit. It's why he's such a dad-blasted stickler for accuracy. So you say nothing more about Phelps. Not a word. This is going to end with lawyers, and we don't want to be on the wrong side of that." Seeing my expression, for once he read it aright. "Don't fret. Your name will be in every piece. Just not in the byline."

Bitterly, I shook my head. But I said, "Fine."

Understanding reporters, the Colonel gave me a sop. "Why not head up to Albany tomorrow night? There's a session scheduled, and I guarantee this is all they'll want to talk about. I can't have you write anything—I have our Albany man for that. Can't be cutting his legs out. But show yourself. Sit in the gallery and scare the daylights out of them."

That, I decided, was a delightful prospect.

MONDAY, APRIL 2, 1888

In a queer coincidence, a different Phelps made the front page on Monday morning. William Walter Phelps, the millionaire congressman from New Jersey, had suffered the loss of his entire art collection when his home caught fire on Sunday evening. Apparently, a defective gas jet leaked enough of the foul stuff that when it found an open grate fire, it rocked his mansion with an enormous explosion.

But the explosion I had set off in Albany took up nearly half of a page all by itself. Phelps's letter was there, making my blood boil anew. In the end, Colonel Cockerill was so enthused that he penned the piece rebutting Phelps himself:

THE LOBBY KING'S BLUFF

"ED" PHELPS'S ABSURD EXPLANATION ABOUT THAT AGREEMENT
TO BRIBE—HE WAS TRYING TO CATCH "NELLIE BLY" ALL THE
TIME—WHY, OH! WHY, THEN, DID HE GIVE WRITTEN MEMO-
RANDA AND HANG ABOUT THE ST. JAMES HOTEL? —TALK OF
A LEGISLATIVE INVESTIGATION—WHY NOT A GRAND JURY
INDICTMENT IN THIS COUNTY?

The remarkable narrative Nellie Bly presented to the readers of THE WORLD yesterday of her visit to the headquarters of Ed Phelps, the "King of the Albany Lobby," and her exposure of how legislation is promoted or destroyed was a startling revelation to the honest citizens of New York. From time to time THE WORLD has heard rumors of an organized lobby at Albany, but tangible proof of its existence has been difficult to secure. To Nellie Bly was intrusted the by no means easy task of not only discovering who was at the head of the "Third House," but of receiving detailed and exact evidence of how bills are killed or forced through the Legislature. This mission Nellie Bly undertook and carried through with success at every point . . .

It suited the Colonel to sing my praises as he recounted the whole affair in two lengthy paragraphs that took up the rest of the column. Next came his commentary on Phelps's response, in which Cockerill took a perverse pleasure in bestowing the wrong Christian name upon Phelps. Instead of Edward, the Colonel called him Edwin. Since the assassination of President Lincoln, the name Edwin had become *anathema*.

I read the whole thing on the afternoon flyer to Albany—quite a different trip than that of the previous Tuesday. It was bright, and we positively hurtled north, with nary a patch of snow in sight. *Out like a lion indeed!*

I was different, too: somehow far more fearful than I had been previously. That was always the way of it. The reality of a story published was more unnerving than the promise of a story in the offing. The Colonel's comment about lawsuits had caught me off guard, and I'd spent the whole night with my brain conjuring courtrooms, reliving Mother's divorce proceeding. I remembered being thirteen and climbing up on the stand to testify, and hearing a click—very like the click of Ford's pistol cocking in my face the day we all left. Telling my story to the court was the bravest thing I had done at that point. I'd felt invigorated. Empowered. It was only afterwards that I had shaken and wept like a child.

With nothing more to do, I pored through the rest of the *World's* morning edition, stunned that there was news other than my exposé of Phelps. There was a story on Spiritualism, which echoed my piece from the week before on the Mesmerist. It closed with an excellent line: "Why is it that a proportion of mankind dearly love to be humbugged?"

One story made me laugh, proving once again what a terrible human being I was:

CRAZED BY HAIR DYE

BARTOW-ON-THE-SOUND, APRIL 2—Samuel C. Doty, a ship carpenter, of City Island, committed suicide last night by hanging himself with a necktie. He was in the habit of dyeing his hair, and it was through the excessive use of hair dye that his mind became deranged.

Another brief story nabbed my attention: a woman named Nellie appearing in court to testify against her husband for shooting her mother. The paper made a point of saying the husband's face was scratched, and that he had feared for his life. *Hmmm.* On the same page, an enormous advertisement caught my eye as it might not have done a week before:

SCOTT'S EMULSION

OF PURE COD LIVER OIL AND HYPOPHOSPHITES

————

ALMOST AS PALATABLE AS MILK.

————

Containing the stimulating properties of the Hypophosphites combined with the Fattening and Strengthening qualities of Cod Liver Oil, the potency of both being largely increased.

————

A Remedy for Consumption.
For Wasting in Children.
For Scrofulous Affections.
For Anæmia and Debility.
For Coughs, Colds & Throat Affections.
In fact, ALL diseases where there is an inflammation of the Throat and Lungs, a WASTING OF THE FLESH, and a WANT OF NERVE POWER, nothing in the world equals this palatable Emulsion.
SOLD BY ALL DRUGGISTS.

The bill that had been killed would have prevented such lunatic claims. I felt unaccountably guilty, which was absurd. The bill had been dead before I had come onto the scene. *Why, then, do I feel like I've failed the credulous souls who will see this ad and invest their last pennies in hope of a cure?* It had been a sound bill that could have protected innumerable citizens from fraud and harm, and it had never stood a chance against the lobbyists.

Arrived in Albany, I again checked in to the Stanwix—this time under my own name. No one connected Elizabeth Cochrane with Nellie Bly, a fact for which I was newly grateful. After unpacking, I dressed in my own normal costume, fiddled with my hair, and basically filled the time until six thirty, when I met the *World's* Albany reporter, Frederick Duneka.

He was younger than I'd expected, not yet thirty, and clean-shaven with a bad case of the squints. In greeting me, he was very grudging. Doubtless, he felt that I had stolen the story from him—regardless of the fact that he could never have broken it himself. Nevertheless, he doffed his bowler hat and offered me his arm as we made our way to the seat of New York government.

"Has there been any sign of Mr. Phelps?" I asked.

Duneka shook his head. "Neither hide nor hair. I talked to one fellow, a former friend turned rival. You've made him very happy, at least. He says that conversation in your piece reads just like him. Though I think he was a tad premature in saying that Phelps has lost his grip, and this is the end of his career as a lobbyist."

"You don't think it is?"

"'No man's life, liberty, or property are safe while the legislature is in session.' Never underestimate the power of corruption, Miss Bly."

"Miss Cochrane, please," I said, as heads turned at the mere mention of my name. "So what do you think will happen?"

Duneka shrugged one shoulder. "Your story has the cat among the pigeons, but they might just fly off until the cat slinks away, and then return to their roost. Now, if another story on corruption broke, well, then they might have to actually do something. Here we are."

The Capitol was suitably imposing, a massive confection of gray stone arches and oversize windows. There were signs of construction everywhere, and I remarked, "What are they building?"

"A never-ending monument to inefficiency," said Duneka. "It's been through twenty-one years, four architects, and untold dollars so far, and bodes fair to take half again as long and cost twice again as much to complete."

I followed Duneka to the gallery, a horseshoe of seats looking down onto the floor of the assembly through enormous arches supported by dark marble pillars. Duneka guided me to a seat near the back, among the early-arriving onlookers. I was surprised—and gratified—to see so many women, and said so.

"Oh, yes," said Duneka. "The ladies of Albany come, especially on Mondays. The theatres are closed, you see. Besides, tonight there promises to be high drama." He started to move off.

"Wait—are you going?"

"Just over there," he pointed, toward the front rail of the balcony.

"Where the men sit." Touching his bowler's brim, he sauntered off.

Segregation of the sexes? Here? Though I wanted to raise a hue and cry, I realized I should be grateful I wasn't to be seated beside the *World* reporter—it would no doubt give away my identity. From my vantage point I could see the central raised podium, enclosed by a wooden horseshoe lower down. Facing the podium were two more horseshoes made up of individual desks, each with its own leather-backed armchair. I watched with interest as young pages rushed to and fro with papers. Their dark uniforms stood in contrast with the pattern of the carpeting, which was far more colorful than I would have imagined: bright diamonds set among symmetrical blobs that looked almost like frogs.

I chatted with the ladies around me, professing to be taking an interest in politics for the first time. I made friends with my neighbors, and as old hands at these things, they promised to answer any questions I might have.

"Who is that?" I asked, pointing to a man helping the pages lay out huge stacks of paper on each desk.

"Oh, that is Mr. Lawrence," confided the woman to my right. "The busiest man in the Capitol."

"And what are those papers?"

"Those are the bills."

Having only ever read the short bill on patent medicine, I was shocked. The stacks of paper were so unwieldy that it was a man's work to lift one. "How many are there?"

"Sixty-two today," said the lady to my left.

"How do they read them all?"

That drew knowing looks from both sides. "Only the most conscientious members do their duty and read the lot, captions and all."

"They vote without knowing what's in them?"

"They decide beforehand, with advice from those they trust in their party. It's shameful," said my new friend with a blasé wave of her hand.

No wonder Phelps has such success! Most of these men need someone to tell them how to vote!

Close to seven o'clock, the uniformed pages were replaced by a parade of pompous facial hair—moustaches, mutton-chops, and beards of all styles and lengths—attached to a pasty collection of gray-haired men with physiques that bespoke sedentary lifestyles.

They all took their places behind their desks, while a fellow who looked like a cheerful, fleshy Thomas Jefferson ascended to the Speaker's chair. His name I had already picked up—Fremont Cole, who in January had replaced the honorable General Husted as Speaker thanks to the machinations of Boss Platt.

As the clerk droned out the journal, I could feel a hum around the great chamber like electricity in a wire. The instant the clerk finished, another clerical-looking gentleman, far older, rose to his feet, literally shaking with fury. Without prompting, my right-hand neighbor whispered, "Mr. Tallmadge."

"Mr. Speaker!" intoned Tallmadge. "A point of privilege!"

Cole nodded. "The chair recognizes the gentleman from Kings."

"Mr. Speaker, I hold in my hand a copy of the *New York World* of yesterday. In this paper there appeared an article under the caption 'The King of the Lobby.'" He then summarized the contents of my article, listing off all the men Phelps said he could buy. With a flourish, he flapped the paper in the air and turned in a circle, declaring, "Is it necessary for me to tell this assembly here that this is all untrue? It is certainly unnecessary for me to tell those present that the bill in question was never in the Committee on Cities. All of you know it. But for every one of us here who knows how silly this matter is, there are thousands who do not know the facts and who are inclined to believe what they read!"

Tallmadge assumed a grave, sonorous air. "I have debated in my own mind what is the proper course to pursue in this matter. It is certainly a serious matter: serious to me, serious to every one of us, serious to the state of New York. I want to say, on behalf of the Committee on Cities—and I think the chairman of that committee will bear me out—that I do not know of any bill that has come out of that committee this year that has cost a man a dollar, either in money or a promise to keep it there."

He turned to face Mr. Cole. "Now, Mr. Speaker, this article, so far as I am personally concerned, is one that I hardly know how to handle. I come from a city where we have three-fourths of a million people. I have been in public life in that city for a decade, and there is no paper in that city that can point to one single thing in my official record that they can throw a shadow upon as corrupt or dishonest. I have made my good name and my reputation there, and when I find that good name—made by public service of years and years—handled in this way, I feel unnerved as to what is best to do in regard to it. The people know me by reputation. They know me by the good name I have established among them. When they read an article like this, they do not know the facts that I know—that you know—in regard to it, and they are unable to account for how such matters can be so."

I admittedly felt a trifle guilty at this point. Sutherland had declared Tallmadge to be entirely honest and, seeing his honest dismay, I regretted the soiling of his name. *But it wasn't me who did it! It was Phelps!*

Shaking his head, Tallmadge continued. "When, coming up on the train, I was engaged in writing out a resolution calling for an investigation of this matter, the chairman of our committee came to me. I told him what I was about to do, and he advised me not to. Mr. Crosby thought it was best to wait and consider the matter, that we might not make any mistake about it. I do see his point. This session of the legislature is now at a point where business requires the utmost attention from all of its members, so an investigation at this time seems impracticable. Nevertheless, something should be done! What, I am hardly prepared to say. But it seems to me that it should not go along without consideration, and I therefore desire to make this motion: that this publication be referred to the Committee on the Judiciary with instructions to consider the matter and report to this house during the present week what, in their judgment, is the best course to pursue in regard to it."

"All in favor of the motion?" said the Speaker.

There were a chorus of "ayes."

"All opposed?"

Silence.

"So adopted. The publication will be sent to the Judiciary Committee for review."

At that moment another man must have stood, but I couldn't see him from where I was perched. "Mr. Speaker, a point of privilege."

"The chair recognizes the gentleman from Kings."

Kings? It had to be the other one, McLaughlin. The one Sutherland said was positively greasy with graft. I craned forward for a glimpse of him, but only heard a deep basso voice say, "I merely wish to say that I saw this article in one of the New York papers, with my name attached to it. I desire to say that in my experience in the legislature, both in the committee and in the assembly, all my actions have been open and above board. I defy and invite the closest scrutiny of every act of mine in this legislature. I hope the Judiciary Committee will indeed inquire into the attack on me."

After that, Mr. Gallagher rose to protest being included in Phelps's list. "The only time I heard tell of the bill was when that hornswoggler Pierce spoke to me, and I told him I would have nothing to do with it. I have never had any dealings with this ratbag Phelps." The women around me all exclaimed at this use of strong language, and Speaker Cole struck his gavel several times.

Mr. Hagan then rose to protest his innocence, he being the first to single me out, though not by name. "I hope action will be taken to protect the reputation of members of this august body from slanderers like this female reporter." I recalled that Sutherland had said Hagan was definitely a Black Horseman.

Mr. DeWitt rose to say it was an "infamous lie" that he had ever been offered or given a bribe. Though he spoke only briefly, he did raise his voice the loudest.

Mr. Prime was next. I could see him, a beetle-browed man whose moustache did indeed dwarf Colonel Cockerill's. It hung over his whole mouth, even dusting his nonexistent chin. I'd always preferred the look of clean-shaven men, but it was this day—observing these haughty men with their greasy moustaches—that instilled in me a lifelong disgust of facial hair.

He took his time clearing his throat, and when he spoke, I heard all the polished smarm of Albert in his voice and was instantly convinced of his guilt. "During my two terms in the legislature, I have never been approached by any lobbyist outside the house, or inside it for that matter, with anything bordering on a proposition or a hint that I should be paid for voting for or against any measure. I may not have the property qualification which entitles me to be classed as unapproachable, as is given to Mr. Crosby. But I am not compelled to resort to that method of obtaining a livelihood and I never have done so. When I decide to accept a bribe to influence my vote, I shall be ready to resign my seat in this house. Further than that, I am willing to let my reputation speak for itself against the word of the notorious Nellie Bly."

With that, he turned and looked straight up at me. My stomach clenched. He continued to stare at me, and though I couldn't tell through the moustache, I think he was smiling. He stared just long enough for the ladies around me to grow alarmed, and when he at last turned to sit, I was surrounded by whispers. Men along the front rail—and even those across the gallery—were all craning to look at me. I considered looking around in confusion, pretending to be as curious as everyone else, but decided to remain still. Duneka gave away the game, however, hurrying over to usher me out when the elected officials proceeded with other business.

"How did he know it was me?"

"Phelps's assistant, Wood, was there."

"Where?"

"On the floor. Phelps must have described you, and Wood passed it along to Prime."

"He's allowed on the floor?!" It was so brazen it couldn't possibly be true.

"Members are allowed to give passes," said Duneka, ruefully acknowledging the absurdity while also judging me for not knowing how the world worked.

I thought of all the parts of the floor I hadn't been able to see. "Was Phelps there?"

"No. He never comes himself, not since the Conkling–Platt affair. He has agents for that. And none more cunning than Woods." Duneka's eye glinted with hidden knowledge.

"What?" I asked.

He shook his head. "You'll see."

Which I took to mean he had his own story cooking. *Well, good for him.* I was tempted to ask, but I was disliked enough for being a woman. No reporter, male or female, would ever forgive someone for horning in on a good story.

TESTIMONY

WEDNESDAY AFTERNOON, APRIL 18, 1888.

EUGENE D. WOOD, sworn, testified as follows:

Examined by MR. SAXTON:

Q. What is your business?

A. Well, I have studied law.

Q. Were you ever admitted to the bar?

A. No, sir.

Q. That does not hardly answer the question, Mr. Wood, as to what your business is, that you have studied law.

A. Well, I have been in the horse racing business.

Q. Selling pools?

A. No, sir.

Q. Buying pools?

A. No, sir.

Q. What way?

A. Owner of race horses.

Q. Have you any other business?

A. Well, nothing that I know of.

Q. Have you any business connected with the Legislature?

A. No, sir.

Q. Have you any business relations with Edward R. Phelps, whom I suppose you know, do you not?

A. Yes, sir.

Q. Have you any business relations with him?

A. None at all.

Q. You are not an agent of his in any way?

A. No, sir.

Q. Do you assist him in the managing or conducting of any business connected with the Legislature?

A. No, sir.

Q. Well, are you yourself engaged then, independently or otherwise, in any business connected with the Legislature?

A. No, sir.

Q. Or have you been?

A. Oh, I have held places here for years.

Q. I guess you don't mean that, Mr. Wood. You do not know what a lobbyist is, do you?

A. No. I have never heard it defined.

Q. You have an idea yourself what a lobbyist is, do you not?

A. I have heard what a lobbyist is.

Q. It is a fact, I suppose, and it is a fact within your knowledge, that it is commonly understood that a lobbyist is a person outside of the Legislature who seeks in some way or another to influence legislation; is not that your idea of a lobbyist?

A. Well, that is what I have heard.

Q. Have you not got a well-defined idea of that in your own mind?

A. No, I haven't.

Q. Then your mind is a blank upon that subject, as to what constitutes a lobbyist?

A. Well, I have seen a great many lawyers, you could not call those lobbyists.

Q. Well, of course, that depends upon your idea of what constitutes a lobbyist. I suppose a lawyer is not a lobbyist unless he has something to do with legislation outside of the Legislature?

A. He tries to influence legislation.

Q. That is your idea of a lobbyist, that he is a person who tries to influence legislation from the outside?

A. Yes, sir.

Q. Then you have an idea of what a lobbyist is?

A. I have an idea.

EIGHT

JUDICIOUS WAITING

TUESDAY, APRIL 3, 1888

O N THE TRAIN HOME THE next afternoon, I considered a career change. *Perhaps I could become a successful murderer.* As I'd boarded, Duneka handed me the early edition of the *Buffalo Evening News*, knowing perfectly well that I would not have time to open it until the train was in motion.

But it wasn't Duneka I wanted to throttle with my own small hands. It was the author of a story about the previous evening's excitement at the capitol.

NELLIE BLY'S LIE

SHE TOOK A BACK SEAT IN THE ASSEMBLY CHAMBER LAST NIGHT.

[SPECIAL TO THE EVENING NEWS]

ALBANY, APRIL 3—Nellie Bly, THE WORLD's detective reporter, is not very pretty, but she is sharp—too sharp perhaps. She received in some way an intimation that her bribery fiasco with Lobbyist Phelps would have a ventilation in the Assembly last evening; so Nellie planked down five cold dollars for her fare and came up here from New York on the "flyer." She had a back seat in the Chamber last evening among 200 prettily dressed women who come every Monday evening to study legislation or watch their own or other folks' husbands. Nellie was *incog*. Nobody knew her except a select few, and they knew enough to keep their mouths shut, for Nellie was terribly afraid that if known, the great big-hearted Ike Scott would dance her before the bar of the house to explain herself. So Nellie kept perfectly still while she heard the clerical-looking Tallmadge of Brooklyn get up and offer a resolution that her story be sent to the Judiciary Committee for them to make a report upon before the week is over as to what was to be done in the matter. This will be the hardest kind of a job for that committee.

Relating my story about Phelps with a decidedly Phelpsian slant, the slanderous piece ended thus:

The game between Nellie and Phelps looks like a draw, but the female detective reporter is having lots of fun out of it, but if dragged before the Judiciary Committee she may collapse at the sight of Chairman Saxton's great big white moustache as he fires legal conundrums at her. What the Judiciary Committee will report will be hard to conjecture. They may decide to go into an investigation, but this is not probable, as the session is too near its end. —G.

A liar, am I! I would collapse, would I? Well, Mr. G., you want to see how sharp I am? This not-very-pretty reporter is going to find your name and—and . . . I couldn't even think of a proper revenge!

I was still steaming like an engine ready to blow when I arrived at the *World*'s newsroom the next day. So I was in no mood to encounter a triumphant staff, crowing like roosters at a particularly bright dawn.

Reaching my desk, I found it piled with the morning edition of the *World*, and I thought for a moment that I was being lauded for something.

But it was quite the opposite. The headline read BRIBERY RAMPANT! Reading on, I saw that two state senators, Ives and Langbein, were accusing Phelps's assistant, Eugene Wood, of attempting to bribe them to introduce a crooked bill on metropolitan transit. This was clearly the story Duneka had been hinting at. I even recalled him saying that my story would only have weight if another accusation cropped up.

Looking around the newsroom, heart in my stomach, I understood the message. *Here*, my male colleagues were informing me, was a story they could be proud of. A story done by a *real* reporter, one of *them.*

But this story would have had no weight without mine! Even further, it likely wouldn't have happened without mine! *Would those two senators have come forward to Duneka if not for my story scaring them straight? Were they not more likely to have taken the bribes, rather than turn in the boodler? Why can't these men admit I had a good story!?!*

My sole consolation was that Duneka didn't merit his own byline. It was just another story in the *World.* And his piece prominently mentioned my name and my own reporting on Phelps. *Cold comfort* is comfort nonetheless.

Later, seated at my desk, I saw Bill Nye approaching, a folded newspaper in his hand. "Oh, no. Not you, too."

He raised his wicked brows in a mockery of innocence, but his smile was kind. "The *Standard Union* is a fan," he supplied, dropping that paper on my desk.

As he left, I read the page two piece, where they took for granted the existence of corrupt legislators, and managed to call Phelps a "corruptionist" five separate times. The piece ended with this:

In the meantime, the thanks of all lovers of good government and opponents of corruption are due to THE WORLD and to "Nellie Bly," its clever and cultivated correspondent, for an exposure of the "King of the Lobbyists" in a way that bids fair to lead to his arrest and punishment.

Clever and cultivated! That's more like it! I felt the sting of tears in my eyes, and sent a beaming smile at Nye, who tipped his hat to me and winked.

That made me think of Nye's friend and mine: Wilson, the Quiet Observer. A typical man, yes, but also a gentleman. I felt a pang so sharp I actually winced. How I missed him!

But it was his turn to write to me. I was not going to break the rules. Not again. As a true gentleman, he deserved ladylike behavior from me.

‹ঞ›

Duneka proved correct in his assessment. The addition of accusations from Ives and Langbein forced the legislature to act, though they spent the rest of week debating how best to proceed. Colonel Husted, the most honest man in the assembly, demanded an immediate investigation by the Judiciary Committee. There were howls of protest from all quarters.

Under cover of the debate, Phelps slipped out of town. The instant Duneka found out, he wrote to the Colonel, who trumpeted our victory across two full columns on the front page:

DRIVEN FROM HIS THRONE

————

KING PHELPS OF THE LOBBY LEAVES ALBANY FOR THE SOUTH

————

THE ATMOSPHERE WHERE "THE WORLD" CIRCULATED WAS TOO HOT FOR HIM

————

[SPECIAL TO THE WORLD]

ALBANY, APRIL 6—"Lobby King Phelps has abdicated," was the rumor that floated through the corridors of the Capitol to-day. It was passed from mouth to mouth and rapidly developed into an apparently trustworthy report. Speaker Cole had heard it before leaving the breakfast table at the Kenmore. He had been told by the clerks of that hostelry that the notorious bill-broker had, to the astonishment of the management, announced that he proposed to leave town indefinitely. The atmosphere where THE WORLD circulated was too hot for him. He therefore would surrender his luxurious parlors and seek, temporarily at least, pastures new and green. Where he would go, he had

not yet determined. He might try Virginia and gloat over his possessions, purchased at the price of many a legislator's character; then, again, he might proceed to Florida and bask in the sunshine or recline beneath the shade of his orange groves. At any rate, he proposed to go somewhere.

————

THE LOBBY KING'S DEPARTURE
And go somewhere he did. The crafty Phelps boarded the 9:55 a.m. train for the south, bag and baggage. His rooms have been closed the greater part of the day. Eugene Wood, his man Friday, remained behind, but business was so bad that he had expressed his intention of taking a trip himself pretty soon. He did not put in an appear-

ance at the Capitol. Indeed, he has given the seventeen-million-dollar elephant a wide berth since the publication of THE WORLD's accusation as to his attempt to bribe at least two members of the Senate. Various reasons are given for Phelps's departure. His son will not talk about it except to say that he will return soon.

Meanwhile, the incorruptible Mr. Crosby introduced a resolution ordering the Judiciary Committee to investigate the matter and report to the Assembly before June 10.

I liked to think I helped spur them to action. Sympathetic to my frustration at having to remaining silent, the Colonel suggested I write a letter to the Judiciary Committee. It went in the mail the same day it was published in the *World*.

New York, April 5, 1888
Hon. Charles T. Saxton
Chairman, Judiciary Committee

Dear Sir,
I have waited almost a week to see what action your committee would take in regard to the statements made to me by Mr. E. R. Phelps touching a certain measure pending in the Assembly. I am ready and willing to appear before the committee and substantiate the statements printed in the New York World *on Sunday, April 1, over my signature.*
I can be addressed, care of the editor of the World.

Very respectfully,
Nellie Bly

The very next day, the Judiciary Committee was assigned to look into the question. I felt quite smug until the Colonel summoned me into his office.

"Oh, they're investigating," snarled the Colonel. "But they're being damned clever about it. They've written the rules so that they're only allowed to investigate the assemblymen we named in the story."

"Not Phelps?"

"Neither Phelps nor Wood." He slammed his hand on his desk. "It'll be a goddamn show trial, designed to exonerate their members!"

"Well, I can tell them what I know."

"You don't know anything that will stand up in a court against those men! No, don't argue, think!" he snapped as I opened my mouth. "You only know what Phelps said. You can damn him, but not the men he named. All you can prove is that he named them. That's the whole point—if they felt safe, they might throw Phelps to the wolves. Instead, they're bent on proving themselves pure as the driven goddamn snow! Should have seen it coming," he mumbled, shaking his head.

"Will they even call me?" I asked in a small voice.

"Oh, they'll call you to ask you all kinds of questions." Lowering his head like a Mexican bull, he leveled his cigar at me. "When they do call you, it's your job to keep bringing Phelps's name into it. Tell the story. Make his name muddier than Mudd's." Slowly, the Colonel smiled, his great walrus moustache turning absurdly up. "They've approved funds for a stenographer. Which means there'll be a record of everything. If you do it right, we can publish the transcript." He made a decision. "I'm sitting you down with a lawyer."

"Why?"

"To rehearse!"

"I don't need to rehearse," I said mulishly.

"Oh, you don't?" he repeated sarcastically. "Remember the hash you made of your time on stage?"

"I'm a good enough actress to fool a parcel of doctors. Good enough to fool Phelps!"

"You're not going in to fool anybody. You're going in to tell a goddamn story. Under oath. One bad question and it all falls apart. What makes you think you can handle it?"

I looked the Colonel in the eye. "Because I'm a clever little liar."

The waiting was the worst part. I had to sit at my desk, answering letters and reading the stories other people brought in. I wasn't even allowed to open my own mail—I found a stack of letters waiting for me each morning. I was told the *World* was waiting for my summons, so we wouldn't miss it.

I was itching to go out and find another story of my own, something to fill the time. But the Colonel forbade me. "I want you focused on this."

"I'll go crazy," I told him.

"No, you won't," he said with a grin. "You've already done that, and it's a bad reporter who repeats himself." Seeing my glare, he added, "Herself."

Since I refused to practice with a lawyer, the Colonel would call me into his office once or twice a day to toss questions at me. Recalling my two experiences with giving testimony—once as a child during Mother's divorce, and again as an adult against the man who had stolen all our money—I found that poise was far superior to passion. Even the Colonel was impressed.

I began to notice some strange behavior around the office. It wasn't just the cold shoulders. Those I understood. No, it was that the men I counted as allies—Nye, the artist McDougall, the repentant Cole, and Metcalfe—they all appeared at my desk just before lunch, or just as it was time to head home. The Colonel even appeared one night. One of them always walked me out of the building, and each offered to share a cab with me. I knew for a fact that Metcalfe lived in the opposite direction. And as much as I enjoyed thinking it was my feminine charms, the unified effort on their part made me suspicious. I kept waiting for the other shoe to drop.

One morning, I arrived to find a note on my desk. It read:

Phelps is back in Albany. He's going to testify. It's war.

—*Col. Cockerill*

I received my summons two days later. I was to appear before the Judiciary Committee of the New York Legislature on Wednesday, April 18, at 10 a.m.—almost a week more of waiting.

To distract myself from the sense of impending dread, I accepted Metcalfe's invitation to another show, this time to see *On the Rio Grande* in Brooklyn. On our way, he guided me around a large puddle. "Don't want you to slip again."

"So you *do* remember!" I exclaimed. "I wasn't certain."

"How could I forget such a smile?"

"Flatterer! You seemed in a great hurry to forget it that day."

"Did I? Shame on me, then. To be fair, though, I had no idea that smile was attached to such a spitfire spirit." He chuckled. "Truth be told, I was afraid you'd fallen on purpose."

"On purpose!"

He shrugged. "It's not unheard of. Do you know the phrase 'catching a mash'?"

I fixed him with a gimlet eye. Then I laughed. "I seem to remember hearing it once before."

After the show, Metcalfe regaled me with the tale of Jim the theatre cat, who'd once survived an eighty-foot fall and recently managed to escape the Union Square Theatre when it caught on fire. I laughed and laughed, and allowed Metcalfe to kiss me goodnight.

Feeling terribly guilty, the next night I accepted Dr. Ingram's invitation to dinner. He was surprisingly adventurous, taking me to Dorlan's Oyster Bar. Though they didn't serve alcohol, I did consume their strongest liquids: tomato catsup and pepper sauce. When Ingram kissed my cheek at my door, I felt like a brazen hussy.

The day before I was due to testify, I was positively climbing out of my skin when the Colonel called me into his office. Expecting another legal grilling, I was surprised when he said, "Conkling's dead."

It took me only a moment to place the name of the former senator who had been stricken with pneumonia. "Oh? That's . . . something."

"Ironic, is what it is. Duneka says Phelps was heard to remark that Conkling got the better of the storm."

"Funny," I said, not laughing. "Do you want me to write the story?"

"Already handled."

I waited. So did the Colonel. When he didn't say anything, I started to go. "If that's all—"

The Colonel cut across me, saying, "After you testify, you should take a vacation."

"A vacation?"

Coming around the desk, he sat on the front edge and leaned close to me. "Bly—Nellie—we ask a goddamn lot of you. I know it's the sort of thing you wanted to do. But assigning you the Phelps story may have been a mistake."

A chill raced the length of my spine. "Did I somehow make a hash of it?"

"No-no, nothing like that. In fact, you may have done too well."
With a sigh, the Colonel waved a hand at the newsroom outside
his frosted window. "It's the men. They're behaving like a bunch of
goddamn spoiled children. They're sore about me giving you this
story. They don't see that the world is changing—our *World* and
the whole world. A delegation was in to see me. They want you to
stay out of what they regard as their field."

The chill turned to fire. *It's not enough that the green-eyed
monsters of the newsroom make their feelings clear every minute
of every day? No, now they have to bother the Colonel, and
complain that a woman's doing their job better than they ever
could!*

Drawing in breath through my nose, I snapped. "*Their* field, eh?
Well, tell them I can handle their field better than they ever—"

The Colonel waved me down. "Don't worry," he said, the hint of
a smile buried under his fat moustache. "I told them I would go on
assigning you any kind of story I thought you could handle."

That brought me up short. "Oh. Thank you. Good. But then . . .
why a vacation?"

"You've earned it!" Laughing, the Colonel returned to his side
of the desk, the fatherly intervention apparently over. "Take your
mother back to visit your family in Pittsburgh. Or go down to New
Orleans for fun. Kick up your heels, let your hair down. Write
another book. Let this sensation cool down a little. Trust me, no
one is going to forget the name Nellie Bly now!"

I eyed the Colonel suspiciously. But he was fiddling with papers
on his desk, a clear sign that the interview was over. Befuddled and
disappointed, I rose to go.

Casually, as if in complete afterthought, the Colonel said, "Oh,
I'm sending a bodyguard along to Albany."

I blinked, confused. "For who?"

He stared at me as if I were dense.

Apparently, I was. "For *me?*"

He nodded.

"Why?"

"Just to be safe."

I laughed. "I made it through Blackwell's without protection! I
think I can handle the lawyers of Albany!"

Dropping the ruse of his papers, the Colonel looked me in the eye. "I haven't wanted to say anything. But we've been getting death threats."

"We have?"

"Well, you have. It's why I've had all your mail read before you got it."

Suddenly, I understood the succession of gentlemen escorts. I had thought they were protecting me from the ire of the newsroom. As it turned out, they *were* protecting me, but from something far more real.

I was immediately transported back to Mexico, with a silent but very real threat of bodily harm. I had run away then. Never again. "Absolutely not!"

The Colonel insisted. So did I. The argument, though brief, grew heated, and in the end, I was loath to admit it but I was glad to lose. No, I wasn't going to run away, but I wasn't so foolish as to avoid sensible precautions. It just grated so hard against my sense of independence that I had to put up a fight.

"The Pinkerton's man will be here at noon to escort you home for your bag. You're on the evening flyer to Albany. He's got your ticket." He pursed his lips, making his fat lip weasel jut out. "Beat him like a drum, Bly."

Snapping my feet together, I saluted as I'd seen soldiers do. "Yes, Colonel!"

Back at my desk, I had three hours to waste before my protector arrived. I glared at my stack of mail, knowing now why it was open and waiting. That secret was out. My ire was still at a boil, and I was tempted to start a fight with the men around me and find out who had been part of the delegation bent on sabotaging my career. But years of Albert had taught me that the thing a bully enjoyed most was their victim showing how much the bullying hurt. So that was out, too. *What should I do?*

Salvation came in the form of Bill Nye, who appeared by my desk with a newspaper. Handing it over, he said, "Thought you might enjoy hearing from an old friend."

It wasn't a New York paper. It was a copy of the *Pittsburgh Commercial Gazette*. Wilson's new paper. I checked. Nye had folded it back to page four. The center column was devoted to my old friend, the Quiet Observer.

Observing my expression, Nye said, "Did I do wrong?"

I made an effort to smile through the fog of nostalgia and—there was no other word for it—the *longing* I felt at the sight of Wilson's *nom de plume.* "On the contrary. I'm touched. And just a little homesick."

Relieved, Nye went back to his desk. My eyes stinging, I thought about how just three years earlier, one incendiary piece by the Q. O. about the role of women had propelled me into my current career. It wasn't that he disliked women. He probably thought he revered them. But his idea of a woman's role in the world had been—well, *outdated* was the kindest way to put it.

Reading through his current piece, I saw he hadn't changed at all:

Women have much to do with molding the moral character of men.

While this is specially true of mothers, it is also true, in a greater or less degree, of all women. They have an influence over men that neither have over those of their own sex.

Were young women more exacting in regard to the moral characters of the young men with whom they associate, we would have a more moral, as well as a better-mannered, lot of young men.

Almost anyone who served during the late war will remember how differently men appeared after passing from the environments of home to the free and unrestrained life of a soldier.

Many of them who had been regarded as the very pink of propriety at home seemed to lose all self-respect, became coarse and vulgar, even indecent in their manners. Others were inclined to get drunk, gamble, and be tough citizens. This is true of not a few who had been raised under the strictest moral discipline. It was such as those who are said to have been ruined by army life.

On the other hand, you found young men whom you would have expected to go wrong, if any did, who not only retained their good habits, but grew and developed into fine, strong, well-mannered men, and now rank as our best citizens and churchmen.

It was simply a question of character. Those who were good for lack of opportunity, or had not the courage to be bad, gave way to their inclinations, and soon showed what manner of men they were. Those whose characters were founded on principle not only retained their manhood, but the scenes and temptations with which they were surrounded served to strengthen them, so that they came home more manly than when they went away.

Hm. After hooking me at the top, he rather lost the thread. Which was a shame, because I wanted him to finish his thoughts about women shaping the morality of men. As always, the Q. O. put the responsibility for men's bad behavior upon women. To him, a woman's role was forever defined by the men in her life.

Yet for some reason, I was smiling. I could hear Wilson in his words, and knew that he was struggling with the concept of morality in a time when it seemed to have become, if not obsolete, at least passé.

I thought of Phelps, and wondered if Wilson would blame the Lobby King's mother or wife for his moral failings. No, of course not. As always, Wilson got there in the end. It was simply a question of character.

There was something in there, though, that caught me. "The courage to be bad." *Does it take courage to be bad?* I would have said the opposite, that it required bravery to be moral and upright. And yet the phrase rang true.

"Those who were good for lack of opportunity" also resonated as strangely correct. But, as my life had proved over and over, it was possible to create opportunity. It took luck, certainly, but also a voice, a determination, a sense of urgent purpose—virtues I liked to think I owned.

What had never occurred to me until that very second was that there were men in this world who had those virtues but, lacking a moral compass, used them for vice rather than for virtuous causes.

According to the Q. O., they had not been influenced by the right kind of women.

Well, if that is indeed so, I'm more than happy to be that right kind of woman. Only, my influence would take a very different form than one the Quiet Observer might deem fit.

I would influence these men by exposing them.

Thinking of what Wilson would say, caught between admiration and disapproval, I laughed. It was the story of our friendship.

TESTIMONY

———————

Pink Cochran, sworn, testified as follows:
Examined by Mr. Saxton:

Q. Did he say something then about these six particular gentlemen? Did he call their names to you at any time in the interview?

A. Yes, sir, of course he did.

Q. What was it he said about those six gentlemen, of any one of them, at that interview?

A. Why, he said it was easier to get the Committee on Public Health— easier and cheaper than it was to get that committee.

Q. He said it was easier, then, to get the Committee on Public Health than it was to get the Cities Committee?

A. Yes, sir.

Q. Well, is that the only way that he referred to those six gentlemen in that interview?

A. Well, I asked him why it was transferred.

Q. I ask you if that is the only way—that is all we care about here. I do not care about Public Health, except as it might have come in relation to those six gentlemen. Was that the only way in which he referred to those six gentlemen upon the Cities Committee whom you have mentioned?

A. No, in another way.

Q. In another way?

A. Yes, sir.

Q. You say he referred to them in another way?

A. Well, he referred to them in connection with a lot more.

Q. Oh, no—

A. Can I divide them from the others?

Q. Did he mention their names?

A. Well, he mentioned the committee.

Q. I do not care about that. I do not care about spreading abroad any further the names of any other gentlemen whom Mr. Phelps mentioned, if he did mention any in that interview. That is not the object of this investigation, and I do not desire you to mention any other names except those of the six gentlemen mentioned in this interview.

A. Well, he did not mention them individually afterwards.

Q. Then if he did not mention these gentlemen individually in any other way except as you have stated, that is as far as I care about going, and that is the fact, is it?

A. Yes, sir.

NINE

THE TRIAL OF NELLIE BLY

WEDNESDAY, APRIL 18, 1888

I ARRIVED IN ALBANY WITH MY Pinkerton bodyguard, a former policeman from Chicago named Greg Kipe. He was certainly intimidating, and I ended up chattering nervously at him on the train up until he had to ask me to stop so he could do his job. He got me to a room in a different hotel, the Carlton. When I asked why we weren't staying at the Stanwix, he said, "You mentioned in print that you stayed there before. Best not make it too easy to find you." Leaving me to dwell on that unsettling thought, he closed the door to my room and told me not to open it again until morning.

Managing to survive the night without abduction or assassination, I dressed in a smart version of my usual uniform, a practical two-piece dress of blue wool with low boots and a small hat, no veil. It had been tempting to don my matron costume, but the point was to appear as myself. I didn't want the committeemen to think I was trying to put one over on them.

At the sound of a knock at my door, I actually jumped. It was only Mr. Kipe, but I made him answer two questions about our journey the previous day before admitting him. I apologized, and he said, "Not at all. I wish other clients were as cautious. Are you ready?"

"As I'll ever be," I said, putting on a brave face. I wasn't sure why I was feeling so intimidated to appear before the committee. After all, I wasn't the malefactor. I was the one who had exposed wrongdoing.

Upon reaching the Capitol, we encountered a vast crowd, including scores of Albany women. Kipe was on his guard as we threaded our way into the building. I was glad we had left early, because it took time to get inside. As it was, we entered the massive chamber at just a quarter to ten.

A very nice clerk approached me. "Ah! You must be Nelly Bly, correct?"

I saw several heads turn my way as I answered, "I am."

"Thought so. I've seen drawings of you in your book. This way, please." He escorted me to a chair near the front, across from an imposing array of desks.

Fidgety and nervous, I said, "Do you have it?"

"Have what?"

"My book. I could sign it for you." I didn't understand why I was being so chatty.

"Oh!" He looked genuinely touched. "I wish I had thought of it. Perhaps next time."

"You'll forgive me, I hope, for saying I hope there won't be a next time."

"Indeed. Well, maybe I can fetch it over lunch. They have decided the order of testimony. You will be last, save one."

"Last?"

"Save one," he told me. "They want to hear from all interested parties."

"Who will be last?" I asked.

"Mr. Wood. His is a different case, but since both he and Mr. Phelps were mentioned in the *World*, they have folded the two together."

"I see. Thank you," I added as I settled into place.

No sooner had I sat down but another man approached me. "Miss Bly. My name is Arthur Hastings. I was sent by the *World* to represent you."

"You work for the *World*?" I sounded more cross than I had intended, but I had told the Colonel that I wanted no lawyers.

"I do. But I used to work for Congressman Cockran," he said. "I understand you know him?"

That mollified me, a little. "We've met, but I wouldn't say I know him."

"Well, he expressed an interest in aiding you, so here I am. Do you want to go over your testimony?" Seeing my expression, Hastings nodded gravely. "The Colonel said you wouldn't, but it's my job to try. Just tell the truth. I'm here to object if there's any trouble. If you're uncertain about anything, look to me. But I expect you to be fine. Would you like a signal?"

"A signal?"

"If you feel you need a break, or don't want to answer a particular question. A signal to let me know to intervene."

"Oh." That sounded like a smart idea. "I don't know. Shall I . . . rub my nose?"

"Perfect. Ah, Mr. Saxton! Allow me to introduce Nellie Bly. Miss Bly, Chairman Saxton."

A man with a moustache so white it might have been made of snow bowed to me very formally. "Miss Bly. Thank you so very much for coming."

I didn't feel like curtsying. Instead, I held out my hand for him to shake. "Mr. Chairman, it is my genuine pleasure." I tried to radiate confidence.

He looked me over. "I'm glad to learn you're not a myth."

"Not even a Missus," I said automatically, echoing a standard vaudeville joke.

Evidently Saxton had not seen that show, or else he disapproved of levity on principle. I helped him by saying, "A myth?"

"It has been reported in several papers that 'Nellie Bly' is a myth, and that the all stories under that byline are prepared in Mr. Pulitzer's office. I'm glad to learn that is not the case."

"I sometimes wish it were. Then I wouldn't require a bodyguard." I gestured to Mr. Kipe.

Saxton's eyes narrowed, and he transitioned from polite hostility to protectiveness in a heartbeat. "You've been threatened?"

"Apparently so, though the World has been careful to not let me read the letters."

"They're serious," said Kipe, and he flashed his Pinkerton badge.

"I'm sorry to hear that," said Saxton. "It makes your presence here today all the more vital. Now, if you'll excuse me." With another slight bow, he moved off as a line of men—and moustaches—trooped into the chamber.

This, I understood, was the Judiciary Committee, as well as the accused men. There were also other senators and assemblymen, drawn out of curiosity. The looks thrown my way ran the gamut from curiosity and polite respect to distaste and disdain.

Mr. Hastings pointed out those he knew. I was particularly interested in General Husted, the man responsible for the incredibly narrow scope of the inquiry. He seemed remarkably complacent, and even waved to me. *The cheek!*

Chairman Saxton got things underway only twenty minutes late, which I imagined was an achievement. He began by calling each of the accused assemblyman in order, starting with the mightily aggrieved Mr. Tallmadge, who admitted to having once met Mr. Phelps on a train eight years earlier. I was interested to hear Mr. Saxton rattle off a list of names of known lobbyists: Eugene Wood, James Caulfield, Thomas Riley, Alexander Moran, Charles Swan, and John O'Brien. I wish I could have taken notes, and I wondered if I might retrieve a copy from the stenographer sitting to the side writing everything down in shorthand with her Blackwing pencil. Interestingly, for all his bluster, Tallmadge admitted to having met with O'Brien and Swan over "certain bills." Mr. Saxton particularly mentioned the New York and Hudson Valley Aqueduct bill, but Tallmadge denied there was any money to be had in such a bill. When the questioning ended, he stated he was eager to answer more. He definitely had chilly looks for me!

Next came Mr. Gallagher, who was immediately asked his age, which welled up all kinds of anxiety in me—they hadn't asked Tallmadge his age! *What if they ask mine?*

The fifty-eight-year-old Gallagher said that he had known about the patent medicine bill, as Dr. Pierce of Golden Medical Discovery fame had written to him about it.

"Is Dr. Pierce one of your constituents?"

"Yes, sir," replied Gallagher smoothly.

"Have you had any conversation, or has your attention been called to the bill by any other person?"

"Yes, sir."

"By whom?"

"Mr. Joseph Lucky of Rochester, representing the Warners."

"Mr. Lucky was here in Albany?"

"In the engrossing room."

"When did you have the conversation with Mr. Lucky in regard to it?"

"I think he and Dr. Pierce appeared here the same day with Dr. Fenner of Chautauqua."

"Did you have an interview with them?"

"I did. Separately."

"With the three gentlemen separately?"

"Yes, sir."

"Not together. They were all opposed to the bill, were they?"

"Yes, sir."

"Did they ask you to oppose it?"

"They did. Asked me what I thought of the bill, and I told them I thought it was a very bad bill."

"Now, at any of those interviews or in any of the letters that you have mentioned—I do not know as you mentioned more than one—was there any intimation, hint, or suggestion of any kind that it was desirable that you should assist to kill that bill, and that there might be some compensation in case you should do so?"

"Oh, not at all," replied Gallagher with a smile.

"Did you make any suggestion to any person that you desired some compensation?"

"No, I think not, sir," said the witness with a show of indignation that did not pierce his smile. "No-no, I think not. I told my friends to go home and pay no more attention to the bill."

Having established the member's complete innocence, Mr. Saxton moved on to the matter of the lobbyist himself. "Do you know Mr. Phelps?"

"Yes, sir."

"Edward R. Phelps?"

"Yes, sir."

"You know him personally, do you?"

"Yes, sir."

"How long have you known him?"

"Well, I have known him off and on while I have been here as a member."

"He has been about the capital how many years?"

"Every year that I have been a member, I think."

"And it was understood that he was here as a general lobbyist?"

"Yes, sir."

Saxton then listed off the names of the other lobbyists. To a one,

Gallagher admitted to knowing them, and denied ever having spoken to them about bills before the legislature. He was excused with the thanks of the chairman.

Hagan was next at bat, and made a point of saying he'd once been a sheriff. He'd never heard of the bill before the *World* article, he'd never spoken to Phelps on any matter, and he'd certainly never asked for or accepted a bribe. They didn't ask his age, which made me hope the question was an outlier.

William H. McLaughlin of Brooklyn said he was on his third term, and served on the Committees of Cities and Indian Affairs. He'd never heard of the bill, but he admitted being acquainted with all the gentlemen accused of being lobbyists.

Mr. Saxton asked, "Now, did any of those men ever—I will confine it first to this particular bill—did any of these men ever speak to you?" Naturally, the answer was negative. "Do you know anything about any other person having been offered any money as a reward for their action?"

"I do not."

"Or as an inducement for their action?"

"No, sir."

"Or anything else. When I say 'money,' of course, I mean anything of value."

Mr. McLaughlin shrugged. "Cigars, or anything of that kind."

I almost burst out laughing, and the chairman had to spend time clarifying that the witness had not accepted paper reward.

Mr. Prime of Essex had heard of the bill, as Mr. Lansing of the *Essex County Republican* had written to ask for a copy of it.

"Did he make any suggestion in regard to your action on the bill?"

"I think he said he hoped I would vote against it." He said he did not know any of the men listed, though he had to have Mr. Wood pointed out to him to be certain.

Mr. DeWitt was the last of those named by Phelps to be called. When he was finished testifying that he knew nothing about anything, he was asked if he desired to make any further statement to the committee. "I do not know that I do. I do not think it is necessary for me to say I am honest and all that."

Next, the index clerk was called to testify as to the history of the J. Wesley Smith bill on patent medicines, and to explain the misprint that claimed it had been sent to the Committee on Cities. "And it was never in that committee?"

"No, sir. It was a pure mistake of the printer."

As they had throughout the morning, other members of the Judiciary Committee rose to ask questions after Saxton had finished. I noticed that Mr. Greene was particularly eager, while Mr. Whipple was fastidious in terms of detail.

Then they broke into what they referred to as "executive session," so Mr. Kipe and I took the opportunity to go to lunch. I was mightily cheered when, heading outside, I received a bombardment of applause from over a dozen well-dressed ladies!

Returning, we were met with such a crush that I was shown in to wait in the room of Colonel McEwan, acting Adjutant-General. He was very complimentary, though his repeated query of, "Are you nervous?" made me nervous.

After the executive session, Mr. Saxton questioned a member of the Committee on Public Health, who said he knew of other bills where bribery had been rumored, but that this was not one. Then, the chairman of the committee, Mr. Mabie, was sworn in to testify as to the voting on the bill itself. It had been adversely reported by a vote of six to one, with one abstention. All of that had happened before I had ever seen Phelps, so it was established that there was no chance that Phelps had influenced the result.

With all hurdles cleared, and all members questioned, it was time for the main event, the prize fight between the two star witnesses: Nellie Bly versus Foxy Phelps.

Only Phelps wasn't there.

Mr. Saxton called for him without response. Indeed, I had been looking out all morning with no luck—though I'd thought I'd seen his son lurking in the back of the gallery above.

We waited nearly half an hour. It was drawing on close to four in the afternoon when Mr. Wood, the other purported lobbyist, finally rose. "I know Mr. Phelps expected to be here, Mr. Saxton. I cannot imagine what is delaying him."

Mr. Saxton did not look pleased. "Well, we cannot wait for him. Miss Bly, are you prepared to testify?"

"Absolutely, Mr. Saxton." And I rose to take the oath.

As the other witnesses had done before me, I took a seat at a table facing the podium where the members of the Judiciary Committee were seated. Mr. Saxton eschewed sitting on the highest point, preferring to pace between the witness and the other members. He was very prosecutorial, and I was glad to have seen the other witnesses before me, so at least I knew he was intimidating with everyone.

The initial questions were uncomfortable, as they were about me. Right out of the gate, Mr. Saxton asked me my name. Until that moment, I had managed to keep the names Bly and Cochrane entirely separate. It was important to me that no one could trace my public persona into my private life. So I when I gave my surname, I hoped it would be enough. There were certainly enough Cochranes in New York to keep at least a little anonymity.

But he desired my first name as well.

"Is it necessary I should give it?" I asked.

That fat white moustache didn't hide his frown. "Yes, I think you had better tell us."

I'm not sure what made me do it but instead of "Elizabeth," I blurted out, "My first name is Pink." Thus Elizabeth Cochrane still held on to one small inch of privacy.

Little good it did me, as he next asked my address, and whether I was married. We discussed my occupation, how long I had been a journalist, and my length of stay in New York. Finally, he picked up a newspaper. "I show you a copy of the *New York World*, or a portion of the *New York World*, of Sunday, April first, page nineteen, and refer you to an article there, the principal article upon that page. Did you write that article?"

Taking the paper, I hardly had to look. "I did."

"And the signature to that is your *nom de plume*, is it? Nellie Bly?"

"Yes, sir. I wrote all of it except the poetry."

I was then asked a series of questions regarding the assemblymen Phelps had named to me as being purchasable: Did I have any acquaintance with them? Had I ever seen them? Had I ever conversed with them? My answers were all in the negative.

"Then, of course, you do not know anything of your own knowledge, that is, know anything yourself, with regard to the integrity of these gentlemen."

"I did not write that I knew it," I said snappishly. It was stupid, but I was starting to bristle.

"No, I understand," he said.

I relented. "No, sir. I do not."

"You have no knowledge, then, as to the connection of any of these gentlemen with any measure pending before this legislature?"

"Nothing. Only what Mr. Phelps told me."

Which brought us to the interview. I rather tooted my own horn about coming up to Albany against Cockerill's will—but it wasn't a lie, exactly. He'd had doubts, and I had been determined to go in spite of them.

Saxton asked me where the interview took place and who else was present. I mentioned the man in the next room, but confessed that I didn't think I could identify him. Mr. Saxton seemed satisfied by that. Then he said, "Will you, please, tell me what Mr. Phelps said in reference to the six gentlemen I have mentioned?"

"Well, I told Mr. Phelps I had a bill—" I began.

"Wait a moment." Mr. Saxton held up a forbidding hand. "I want to tell you right here that our investigation limits us to the charges that are made in this paper against these specific gentlemen. I desire simply to ask you what Mr. Phelps said in reference to those particular gentlemen."

"He said he could buy them for a thousand dollars to kill the bill."

A cry from behind me made me bolt in my seat. "Did I say b-buh-buy!? Did I say buy!?!" Turning about, I saw that Phelps had arrived while my back was turned. His lateness had been deliberate: the rascal wanted to hear my testimony before swearing his own oath.

I noticed that Mr. Kipe's hand was in his coat, and I wondered if he had brought a pistol into the Capitol—and if it might prove necessary. But Phelps quickly calmed himself and allowed Wood to pull him back into his chair.

At his shout, I'd practically jumped out of my skin, and I was starting to worry that it made me look guilty. Which was exactly what he wanted. Trying to compose myself, I continued my testimony, telling Mr. Saxton about the paper that Phelps had marked.

"Have you that paper present?" he asked. "Will you show it to me, please?" Hostile as he seemed to me, the transcript would show him as unfailingly polite.

Opening my bag, I handed the paper over. "It has been cut since I took it away from Mr. Phelps."

We did a brief vaudeville routine about where he got the paper—"Not exactly a table, a little ledge between the windows"—followed by another on lead pencil marks. "The marks that he made, are those the ones that appear there now, opposite the names?"

"Well, not exactly. They were made with a lead pencil, but in order to reproduce them in the paper we had to make them blacker so they would show to be photographed, and the artist on the paper, McDougall, he covered them with ink. Just as they were! But covered with ink."

"Then you mean to say that the marks that are there now are the same in shape that they were then?"

"Yes, sir."

"But they are now covered with ink."

"Yes, sir."

"And then they were in pencil?"

"Yes, sir."

"Did you do that yourself?"

"No, sir."

"The artist did that?"

"The artist did that."

"What is his name?"

"McDougall. He is the artist for the *World*. The head artist."

"What is his first name?"

That derailed me completely, as I realized I didn't know. No one used first names at the office. He was just McDougall. "I—I don't know that," I said, rubbing my nose furiously.

Mr. Hastings was smiling as he half-rose. "Walter."

"Thank you," I said.

"Thank you," said Mr. Saxton. And we were off again. "As a matter of fact, when you told Mr. Phelps that you wanted to show this to your husband, that was not true, was it?"

"No, sir, it was not true. Told a story to catch a story."

Entering the paper as Exhibit A, Mr. Saxton glanced at Phelps. "Did Mr. Phelps, in that interview, when he was speaking of these six gentlemen, use the word 'buy'?"

"Use the word 'buy'?"

"Yes. I wish you would give his exact words if you can, his exact language."

I was getting flustered. *Did he say 'buy'? Of course, he did! But did he? What game is he playing? Can they prove he didn't say 'buy'?* Perhaps the person next door had been listening after all, and was prepared to act as a witness. "I don't think I can remember his exact words."

Phelps gave a crow of satisfaction. Saxton shot him a quelling glare. "Well, give them just as near as you can recall them now."

"In the first interview he said—he said he could get the six men for a thousand dollars."

Saxton's brow furrowed. "Now, let us see if that is correct. He said he could get the six men for a thousand dollars?"

"He could get their votes."

"Get their votes for a thousand dollars?"

"A thousand dollars," I agreed.

Phelps looked smug as Saxton said, "Then, if that was the case, and that was the language he used, he did not say 'buy those six votes for a thousand dollars'?"

"No," I said. Then, before Saxton could ask his next question, I added, "But he said so the second time."

Flustered, Saxton said, "That is at another interview. That isn't down here in the paper, is it?"

"Oh, yes," I told him. "It's in the paper."

Phelps looked like he had swallowed a toad. Clearly, Phelps had hung his hat on the fact that he'd never used the word *buy* in our first interview. Now I was certain either Mr. Wood or another confederate had been ready to swear he'd never said "buy," and that by "getting them," he only meant he would convince them, and the thousand dollars had been for him, not them.

But I had foiled that game. He could have his son testify, but according to my story, Phelps junior had not been with us the whole time. It was still my word against Phelps's.

Saxton looked less queasy than Phelps did, but he was definitely annoyed. I wondered at the level of collusion here. He had been ready to use the man in the next room to impeach my credibility— I was sure of it. But since I'd avoided that trap, he did not seem overly intent on chasing me. I arrived at the opinion that, having proven the assemblymen guiltless, Saxton did not care about Phelps one way or the other.

I, however, wanted to sully Phelps's name with as many members of the legislature as possible. If I were to get my way, he would have no friends remaining. To that end, three times I tried to mention how Phelps implicated the entire Committee on Public Health, saying they were easier to buy.

Each time, Saxton cut me off. Finally, he said, "I do not care about that. I do not care about spreading abroad any further the names of any other gentlemen whom Mr. Phelps mentioned, if he did mention any in that interview. That is not the object of this investigation, and I do not desire you to mention any other names except those of the six gentlemen mentioned in the interview!"

I folded my arms and pouted. But I obeyed. Behind me, I heard General Husted chuckle at the impotency he had inflicted upon this inquiry. *I wonder if there's a story to be done on him . . .*

After another few minutes, Saxton's questions wound down and a different member, a Mr. Roesch, approached. He had been openly conferring with Phelps, which I thought to be shameful, and now tried to catch me out. "I read here, in this article that you wrote, that he said the following, using your own language: 'Mr. Crosby of New York is a rich man, and cannot be bought, but we can buy Gallagher, Tallmadge, Prime, DeWitt, and McLaughlin. The rest are no good.' Now, which answer is the correct one? The one you make here today, or the one in the article?"

He *had* said "buy" in the Kenmore! "They were both correct," I replied, chin high, "because we talked it over repeatedly."

Disappointed at failing to make me burst into a tearful confession of falsehood, Mr. Roesch kept after me: about the whereabouts of the rest of the list that had been cut off, my reason for starting the investigation in the first place, and the false name I had given. "This telegram from Philadelphia was fictitious, was it?"

"Fictitious?" I echoed. "How? I sent it."

"You actually sent the telegram?"

"Yes, sir." *Well, I gave it to Nye to send.*

"But the contents of the telegram were fiction?"

"Yes. As I said, tell a story to catch a story."

"Anything for a story, eh?" asked Roesch with a salacious sneer.

"Anything to expose a liar and a boodler," I replied. Roesch objected, and had that remark struck from the record.

After me, it was Phelps's turn.

When asked what his business was, he answered, "Well, I am engaged in railroading. I deal in stocks, grain. Speculator."

"What is your business in Albany?" clarified Mr. Saxton.

"When I have been in Albany, I have been looking after bills I've been interested in."

"You have been in Albany, I suppose, principally engaged upon business relating to legislation?"

"Well, yes, sometimes," admitted Phelps.

"You are commonly known as a lobbyist?"

"Yes, sir," said Phelps. He then went on to say he knew four of the six men quite well. I wondered how Mr. Tallmadge felt when Phelps said they had a speaking acquaintance. When it came to me, he did not use the argument he had in the *World*, that he was trying to catch me. He simply said that there was nothing wrong in what he did. He did name two of the men who had been in the other room, both former members of the legislature. And the others? "I am not certain who the other gentlemen were. I would not like to swear who they were." Mr. Saxton spent a great deal of time establishing how far we were from the door to the other room, presumably to determine if we could have been overheard. But since I had foiled the plan to catch me out over the word "buy," it came to nothing.

I got the distinct impression that Chairman Saxton did not much like Mr. Phelps. Every time the lobbyist would start to relate the tale, he received the same treatment I had. "I don't care about going into all that now! You don't answer the question, which was whether you said anything to her about any of those gentlemen by name?"

"I am certain I never said anything to her about any of those gentlemen by name. She spoke about buying. I never used the term *buy* in my life."

"Oh, what a whopper!" I exclaimed, to the consternation of all present. Mr. Hastings put his hand on my arm and I subsided.

Phelps lied, and lied, and lied. Oh, how he lied! And the chairman allowed it! "Did you make those marks?" "No, sir." "In pencil?" "No, sir." On and on it went.

I was fairly angry by this point, and had to be hushed twice more. However, when Saxton finished and another member rose, Hastings whispered in my ear, "That's Steven Coon. One of the keenest prosecutors in the state. Fellow Yalie. Watch this."

A clean-shaven man with a pointed chin, Mr. Coon did not pace, but stood and looked directly at Phelps as he posed his questions. He began by asking about Phelps's business, the buying and selling of wheat and oats. Then he got to the lobbying. "You said you kept files in your rooms of bills?"

"Yes, sir."

"And you had lists of the committees?"

"There were lists of the committees, files, and all those things in my room." Coon stared, and the shifting Phelps felt compelled to fill the silence. "If a gentleman calls and wants a bill, if I can give it to him, I will do so. If he wants a list of the committees and I can give it to him, I will do so."

Mr. Coon's mouth curled in an ironic smile. "Is that your object in getting those bills?"

"Yes, sir."

"To supply any gentlemen that might call?"

"Yes, sir."

"A sort of an—"

"Accommodation."

"Assistant to the document room here?"

"Yes, sir."

"Was there any talk between you and this lady about influencing these six gentlemen in regard to that bill?"

"No, sir."

"No conversation of that kind?"

"No, sir."

"On that subject?"

"Not at all."

"That you could influence those six gentlemen?"

"N-n-not at all. It was not talked about."

The stutter had appeared. Evidently, Coon's repetitive style was making Phelps more and more uneasy. It was a delight to watch.

"Was there anything said that Mr. Crosby was a wealthy man and could not be bought?"

"N-n-nossir! I n-never said anything about Mr. Crosby's wealth at any time. I did not know that Mr. Crosby was w-w-wealthy, any more than any other members of the committee. There may be other members of the committee as wealthy as him."

Evidently this was a lie too far, for the entire room erupted in laughter. I wondered how wealthy Mr. Crosby was.

But it was on the question of our second interview that Mr. Coon made a true fool of Foxy Phelps.

"There was a little talk, then, about paying you something?"

"Yes, sir."

"Was any amount talked about?"

"Yes. She talked about a thousand dollars. I said no, I did not wish anything. She said she wanted to give me something. 'Give me two hundred and fifty dollars,' I said."

Mr. Coon's eyebrows shot up. "Why did you suggest to her to give you two hundred and fifty dollars?"

"She was so persistent to give me something." Again, there was a ripple of laughter. I wondered if it might not be partly at my expense.

Mr. Coon remained entirely calm. "You did not claim that you had done her any particular service at that time, did you?"

"No, sir."

"Did you say to her that you had not done her any particular service?"

"Yes, sir."

"That you had not secured any votes for her?"

"I did not say anything!" cried Phelps, contradicting himself entirely before catching himself. "I did n-nuh-not talk about the votes."

"You said you had not exerted any influence for her?"

"Exerted any influence? I m-m-merely said I had done n-n-nothing toward the b-bill. The bill was reported adversely, and I understood it was reported adversely when she was in Albany."

"And that you had done nothing at all about it?"

"And that I had done n-n-nothing at all about it," agreed Phelps.

Coon struck with calm curiosity. "But you were willing to receive this two hundred and fifty dollars as a little—what, a little souvenir of the occasion?"

There was more laughter, not at all at my expense. Phelps answered in a very small voice. "Yes, sir."

Then yet another member, a Mr. Magner, rose. I instantly recognized an ally when he started to question the lobbyist as to how he made money. "You say you have been up here twenty years. During all that time have you furnished bills for persons who inquired for them?"

"Who wanted them," echoed Phelps.

"In an accommodating spirit?"

"Yes, sir."

"Never charge anything for them?"

"No, sir."

"Did you neglect your own business during this time?"

"My own business?"

"Your own business in New York. This grain business."

"Oh. No, sir."

"You do not carry it on up here?"

"You can buy all the grain you want here by telegraph."

Magner cocked his head, as if concerned for Phelps's well-being. "Do you not inconvenience yourself by being up here?"

"Not at all."

"Were you employed by any person up here?"

"Not at all."

"Were you in the habit of furnishing such information as Miss Bly called for without *any* charge?"

"Yes, sir."

"Have you done it heretofore for charge?"

"No, sir."

"Never received *any* consideration for doing it?"

Phelps must have known himself close to perjury, for he waffled. "Sometime I have, and sometimes I haven't."

Magner honed in like Robin Hood at the butts. "Have you ever this year?"

"N-n-no, sir."

"From whom have you received consideration heretofore?"

His side whiskers wilted with sweat, Phelps squirmed. "I don't recollect."

Mr. Coon, whom I had come to regard as my personal hero, then rose—not to question the witness, but to address Chairman Saxton. "I am frank to say if the legislature did not limit us to a particular line of thought, we could make a much more interesting inquiry, probably." His slow speech emphasized the magnitude of his understatement.

Mr. Magner clearly agreed. "I am of the opinion that they instructed us to make further inquiry."

Chairman Saxton shook his head emphatically. "No. It is in regard to the charges published in the *New York World* previous to May 1, 1888. That is all of this resolution, and that is all we have to do."

Frustrated, Magner and Coon sat down as Saxton redirected the questioning once more to safer ground. Nevertheless, Phelps looked chastened by the end of the questioning. His skin had turned a sickly yellow and he kept dabbing his brow, though it was not at all warm in the chamber.

The moment Mr. Saxton excused him, Phelps approached my chair. Mr. Kipe stood, and I was grateful for the force of his presence. Checked, Phelps modulated his voice as he leaned close to me. "You are a c-cuh-clever girl," he said, taking my hand. "A very clever girl."

"But Mr. Phelps," I said, "*you* are very clever. Only, you made a great mistake in not acknowledging the truth of our entire interview. If you'd done so, people would have believed that you were indeed trying to fool me. But when you deny half of the story and admit the other half, you open yourself up to being called less than honest."

His jaw worked for a time, but whatever words he was chewing upon did not emerge. Finally, he said only, "You are a good one. You are a good one." Glancing at my bodyguard, he dropped my hand and departed the chamber.

And, as it turned out, Albany.

THE DAY ENDED RATHER HILARIOUSLY with the testimony of Mr. Wood, whom I'd never met. It was he, Phelps's underling, who had been accused of trying to bribe two senators. He testified about his interest in race horses, and how he had an interest in the law, but had never passed the bar. Asked by Mr. Magner if he was a lobbyist, Wood replied, "I don't know what that is."

Amid the chuckles from the crowd, Chairman Saxton intervened. "I guess you don't mean that, Mr. Wood. You do know what a lobbyist is, don't you?"

"No," said Wood cheerfully. "I have never heard it defined."

By the bristling of his white moustache, Saxton was furious. He was attempting to exonerate his elected brethren, and his hearing was devolving into a farce. "It is a fact, I suppose, and it is a fact within your knowledge, that it is commonly understood that a lobbyist is a person outside of the legislature who seeks in some way or another to influence legislation. Is not that your idea of a lobbyist?"

Wood shrugged. "Well, that is what I have heard."

"Have you not got a well-defined idea of that in your own mind?"

"No, I haven't."

"Then your mind is a blank upon that subject, as to what constitutes a lobbyist?"

Cool as ever, Wood spread his hands. "He tries to influence legislation."

"Then you have an idea of what a lobbyist is?"

Wood smirked. "I have an idea."

Mr. Magner was grim as he said, "From that idea, are you such a person?"

Wood put a hand to his heart, as if wounded. "No, sir!"

The crowd dissolved in mirth, and Chairman Saxton was forced to dismiss the witnesses and return the committee to executive session. Wood seemed ready for the peals of laughter his testimony elicited. He was certainly more poised than Phelps, and of the two, I decided that the villain who laughs is far more dangerous than the villain who sweats.

As members filed out, Messrs. Coon, Magner, and a fellow named Whipple approached to shake my hand and thank me, the latter saying, "I wish every witness before us were as enlightened and as explicit as you are."

It was quarter to six by this time. A press of reporters wanted a statement from me, and I was tempted to hunt up the fellow from the *Buffalo Evening News* who had said I wasn't pretty. But Kipe whisked me out of there and into a cab heading straight for the train station. He was particularly attentive to our surroundings, and I understood that this would be the best opportunity for someone feeling aggrieved to make their grievance known. Even when we were aboard the evening train home, he stood smoking at the end of the car, watchful.

For my part, I sat by a window at the center of the car and stared at the passing landscape until the light faded. I was exhausted and sore, as sore as any night I'd spent in the insane asylum—a reaction to all that tension and the pounding of my heart.

Perhaps the exhaustion was the cause, but I felt horribly depressed and wondered if what I had done mattered at all. I had never thought much of lawyers, especially after one robbed me of my inheritance. Like every other human not admitted to the bar, I'd often joked about the profession, echoing Shakespeare's line, "The first thing we do, let's kill all the lawyers."

And the proceedings in Albany only served to reinforce my opinion that many lawyers used the law the way preachers used religion: making of it what they would, twisting and contorting it to serve their own ends. For every Bourke Cockran, there were five Phelpses. It was just like on Blackwell's Island, how the good physicians like Dr. Ingram were far outnumbered by the bad ones.

Thinking of the comparison, I begin to see a parallel. Law was the medicine of society. If a society is sick, its ills must be fixed by the law. And just as there were quacks peddling their fake patent medicines to enrich themselves at the cost of the health of innocent people, so there were lawyers peddling their own snake oil in the form of bills and lawsuits—not to redress wrongs, but to commit them.

Yet even if the patient had good doctors, death overtakes everyone in the end. I wondered if the same was true for societies. Rome had fallen. Had its laws grown so degraded that they'd ceased to function? If I knew more about history, I might have known the answer.

I then thought of the future, and in my bleak frame of mind I decided that someday America's laws would fall victim to all the Phelpses and Woods out there, and grow so sick on the snake oil they sold that the heart of the body politic would cease to beat. When the law-makers became the law-breakers. When the disease was more attractive than the cure.

There was something in that. It was a philosophy almost worthy of the Quiet Observer. *I'll have to talk to Dr. Ingram about it—if I can ever get over calling him "Doctor." Or maybe Metcalfe?* He seemed amused by life, which probably meant he enjoyed philosophy.

I did not. *There are thinkers, and there are doers—I'm best when I'm doing.* And where there were rules, I was always interested in doing the opposite.

In that way, perhaps I had more in common with a man like Phelps than I cared to admit. A lobbyist twisted the law to serve his client. And my client was Nellie Bly. I would lobby for her against all things. I would even burn down the *World* if I needed to.

Am I any better than Phelps?
There was a philosophical question.

A S HE SAW ME HOME, Mr. Kipe asked if I was in for the evening. I said I was. Then he asked if I was planning on taking
the trip the Colonel had advised.

"I'm not going anywhere," I told him.

"Then I'll see you tomorrow morning," he said, tipping his hat.

Inside my apartment, I discarded my coat, hat, and gloves on the
telephone table and leaned against the wall, head first. That was
how Mother found me. Emerging from her bedroom, she said,
"Welcome home. How did it go?"

I shrugged. "It was fine. But I don't know if it will make any difference."

She made a sound that was part sympathetic and part cynical.
Then she held up a newspaper. "Did you subscribe to the *Commercial Gazette?*"

Struggling out of my boots, I nodded. "A taste of home."

"Why not the *Dispatch?*" she asked, referring to the paper that
had given me my start.

I decided not to be coy. "My friend Wilson writes for the *Gazette*
now."

"The Quiet Observer," said Mother.

I nodded. "I miss him. Even if he drives me mad with his outdated
opinions."

"Mm. Good thing you have Dr. Ingram to fall back on."

I froze with one boot off. Slowly, my head swiveled to look to
her.

Mother added innocently, "In case you *do* go mad." She handed
me the paper as she passed to her bedroom.

I pulled off my other boot and went to sit in the living room.
Flipping to page four of the *Gazette*, I read the perfect words heading that day's Quiet Observations. Wilson began with a quote from
the play *Cato*, by Joseph Addison:

"My voice is still for war." —Addison

Below that was this statement, Wilson's own:

It has been said that a woman may be beaten, whipped or routed, but never vanquished.

Amen, Q. O. Amen.

REPORT

JUDICIARY COMMITTEE, ON THE INVESTIGATION ORDERED BY THE ASSEMBLY, IN REFERENCE TO CHARGES MADE IN THE *NEW YORK WORLD,* OF APRIL 1, 1888, TOUCHING THE LEGISLATIVE INTEGRITY OF CERTAIN MEMBERS OF THE ASSEMBLY.

CONCLUSION

Even conceding that Phelps made the declarations attributed to him, the committee are decidedly of the opinion that the unsworn statement of a self-confessed lobbyist, made for the manifest purpose of inducing a supposed customer to believe that he could aid her in an unlawful undertaking for which he expected to be paid, ought not to bear a feather's weight against the character of any reputable person. The stock in trade of a lobbyist consists of making a person believe that he can influence legislation by buying up legislators. He trades upon the wickedness of the few and the gullibility of the many. A professional lobbyist is a plague spot upon the body politic. His calling is the most nefarious that can well be imagined. His object is to promote bad legislation and to defeat good legislation, thus striking at the vital interests of every citizen who lives under the authority of our laws. This object he accomplishes or seeks to accomplish by means of fraud of corruption. Thus he becomes a center from which emanate the worst influences; a putrid mass from which go forth those germs of disease most fatal to a State.

It certainly is commendable for a paper to call public attention to such a source of contagion, to the end that some remedy may be applied. But we do not think that any paper is justified merely as a matter of journalistic enterprise in spreading before the whole nation charges against the integrity of esteemed public servants, who are honored and trusted by the people among whom they have long dwelt, which rest upon so slender a foundation as do the charges against the gentlemen named above.

The committee, therefore, do not hesitate to say that there is no evidence whatever even tending to impeach the character of any legislator named in the *World* article. We go further than that and say that the testimony of witnesses and the circumstances surrounding the transaction prove beyond the possibility of a doubt that the statements or what purported to be the statements of Phelps concerning the legislators mentioned, as published by the *World* newspaper, are absolutely false in every particular.

The resolution under which the committee are acting did not require any recommendation or advice at our hands. Therefore, none is offered.

Dated, Albany, May 1, 1888

AFTER WORD

This is the second of a series of short works based on Nellie Bly's articles (I say "short." As with most of my projects, it turned out much longer than I expected). This story takes place five months after the close of my first Nellie Bly novel, *What Girls Are Good For*, and the follow-up novelette, *Charity Girl*. Time and interest may spur me to tackle other such stories; we shall see.

As I said in the note to *Charity Girl*, my aim is not to simply regurgitate Nellie's articles. I mean to flesh them out, adding both the larger world in which she lived, and more of her as a person. So far, I'm choosing from her stories those that seem to resonate with societal ills still with us today.

Which brings me to lobbyists. Obviously, there's nothing wrong with going to speak to elected representatives about issues that matter to you. In fact, it's a civic duty, right alongside voting. The trouble is that when you have a professional class based upon doing just that, you are no longer appealing to your representative. Now you're wining and dining dozens of congressmen on an unlimited expense account, promising donations to their campaigns, and maybe a job in your industry when they leave office. Even if it is legal, it is the definition of corruption. It's what Nellie Bly set out to expose, and she succeeded, banishing Phelps from Albany for almost three years. He only came back when both Bly and Cockerill had left the *World* and there was no one left to hold him accountable.

That's the way with cockroaches. They flee from the light. But the moment the light turns off, you can hear them scuttle back across the floor.

One of the wonderfully frustrating things about writing fiction based on Nellie Bly is how often she is an unreliable narrator in regards to herself. This raises all kinds of problems, for her readers, her fans, and anyone trying to capture her in fiction. For example, she wrote three different versions of her Mad-House exposé, all with slightly differing facts. In *What Girls Are Good For*, I aimed for a blending of those facts, combining them with the other reporting that went on around her at the time.

This provides me a certain amount of freedom. Unless I have evidence to the contrary, I assume Bly is not fibbing. But when she is caught out by some stray fact, I have to figure out why. I never want to imply that it's shoddy journalism on her part. It's much more fun, and more in character, to make her cover up something personal about herself. Take, for example, her false testimony here about her name. While she was certainly called "Pink" by her family, there is no evidence at all that Elizabeth Cochrane was ever legally named after a color. But she knows that to give her proper name would both expose her and ruin her unique persona, one carefully crafted over the previous three years. "Pink" is a much more suitable name for Nellie Bly, far better than Elizabeth. And no one would be able to track her down using it.

A couple of years down the road, she lies again under oath, this time about her age, knocking a few years off to stay consistent with the public reporting of how old Nellie Bly was. After all, it's so much more tantalizing if she went into the madhouse at nineteen rather than twenty-two. If she could have managed it, Nellie Bly would have stayed seventeen forever. Vanity? Partly. But she was keenly aware that her youth made everything a better story. It was her brand. Even in her forties, she kept herself drawn in the papers as a young lady, and avoided ever having her photo published.

Nellie Bly understood that the one story she was telling across her entire career was the story of herself. Yes, we could call it vanity. Or we could acknowledge that from the start, this slip of a girl from Pittsburgh had an instinctual understanding of how an audience craves a narrative, and she knew how to fill that craving. To her, reporting was never some lofty ideal. It was a means to an end.

She saved her ideals for causes that struck her as worth reporting, and she would beat her readers with a story until they cared about it as deeply as she did.

Because that's the truth behind Elizabeth "Pink" Cochrane: she cared, deeply. There was no journalistic detachment. There was a wonderful combination of sympathy and rage—sympathy for the downtrodden, rage at injustice.

In the case of "Foxy" Phelps, no one required her sympathy. So she could give full vent to her fury.

Clothes are often part of Nellie's investigations. Her description of her costume for Blackwell's is quite detailed, as is her recitation of being outfitted for her trip around the world in 1889. So it seemed a fun digression here to explore another outfit, with more detail about her daily preferences than I have used before. I confess that a great deal of it is conjecture—I have no idea what corset she preferred. But since I had her roller-skating in *What Girls Are Good For*, it seemed perfectly sensible to me that she would have tried and liked a skating corset, as it would have granted her more mobility.

The same is true of the bustle. We don't have many full-length photos of her, and those we do are, naturally, from the front. But examining these, I can see no evidence of a large bustle, if there's even a bustle at all.

Two different sources reference the bombazine dress, though she herself makes no mention of it. The dolman, on the other hand, is straight from her account of her costume. Sealskin was all the rage in 1888.

The ill-natured hazing of Bly at the Albion by her fellow *World* reporters is maddeningly true. It seems to have happened earlier in her time at the *World*, but as I couldn't find a date, I have transplanted it here to set up relationships for the next full-length Nellie

Bly novel. Based on their future animosity, I added Nym Crinkle to the scene, though he was not mentioned in the original account.

I have to say, reading about that episode, my opinion of the Colonel improved. And, since the humorist Bill Nye really was there, this seemed the perfect opportunity to properly introduce him into Nellie's life. Bill Nye and Nell Bly: a friendship preordained by wordplay alone.

This story was also the perfect moment to bring James Stetson Metcalfe into Bly's life. Historically, they did meet when she slipped on the street during the blizzard of '88—he makes much of that meeting, and his original disinterest, later in their relationship. But though their names would be connected for years to come, often in a romantic sense, we have no idea how their courtship actually began. Since she opens her piece about Phelps with a bastardized version of Gilbert and Sullivan's "I Am A Pirate King," having her attend the theatre to hear the song seemed apt. Since Metcalfe was a theatre reviewer, who better to escort her?

Speaking of theatre, at the eleventh hour I remembered this was exactly the time Colonel Cockerill began courting Leonora Barner. It's a minor story, but as she becomes a fixture in the Colonel's life for the next few years, it seemed too ripe a moment to resist plucking. I also left myself room to go back to Bly's March 4 story about being a chorus girl, in case I need to further explore Leonora's character. Bly and Barner (or, as she's known by then, Mrs. Cockerill) do have at least one scene together in the next book.

Phelps did not return to Albany—at least, we have no record of him there—until 1891. Even after that, he was a spent force.

Eugene Wood, on the other hand, was just getting started. He went on to usurp the title of "King of the Lobby," and had a long and prosperous career as a lobbyist until his name was linked with Tammany Hall during a corruption trial in 1913. If there was a scandal in Albany from 1890 to 1910, Wood was invariably part of it. In 1892, the *New York Times* claimed he was bribing voters in Albany. He was named as part of an operation involving the purchasing of judgeships through Tammany Hall. He plotted with

Tammany leaders and Lieutenant Governor Glynn to have Governor William Sulzer impeached. He was alleged to be part of a plan to dole out bribes to legislators to defeat Governor Hughes's anti-gambling bill in 1908, and subsequently to arrange for a judge to have the act found unconstitutional. It was all great business. When he died in 1924, his estate was valued at $1,216,013.

Wood was a significant fan of horse racing. Fifteen years after this story, in April of 1903, Wood helped to found the Jamaica Racetrack and served as president there. To this day his eponymous race is seen as New York's main prep for the Kentucky Derby.

A few minor notes:

—In both the state transcript and in print, Phelps's first name alternates between Edward and Edwin. I have stayed with Edward.

—Assemblyman Daniel Tallmadge took the *New York World* to court for libel and in 1890 won a whopping twenty-thousand-dollar award, mostly due to Bly's refusal to testify, as she was at that point decrying her shabby treatment by Pulitzer's paper and unwilling to help them out. Rumor says the reason Pulitzer was not more effusive about her trip around the world was this lawsuit. So, in a very real way, this story sows the seed for her departure from the *World*.

—Frederick Duneka went on to be city editor at the *New York World*, and for a while was in charge of its London office. In 1900, he left journalism to go into publishing, joining the firm of Harper and Brothers. He is probably most famous for undertaking, along with Twain biographer Albert Paine, to collect and complete the unfinished works of Mark Twain into the contentious novel *The Mysterious Stranger: A Romance*.

—Nearing completion of the piece, I felt the need to compress time just a little. As a result, I moved Congressman Cockran's speech on Irish Nationalism ahead by one week. It was given Sunday, March 17, not March 24. As I could not find the text of that speech itself, I have constructed one from several other speeches he gave on the topic over the course of his career. I must thank the Brooke Russell Astor Reading Room for Rare Books and Manuscripts at the New

York Public Library for their assistance in hunting down the congressman's speeches.

—Similarly, I have compressed the testimony into a single day so that Bly could witness the proceedings. In reality, the testimony of all the members was spread out over a week, starting on April 12.

This story has a wealth of sources.

Naturally, we begin with Bly herself. Her article, "The King of the Lobby," was indeed a sensation, and went off like an anarchist's bomb in Albany.

Just as valuable was the writing *about* her article in the weeks that followed, most especially Phelps's reply in the *World* and the pieces in Albany papers excoriating her for daring to interject herself into their well-ordered world. The testimony of both Bly and Phelps is fascinating.

I spent hours upon hours on Newspapers.com, looking at the papers of the time for period color, from weather reports to clothes to what plays were being performed where, when, and by whom.

Hudson C. Tanner's 1888 book *"The Lobby," and Public Men from Thurlow Weed's Time* was a terrific find. From 1876 to 1885, Tanner was the official stenographer of the New York State Senate. Thurlow Weed was a publisher and politician who died in 1882. After having been a staunch Whig Party member, Weed helped organize the nascent Republican Party, though he opposed Abraham Lincoln and supported Andrew Johnson. The book has a lengthy, gossipy section on Phelps, including his stutter and rheumatism.

Other sources were my friend Matthew Goodman's *Eighty Days: Nellie Bly and Elizabeth Bisland's History-Making Race Around the World*; Homer W. King's biography of Cockerill, *Pulitzer's Prize Editor*; Frederick Van Wyck's *Recollections of An Old New Yorker*; Frances Elizabeth Willard's *American Women*; Ishbel Ross's *Ladies of the Press*; Iris Noble's *Nellie Bly: First Woman Reporter*; and *New York Criminal Reports: Reports of Cases Decided in All Courts of the State of New York Involving Questions of Criminal Law and Practice, with Notes and References, Volume 4*.

The best resource, of course, remains Brooke Kroeger's excellent biography *Nellie Bly: Daredevil, Reporter, Feminist.* This is my first and most trusted stop for information on Bly.

For this edition, I have included an appendix containing all the articles revolving around Bly and Phelps from April and May of 1888, as well as the transcript for both of their testimonies before the New York State legislature. I have not included the testimony of all the men Phelps named. I did include Wood's testimony, mostly because I find it hilarious.

Some of these articles are repetitive, of course, retelling the story, sometimes in Bly's own words. But just as often they attempt to smear Bly, and openly speculate as to if she might be charged with libel.

The pertinent information I included within the story, and you will miss no significant details if you stop reading right here. But there's always something exciting to see a story unfold as it did through contemporaneous reports, without my personal storytelling biases. If you are so inclined, have at, and enjoy.

Huge thanks to my editor Robert Kauzlaric for helping me shape and hone both this and *Charity Girl.* He's now nearly as steeped in Nellie Bly as I am, hunting up related articles on his own to explore aspects of her research and her thoughts in order to push me along.

Nellie Bly will return in *Stunt Girl.*

Ave,
DB

APPENDIX
PRIMARY SOURCES

BLY'S ORIGINAL STORY IN THE NEW YORK WORLD.
PUBLISHED SUNDAY, APRIL 1, 1888:

THE KING OF THE LOBBY
NELLIE BLY

EDWARD R. PHELPS CAUGHT IN A NEATLY LAID TRAP
————
NELLIE BLY'S INTERESTING EXPERIENCE IN ALBANY
————
HOW THE LOBBY KING CONTRACTS TO KILL BILLS FOR CASH
————
DEALING WITH LEGISLATORS AS WITH PURCHASABLE CHATTELS
————
PHELP'S FURNISHES THE "WORLD" REPRESENTATIVE WITH A LIST OF
ASSEMBLY COMMITTEEMEN WHO ARE BRIBABLE—HIS AGREEMENT TO
KILL ASSEMBLY BILL NO. 191 FOR $5,000—AFTERWARDS CONCLUDES TO
TAKE LESS—THE CHECK TO BE MADE OUT TO HIS SIDE PARTNER, J.W.
CHESBROUGH—"I PASS OR KILL ANY BILL"—A REVELATION OF BASENESS
WHICH SHOULD FILL THE STATE WITH INDIGNATION—THE WATCH HERE

For I'm a Pirate King!
I'm in the Lobby Ring!
Oh! what an uproarius
Jolly and glorious
Biz for a Pirate King!

I was a lobbyist last week. I went up to Albany to catch a professional briber in the act. I did so. The briber, lobbyist and boodler whom I caught was Mr. Ed. Phelps He calls himself "King of the Lobby." I pretended that I wanted to have him help me kill a certain bill. Mr. Phelps was cautious at first and looked carefully into my record. He satisfied himself that I was honest and talked very freely for a king.

He said that he could buy up more than half the members of the Assembly. It was only a question of money. I pretended to doubt his ability to do this. To prove his strength he took out a list of members and put a lead pencil mark against those he swore he could buy. In his scoundrelly anxiety to provide his strength and to get my money he besmirched the character of many good Assemblymen.

Everybody knows Ed. Phelps, the lobbyist. He has been in trouble before, but his assurance has carried him through. During the celebrated Conkling-Platt Senatorial fight I am told that Phelps, in company with Lo Sessions, was indicted for bribing a member, who took the money up to the Speaker's desk and exposed him.

Again, Mr. Phelps had the assurance to sue one Jones, who lives at One Hundred and Thirty-fifth street and Alexander avenue, for $5,000 on a note which Jones gave. The suit was brought in the Supreme Court here. He even tried to get the courts to sustain his wrong-doing. Jones claimed that he had given Phelps the note because the latter claimed to be able to buy certain Senators in aid of a bill. He found that the Senators were already in favor of the bill and so refused to pay. The suit was afterwards dropped, because Phelps was threatened with exposure.

But enough of Phelps. He is notorious. Anything I can say cannot blacken his character more. I can only tell what I did.

I selected a bill that I pretended to be interested in. It was Assembly bill No. 191. I said that if it passed it would ruin my husband's patent-medicine business. He said he could suppress it.

The bill itself is not very interesting, but here it is:

STATE OF NEW YORK
No. 191, Int. 298
In Assembly
January 27, 1888

Introduced by Mr. J.W. Smith—Read twice and referred to the Committee on Public Health—Reported from said committee for the consideration of the House and committed to the Committee of the Whole—Ordered, when printed, to be recommitted to the Committee on Affairs of Clinics.

An ACT

For the better protection of the public health in relation to the sale of medicines and medicinal preparations

The People of the State of New York, represented in Senate and Assembly, do enact as follows:

SECTION 1. It shall be unlawful for any person, firm or corporation to sell, offer or advertise for sale in this State any secret or proprietary medicinal preparation or any substance, fluid or compound for use, or intended to be used, as a medicine or for medicinal purposes, unless the person, firm or corporation preparing or putting the same up for use shall first file with the State Board of Health a formula or statement under oath showing all the ingredients and compound parts of said preparation, and the exact proportion of each contained therein, which shall be of standard strength, and also the name under which it is intended to be sold. If said Board of Health shall be satisfied that said preparation or its ingredients are not detrimental to public health or calculated to deceive the public, they shall issue a certificate, under the seal of said Board, authorizing the sale of said preparation in this state, setting forth the formula under which the same is to be prepared, and stating the name under which the same is to be sold, and it shall be unlawful for any other or different article to be placed in or added to said preparation, or of a different article to be placed in or added to said preparation, or of a different degree of strength, or to sell the same under any different name than as set forth in such certificate, and there shall be paid to said State Board of Health for each certificate so stated the sum of $1 for the use of said Board.

SEC. 2 It shall be unlawful to sell, offer or advertise for sale in this state any secret or proprietary medicinal preparation of any substance, fluid or compound for use or intended to be used for medicine or for medicinal purposes, unless the bottle or other vessel containing the same shall have plainly printed upon the outside of the wrapper and label thereof, in the English language, statement of each and all of the component parts and ingredients of the same and the proportion of each contained therein, and in addition thereto the name ad place of business of the person, firm or corporation manufacturing the same, and also the words "Sale authorized by the New York State Board of Health."

SEC. 3. Every violation of the provisions of this act shall be deemed a misdemeanor, and in addition thereto the person, firm or corporation violating the same shall forfeit the sum of $200, to be recovered by any person who will sue for the same in any court of competent jurisdiction, one-half thereof to be paid to the person bringing suit and one-half to the State Board of Health for the use of said Board.

SEC. 4. Nothing contained herein shall be construed to prohibit the sale of compounds or medicines put up by a licensed pharmacist in accordance with a physician's prescription, delivered at the time of such sale.

SEC. 5. This act shall take effect immediately.

————

THE TRIP TO ALBANY

Armed with this little bill and what I had learned, without confiding in any one, I took the train for Albany. The day (last Tuesday) was not bright, so I spent the time reviewing what I had learned. The only thing that amused me was my list of lucky odd numbers. It was the 27th of March, the train was an odd number, my chair was No. 3 and there was an odd number of passengers. Even when I reached Albany this odd streak did not desert me. I walked to Stanwix Hall and was given room No. 15, and there were only three chairs in the room. I did not look any further for odds.

The next day about noon I made my appearance at the Kenmore Hotel, where Mr. Phelps resides and keeps his legislative office. A half-grown boy in uniform met me at the door ad politely escorted me through the lobby of the hotel to the elevator. A number of men who sat around glanced at me curiously.

"I want to see Mr. Phelps, please," I said as the boy started the elevator on its upward flight.

"Do you want to send your card up?" he asked. I had intended to send up a card—not Nellie Bly's, of course—until the boy unwittingly let me know that it was possible to get in without the use of that modern passport. I immediately decided to storm his castle.

I followed Buttons along the softly carpeted halls until he stopped at a door which bore on a little china plate the number 98.

At the boy's second knock an invitation to enter was given in a gruff voice. I stood at the half-opened door and saw a gray-haired man busily writing at a desk which occupied the center of the room.

"He's in the other room," he replied to Buttons's inquiry for Mr. Phelps, without lifting his head. The boy knocked on the door which separated the two rooms, as he said, "A lady to see you Mr. Phelps."

"Very well, show her to the other door," was the answer, delivered in a rather smooth and not disagreeable voice.

THE MEETING WITH PHELPS

"Are you Mr. Phelps?" I asked, only to make him confess the fact.

"Yes, madam," he replied, smiling slightly, while he offered me a chair, with the request to "please be seated."

I sat down and looked about me. This was not what I had pictured to myself. This self-possessed, smiling man could not be the vampire I had been made to believe him. As he sat in the chair close by me with a reassuring smile on his face he did not look more than fifty-five years old. He is not a robust man, yet he is not of delicate build. He was dressed plainly, but with taste. There was nothing gaudy or loud about him, as one might imagine from his position. His hair and his side whiskers are gray. His upper lip and chin are clean shaven and he has something of the parson in his appearance.

The room in which we sat was comfortably furnished. It was apparently fitted up for an office; the only piece of furniture which looked out of place was a wardrobe which stood against the centre wall.

I thought my surest bait for this occasion was assumed innocence and a natural ignorance—not entirely assumed—as to how such affairs are conducted.

"Mr. Phelps, I came to consult you on a matter of importance," I began nervously, as if afraid of my position. "I—I hope no one can overhear us?" and I looked at him imploringly.

————

WINNING HER CONFIDENCE

"Oh, no, you are safe to speak here," he assured me with a pleasant smile. He drew his chair closer to me and adjusted his glances carefully on his nose, meanwhile looking me over critically.

"I have come to see you about a bill," I began to explain. His face lighted up a girl's will over strawberry soda on an August day. He smiled encouragingly and rubbed his hands together gently.

"What bill is it?" he asked eagerly.

"A bill about patent medicines," I answered. "My husband is ill and he sent me to New York from Philadelphia to place some advertisements and a friend, who also has a patent medicine told me of this bill, so I came up to see if anything could be done."

"Have you the bill with your?" he asked in a low tone.

"Yes, my friend gave it to me when he told me about it," I replied. He got up and walked over to the door, as if to be positive it was tightly closed. Then he came back, and taking the bill, which I held in my hand, he quickly scanned it.

"Do you think you can kill it?" I asked, with a proper amount of enthusiasm

"Oh, yes," he responded heartily. "Never fear, I'll have it killed."

Excusing himself he went to the other room. When he came back he had a large ledger in his hand and a large smile on his face. He sat down and, resting the book on his knee, he ran his finger down the alphabet. He turned to a page which was filled with data of bills—a sort of a memorandum. He grew very happy after this and closed the book in order to pay all attention to the poor little lamb who had come to be fleeced.

"What made you come to me?" he asked. I hardly knew what was my best reply, so I said:

"Well, I had often read of you, you know; so when my friend told me about the bill I did not want to place the advertisements and so lose all my money. If that bill passes, you know it will ruin our business."

"That is true," he assented warmly. "It will kill patent medicines. But who sent you to me?" he still urged.

"My friend said I might consult Mr. Phelps," I answered evasively.

"Who is he?" he asked sharply.

"I would not like to give his name without his authority," I said, while I wondered what I would do if he pressed the subject.

"I only wanted to know, because we have had lots of people up here paying to have that bill killed. Do you know Pierce of Buffalo? He is trying to get it killed," he said.

"I never heard of the bill until recently," which was true. "I concluded not to go home, so I telegraphed my husband and came on here."

"Where are you from?" he asked.

"Philadelphia. We make a patent medicine there but it sells all over New York state. Do you think you can kill the bill?"

IT WILL TAKE MONEY

"Oh yes; I assure you of that. Now you keep up your nerve," he said, seeing my assumed nervousness. "I'll kill that bill. It will take money, you know." It was a shock, this cool assertion. I clutched at my umbrella.

"I am willing to pay anything up to $3,000," I said faintly, "if you assure me it will be stopped."

"I can assure you that," he replied confidently. "Of course, you don't need to talk of $3,000. You see there will be my expenses, and then I will have to pay some Assemblymen."

He went to the end of the room and took from there some pages containing the names and classifications of Assemblymen and Senators—a list of committees. Under the title of "Affairs of Cities" he showed me the twelve names of the men who he said would kill or save the bill.

"Mr. Crosby," of New York, is a rich man and can't be bought, he said calmly. "But we can buy Gallagher, of Erie, Tallmadge, of Kings; Prime, of Essex; DeWitt, of Ulster; Hagan, of New York, and McLaughlin, of Kings. The rest are no good."

Oh, Mr. Phelps, I thought sadly, you are into the trap with both feet, for he had marked with his lead pencil the names as he read them off.

"But if the rest are opposed?" I urged quietly.

"The majority gains," he said sweetly. "There are six out of eleven I can buy."

"How much will it take for them?" I asked, innocently.

"You can get the lot for $1,000."

Great goodness! just imagine, the whole lot for $1,000!

"I must never be known as connected with this," I began to cry. "It frightens me. I wouldn't have it known for anything; though," I added, "I'm willing to pay all it may cost to have the bill killed."

"That is nothing," he said lightly. "That's my business. I just stay here to watch bills for railroad presidents, insurance companies, &c. I'm kept here just to do this," he said firmly. "There is a lawyer of the name of Batch in New York who is also assisting me in getting people who want to fight the same bill you are here about. I've had my agents send out hundreds of copies of it."

SHE CAME TO THE RIGHT MAN

I felt inclined to ask if it were to bleed the public, but I was afraid. I had not finished yet, so I said, "I thought when I came up that I would go to see Mr. J.W. Smith, who introduced the bill, but I did not know where to find him, so I came direct to you."

"It's a good thing you did," he said warmly. I wondered if he would feel so sure of that in a few days. "Smith is a dissipated and unprincipled fellow. He would have taken your money and given you no returns. You came just to the right one to help you this time."

"You are sure then for about $3,000—which I would rather spend this way than lose it in advertising—you can kill the bill?"

"I can have it killed for that amount or near it," he replied confidently. "Now, where can I see you again to make final arrangements?"

"Any place you state," I replied.

"Well, when you come from Philadelphia could you come Friday. Well, you telegraph me to meet you at your hotel in New York. Where do you stop?"

"Sometimes at the Sturtevant and again at the Gilsey," I answered. "But then I dread exposure in this affair. Could you not appoint a place where it would attract less attention? Have you no place I could see you?"

"You might come to my office," he said, falling easily into the trap I had laid for him. That's where, of all place, I wanted to go, but I said with well-feigned surprise:

"Oh, you have an office in New York also?"

"Yes in the Boris Building. Do you know where that is? Well, when you cross the Cortlandt Street Ferry you cross to Broadway, and it is about two blocks below. No. 115, room 97. Wait, I'll write it here for you on the bill." And he thereupon took the bill and wrote on the margin, "E.R. Phelps, 115 Broadway, Room 97, Boris Building."

"How very kind of you," I said.

"Now you come down Friday; meet me there between 12 and 1. If I'm not in when you arrive wait for me. I'll be there as soon as possible. I live out of the city. Come down prepared to make final arrangements (this meant pay the price) and I assure you I'll kill the bill afterwards."

"Then I can place my advertisements on Friday, on your assurance that the bill will be killed?" I asked.

"Don't place them until you see me." This was for fear I would resent the price after my advertisements were safely placed. "I assure you, after you see me you can safely place them. The bill will then be dead, or just as good, it will be harmless."

————

TRYING TO GET RID OF HER

"Why stay in Albany any longer?" he asked. "Why not take the 1.30 train for New York?" It was close on to that time, and I wanted my dinner, so I told him.

"They carry an eating car," he urged. "Take that train; it will get you in at 5 o'clock."

"That will allow me to go on to Philadelphia," I said, apparently falling into his plans, while I had no intentions of going.

"There is no use in waiting any longer," he urged. "You'll be seen, and that will raise comment. You might as well go now, and be sure to meet me Friday." I began to suspect that he feared if I remained longer some other boodler would get hold of me and rob him of his prey, or that I would discover that which I already knew, i.e., that the patent-medicine bill was really dead and had been for some time. So I promised to go.

"I'll take that list home to show my husband," I said, as I reached for the list he had marked of buyable assemblymen.

"Give it to me," he exclaimed hurriedly, as he took it from my grasp. "Your husband may know some of these men and may tell them. It wouldn't look well for me to cross off those that can be bought. I'll cross out all the names."

THE LIST OF HONEST MEN

My heart sank. I really believe if hearts could faint mine fainted. Here was my only clue to those who, Mr. Phelps alleged, could be bought. If he crossed out all I could not tell one from the other. I shut my eyes and thought of several nasty things against cunning men and odd numbers. Then I opened them and looked blankly as he started to destroy my clue. He placed the sheet on a book on his desk and made crosses against the remaining names, excepting Mr. Crosby's, and then he handed it to me. I glanced at it, and with a prayer of thanks folded it hurriedly and placed it in my purse.

The rough covering of the book had caused the lead pencil to make a peculiar spotted line against the second lot of names marked by Mr. Phelps.

When marking the original ones the committee list was on a flat, smooth surface, and as it had pens that the lines are as distinctly recognizable as though they were in difference colors.

Here is a fac-simile of the list just as he marked it.

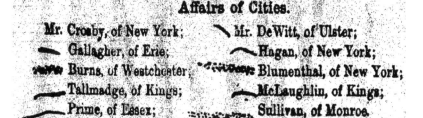

After dining at my hotel I started for the city. I had told Mr. Phelps that the name I gave him—Miss Consul—was an assumed one, taken because my own and my husband's name was so familiar that everybody would recognize it at once So I went under my maiden name.

As soon as I got to New York I sent a telegram to a friend in Philadelphia, instructing him to forward it from there to Mr. Phelps. It was done to ease any doubts he might have. This ran as follows:

PHILADELPHIA, MARCH 28.
E.R. PHELPS, ROOM 96 KENMORE, ALBANY, N.Y.
HAVE MADE SATISFACTORY ARRANGEMENTS WITH HUSBAND. WILL SEE YOU AS AGREED.
MISS CONSUL

THE SECOND MEETING

Friday came and with it the disquieting intelligence that the bill I professed to be interested in had been reported adversely by the committee on Thursday.

How would Mr. Phelps act under this news? However, I borrowed a long sealskin dolman to give me a matronly look, and hiring a hansom I was driven to No. 135 Broadway, the Boris Building.

Mr. Phelps name was on the boor of No. 97, and before I could knock the door was opened, and he, smiling sweetly, stood before me and invited me in. "My son," he said, introducing a rather handsome young man who sat behind the solitary desk the office contained. I was wondering how Mr. Phelps knew I was at the door, when I glanced out and saw that from his window he could see everybody who came up on the elevator. The door of the office was darkened.

"I suppose you know about the bill?" he inquired sharply.

"Oh, no," I said, in assumed voice of alarm and ignorance. "Can't it be killed?"

"Yes, that's it," he said smiling, "it has been killed."

"So soon. How clever you must be!" I remarked flatteringly.

"Well, I saw that you were anxious to kill the bill and I told you that it should be killed. It's done. That will never bother you again." Mr. Phelps's son here took his silk hat and left the room.

"How did you ever manage it?" I asked simply, with a world of admiration in my eyes.

————

HOW CLEVER MR. PHELPS WAS

"Why, you see"—he talked in a confiding whisper—"I went to work on it right away. You see I had it transferred from the committee that first had it. As I told you, Mr. Crosby could not be bought, and I knew he and some others determined to pass it, so I went to the ones I told you I could get and told them I wanted that bill killed. They said they were anxious to get rid of it, so I had it reported back to the Committee on Public Health. I knew I could get them easier."

"Oh, how very clever!" I breathed rapturously, "and they did not refuse?"

"No, they asked me what it was worth," he said boldly, "and I told the $1,000, and so they promised to do it."

"They did not dare refuse," I murmured again.

"No; I should say they did not," he said laughingly. "You see that's my business. I'm the head of the Lobby."

Oh, indeed! What a good thing I went to you. How can you ever do all the work?"

"Why, I keep a lot of runners who watch and know everything that happens I am head. They report to me, and I have books in my rooms where entries are made of every bill and notes of every incident connected with it. You noticed when you gave me the bill in the Kenmore I went into another room and got a large book? Well, by that book I at once saw all about the bill and knew just what to say to you."

"What did you say to the committee about the bill?" I asked, curiously.

"I just told them the bill had to be killed, and I told them it was worth $1,000. I had to give my check for it right off, but I told you that I could have it done for $1,000 for the committee, with my expenses extra.

"My husband could not understand how you could buy the whole committee for $1,000. It seems so little," I suggested.

"I couldn't if that was my only case, but you see this is my business. I spend all my time at it. I pay these men heavily on other bills, so that makes some bills more moderate."

"Then you can have any bill killed?"

HE OWNS THE HOUSE

"I have control of the House and can pass or kill any bill that so pleases me," was Mr. Phelps's astounding reply.

"Next week," he continued, "I am going to pass some bills and I'll get $10,000 for it. I often get that and more to pass or kill a bill."

I was stricken dumb. I did not know what to say. The brazen effrontery of this appalled me.

"You can take this," handing me the Albany Journal, "to show your husband that the bill was killed. You will also see an account of it in today's WORLD."

"I would like you to tell me who sent you to me," continued Mr. Phelps. "Not that I want to pry into your affairs, but it may be one of my agents and I want to pay him."

The only agent had been my own sweet self, so I demurred and said I feared to give the name without the man's authority.

"I have to pay the money for killing the bill to the committee this week," Mr. Phelps began, returning to the subject of money, "and as I got it done so quickly I thought I would deal honestly with you and only charge you $250 for my expenses. That will make a total of $1,250. Could you write a check here for that amount?" he asked boldly.

FENCING ABOUT THE MONEY

"I—oh, dear, I'm dreadfully frightened," I exclaimed, to give myself time to think. He smiled, as if well pleased. "You see, my husband told me not to do anything that would connect me with this affair." I breathed easier. "For that reason I do not want to give a check."

"Well, you could write out a check payable to J.F. Chesbrough. He is a relative of mine, and it's just the same as giving it to me; or you could make it out in my son's name."

"No, I don't want it made out to Phelps, I'm afraid," I said; "but if you send your son up to the St. James Hotel, where I am stopping, I will give it to him there."

"That will do," he said carelessly, and then he called "Johnny! Johnny!"

"Aha! Johnny is waiting on the outside," I thought, "and comes at the call when the poor lamb is fleeced. I began to fear that really, somehow, they would compel me to pay the money.

"I'd rather make out a check," I began, hastily.

"Very well, I'll write the name for you," and suiting the action to the word he took from his desk a white envelope, smaller than the ordinary envelope, and made the check payable to. He then wrote in the corner the amount, $1,250.

"My son will go up with you and get the check," he said, and again began to call "Johnny."

"Oh, then I might just as well get the money and hand it to him," in half hopes of getting him to abandon the idea of sending someone with me. I wanted a chance to escape. He took the envelope from me and tore the ends and back off it. I wanted to save that name, so I said quickly: "Give me that, I'll write the check after all and give it to your son."

He handed it back. The name was yet clear, but the numbers were partially torn away, only "50" remained. Here it is:

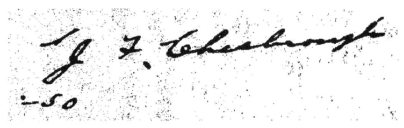

Mr. Phelps showed me the telegram, which purported to come from me in Philadelphia, after he had called his son in to tell him to accompany me to my hotel.

––––

SUCH AN HONEST LITTLE WOMAN

"I felt queer about you at first," he said. "It is the most natural thing in the world for a woman to come to me for such work. First I thought it was a trap to catch me." I looked at him and then at his son in a hurt manner. "But then I saw how innocent you were and how honest I must stay I was surprised though."

"Well, you see, I did not know what to do," I urged, as if I had blundered. "I was so ignorant of it all."

Mr. Phelps, Jr., leaned on the desk and glanced at me admiringly. My cheeks began to burn and I began to long for freedom. Would I never escape them?

"Madam is going up to the St. James," Phelps, Sr., explained to Phelps, Jr., "and you are to go with her. She will give you a check there for some work I have been doing for her."

"Can't you come along?" I asked Mr. Phelps, Sr. "I hate to have your son connected with this; besides I am better acquainted with you." I was getting deeper and deeper into it and I didn't know what to do.

"Father, you go," urged the young man. "You might as well. You would leave the office in a half hour, anyway."

I said I had a cab at the door, but that I would not like to be seen taking Mr. Phelps away in it. They urged, but I was firm, and at last Mr. Phelps sad his father would go up on the Elevated Railway and would get there about the same time I did.

––––

FAREWELL WORDS

"He can wait for me in the parlor," I began, joyously, now that I could escape. Wait for me? Well, he would wait years before I would come.

"I'll get the money, and when I go in the parlor I will hand it to you. No one will see me there." He could be sure, no one would ever see me give him money.

"Where will you get the money?" he asked, impudently.

"Father, that's nothing to you, so she gets it," the young man remarked, for which I looked my heartfelt thanks.

"In a half hour, in the parlors of the St. James Hotel?" said Mr. Phelps, as I arose to start.

"Yes," I replied, and walked smilingly with the young man to the elevator.

"I was extremely nervous over this," I said, half apologizing for my hesitating manner.

"You'll get over that by the time you have had more bills to kill," he said, encouragingly. I laughed and said that I thought I should.

I got into the cab, gave the driver instructions to go a thousand different ways and to stop at the WORLD office, where I could write my story. He was a man who knew his business and I felt confident in a short time that I was not followed.

So far as I personally know, Mr. Phelps is still waiting my arrival in the parlor of the St. James Hotel.

❧

FOLLOW STORY IN THE NEW YORK WORLD THE SAME DAY
PUBLISHED SUNDAY, APRIL 1, 1888:

MR. PHELPS'S VAIN WAITING

———

HE KEEPS HIS ENGAGEMENT WITH THE PATENT-MEDICINE LADY AND THE $1,250.

As soon as Nellie Bly reached THE WORLD office a reporter was sent out to watch Mr. Phelps and to see whether he kept his engagement to meet the young woman at the hotel. Sure enough, Mr. Phelps was on time. He arrived at the St. James Hotel a few minutes before 2 o'clock and took up a position against one of the front pillars of the hostelry. He leaned against his heavy walking cane while his eyes kept wandering up and down Broadway. Presently a nattily dressed young man, rather slim of build and wearing a dark brown moustache, came up and engaged in conversation with him. The young man was Mr. Phelps's son, who is in training to succeed his father when the latter grows too old, too wicked or goes to the land where the lobby has no control or influence.

The son and father held a short conference, which ended in the father, no doubt, appointing the son a special committee of one to ascertain if the lady had kept her engagement, for the son hurried into the lobby and went straight to the ladies' parlor. He returned in a few minutes and held another conversation with his father. Then the father and son adjourned to the southwest corner of Broadway and Twenty-sixth street, where they stood in caucus for five minutes. A WORLD reporter, who knew both and had kept track of their movements, now located himself in Delmonico's. At twenty minutes past 2 young Phelps made another pilgrimage to the hotel, and entering it did not return to his father for fully ten minutes. They conversed together only a few minutes, when both walked to the Broadway entrance of the hotel. The father remained outside, while the son darted in once more. The WORLD reporter walked out of Delmonico's, proceeded to the Hoffman and then, retracing his steps, was soon in the presence of Phelps, sr. Mr. Phelps shook hands with the reporter and remarked that it was a beautiful day. The reporter entered the hotel and met young Phelps coming out. Five minutes later Phelps, sr., and Phelps, jr., had gone into executive session on the northwest corner of Broadway and Twenty-fifth street. The session was adjourned every five minutes to allow the junior member of the firm to visit the St. James Hotel. At 3.10 o'clock an adjournment for the day was evidently taken, as father and son were seen walking down Broadway.

PHELPS REPLY IN THE NEW YORK WORLD
PUBLISHED MONDAY, APRIL 2, 1888:

THE LOBBY KING'S AMUSING EXPLANATION

————

IN ANSWER TO THE DETAILED, CIRCUMSTANTIAL, AND EXPLICIT STORY OF NELLIE
BLY, EDWIN R. PHELPS OFFERS THE FOLLOWING ASTONISHING EXPLANATION:

————

To the Editor of THE WORLD:

I have read with some amusement from time to time the remarkable stories got up by your smart female confidence correspondent, Nellie Bly, who must be admitted to be the champion story-teller of the age. I have no objection to the attention she has now paid to me, but I do object to her resort to groundless statements that affect other people in her efforts to concoct a sensational romance such as you seem to suppose your readers relish.

The fact is that I had a visit at my hotel in Albany last Wednesday from the fair Nellie, who came to tell me gravely that she wanted my services to kill a bill relating to quack medicines, then in the Assembly. Naturally I asked the dear girl what she knew about legislation, how she became interested in quack medicines and who sent her to me. On the first question she professed an interesting verdancy, to the second she pleaded a husband, which for her sake I hope will not long be a false pretense, and to the third she objected to say what valued friend had mentioned my name to her as what you call the "King of the Lobby," but professed to be eager to pay me $4,000 or $5,000 to kill the bill. While I did not know your bogus lunatic, I was well aware that she was an imposter, and I at once set her down in my mind as one of two things—a blackmailer or a newspaper decoy. My usual course would have been to tell her that I had no business transactions with women and that her husband must call on me if he wished to obtain my services. As it was I resolved to lead my fair visitor on as far as she would go. All my actions were with that object and I intended when it came to the crisis to give her a lesson that would teach her better sense hereafter.

Now, some portion of what Nellie says about our conversation is true. I met her at her own game and certainly indulged in some tall lying to astonish her. But it is utterly, positively a whole-cloth lie to say that I mentioned the name of a single Assemblyman or even hinted at "buying" anybody. Not a legislator was named while Nellie was in my room, and as a matter of fact I never talked with any Assemblyman on the Patent Medicine bill, never heard it mentioned by a member, and with two of the members name by Nellie I have no acquaintance whatever. The marks put on the committee list produced by Nellie must have been the work of her own fair hands. The story that a portion of them were made by me on a smooth surface and the others on the rough cover of a books is "too thin." No one who wanted to cover up his tracks would be guilty of such folly outside of the lunatic asylum where Nellie played her tricks. Besides, the dear girl in her story says that I "placed the sheet on a book" on my desk and "made crosses against the remaining names." Fibbers should be more careful not to confound straight lines with crosses, or Nellie ought to have made her tally-sheet correspond with her text. Besides, nobody who knows me would for a moment believe that I would talk to any living soul, in jest or in earnest, about "buying" votes. I have had some experience and am not quite a fool.

The plain truth is, that while poking fun at the sweet girl, I gave her a list of the committee having the quack medicine bill in charge and advised her to go and see all the gentlemen on the committee. At which dear Nellie started and said, "Oh! I'm afraid of the men, I'd rather do business with you." If I had been a young man probably I should have considered the look that accompanied the words quite fascinating.

I did give Nellie my address in New York. She had to hurry away from Albany, she said, and wanted me to call at her hotel in New York. I was not to be caught (but was trying to do the catching), and so allured Nell to my own office. I instructed my son to be on hand. He heard every word of conversation that occurred in my office, and I took him with me to the St. James Hotel, intending, as soon as Nellie gave me a check, he open spot her and threaten her with arrest unless she made a clean breast of her fraud.

The piece of paper with the name of an old friend of mine, J.F. Chesbrough, on it, must have been picked up by Nellie in my office, and the "—50" on it seems to indicate that it was a memorandum of some business transaction.

I may say, in confirmation of my statement, that immediately Miss Nellie took herself and her satchel and her sweet smile out of my apartment at the Kenmore Hotel I stepped into the adjoining room, related the whole story of the remarkable visit to Mr. Crenell of Rochester and another gentleman, who were waiting for me and told them I had made an appointment with the mysterious female quack actress at my office in New York and intended to catch her in a trap while she was supposing she was catching me.

I have been twenty years in business. I make no disguise of my occupation and have nothing against being called a "lobbyist." I do business as legislative against for persons who can better afford to pay me than to waste time in Albany. But I never in my life paid nor offered a dollar to any Senator or Assemblyman to influence him in legislation, and, despite the thoughtless and uncharitable assertions of some newspapers, I have never known a Legislature in which there were not a sufficient number of honorable, upright men to uphold a meritorious measure and to kill any attempt at injustice or blackmailing.

EDWARD R. PHELPS
115 Broadway, New York

––––

AN ANALYSIS OF THE EXPLANATION.

In view of the ingenious plan resorted to by the "king of the lobby" to combat the unquestioned accuracy of Nellie Bly's narrative, it is interesting to analyze the foregoing astonishing document. Mr. Phelps at once admits the fact that the representative of the WORLD called on him at his headquarters and that her whole interview was in relation to the killing of the quack medicine bill. He says he asked Miss Bly about her interest in the bill, who sent her and what she knew about the legislation. These are precisely the questions any lobbyist would ask one who approached him on "business," and they are the questions which Miss Bly not only gives but relates her answers. Mr. Phelps is in error when he says his visitor professed to be willing to pay $4,000 or $5,000 to kill the bill. She offered "up to $2,000." But the "king of the lobby" knew at once that he was dealing with either a blackmailer or a newspaper decoy. Then comes the inadvertent admission that Mr. Phelps was no stranger to such business transactions, for he writes, with truth "my usual course would, &c." There is no doubt that the greater part of customers who come to Mr. Phelps to offer money to have bills killed are men, and they are able to show good and sufficient reasons why they are not imposters. As it was, however, Phelps resolve to lead his fair visitor as far as she would go. This is precisely what Nellie Bly demonstrates by the successful efforts the king made to kill the bill and his prompt request for his pay. The absurd statement that his ultimate intention was to expose his visitor—blackmailer or newspaper decoy, he and not made up his mind which—is rather gauzy, in view of the fact that he does not pretend that he made any effort to follow Nellie Bly and inform himself just whom he was dealing with or ascertain how far she was likely to go. In other words, he would have it understood that he was playing a very deep game, and yet at the same time was taking none of the precautionary measures that might have been expected of so shrewd a man.

––––

At almost the outset Mr. Phelps is a self-confessed liar. This bold statement tallies very well with the shameless way in which he told of the men he could buy, and exhibited the proofs of the truth of what he said. Mr. Phelps, however, is not slow in seeing that the men whom he has so basely slandered, if he was not telling the truth, will make trouble for him, and this part of the narrative he wisely denies in positive terms. He did do some "tall lying," but he drew the line on his lies at mentioning any names. Is this reasonable?

The next dangerous thing in Nellie Bly's history of the interview is the annotated list of the members of the affairs of cities committee. This is, according to Mr. Phelps, a pure invention, even to the marks on the margin. His first impulse is to make such a sweeping denial that the uncomfortable bit of paper is at once eliminated from the discussion. Therefore, he says that he did not even mention the name of any of the members of the committee. But the paper must be accounted for in some way and the suggestion is made that Nellie Bly fixed up the marginal notes herself. If she were doing this and inventing this bit of proof, what would put it into her mind to conceive a complex and confusing set of marks—some of them smooth and some of them ragged? It would have been much easier to have checked off what she wanted with the dash of the pen. But no, she goes to the needless and absurd length of marking out and then telling the story of how the different kinds of marks happened to be made. This single incident of the committee list and the two sets of marks bears the indisputable stamp of genuineness. It is a problem that Mr. Phelps could not get over. But the king says in one place that nothing was said about the members of the committee and yet in another place he inadvertently declares that he gave her the list, told her about them and advised her to "go and see all the gentlemen on the committee."

––––

Mr. Phelps did give Nellie his address in New York. Well, of course. The WORLD published the fac-simile of that particular address just as he wrote it. And now comes a most interesting bit of evidence of Mr. Phelps' "tall lying." In his "explanation" he writes this sentence: "I was not to be caught, and so allured Nell to my office." On looking it over afterwards, he happens to think of his adopted plan of explanation and puts in his afterthought in this significant parenthesis "(but was trying to do the catching)." Yes, Mr. Phelps has been "in the business," as he says, a good many years and he is "not exactly a fool." Just what the business of a self-confessed "lobbyist" would be an interesting subject for an essay by an acknowledged "king." If he handles no money how does he give birth to bills which he smiles upon and blight and wither measures which receive his frown? Whence comes his influence, and where lies his mysterious but mighty power? Has the "King of the Albany Lobby" in very truth discovered a force more potent than gold and is there now locked up in his breast a secret more to be desired than Ponce de Leon's "Fountain of Youth?"

––––

WILL HE BE INDICTED?

The question whether Mr. Ed Phelps has not thrown himself open to indictment for bribery was yesterday submitted to several well-known criminal lawyers in this city, and the views of a number of Senators and Assemblymen upon his ----- proceedings were also obtained. A lawyer, who is one of the best authorities on the question of bribery, but who was not desirous of having his name seen, said:

"The confession of Phelps to Nellie Bly that he had bribed certain members of the Legislature is full, complete and convincing. A confession alone, however, is not sufficient to convict a defendant; there must be some corroborating proof that the crime charged has been committed. The Court of Appeals said, in the case of the People against Jaehne, that the confession itself was some proof that the crime charged had been committed and sufficient proof that the defendant had committed the crime, and that only some corroborating evidence was required tending to make the confession appear to be probable and true. In a very early case, which was approved by the Court in the cast of the People against Jaehne, Chief-Justice Nelson, of the State, said: "Slight corroboration is sufficient." Now, the corroborating facts in this case are the transfer of the bill from one committee to another, certain of whose members Phelps admitted he had bribed; second, the various memoranda which Phelps gave to Nellie Bly, including the clipping containing his office address, and the cutting from the check with the name of Cheesborough upon it; and third, his appearance at the St. James Hotel to get her money, all of which can be proved by independent evidence. I am thoroughly convinced that there is sufficient evidence to go to a jury and convict Phelps."

PHELPS' LETTER TO THE NEW YORK TIMES.
PUBLISHED MONDAY, APRIL 2, 1888:

HE IS A "LEGITIMATE AGENT."

————

AND HE WORKS FOR PAY, BUT HE IS A TOLERABLY SHARP PERSON.

————

To the Editor of THE NEW YORK TIMES:

Will you permit me to say through the columns of your paper that the yarn printed about me in the WORLD of to-day is a romance, with the single exception that a female scribbler, signing herself Nellie Bly, did call on me at Albany in reference to killing a patent medicine bill in the Assembly. I thought she was a female decoy of some sort and accordingly drew her out by pretending to fall into her proposition to try to corrupt some one.

I do not deny that I am a legislative agent in which I do legitimate work for pay, but do unequivocally deny that I have ever said to any one that I could purchase any member of the Legislature, either of the Senate or Assembly. I am not quite fool enough for that, and no one who knows me will take me to be such an idiot as this sensation-monger has painted me. I also desire to say that I did not mark any committee list of members who could be purchased. If such a list was marked it must have been done by the enterprising young woman herself.

EDWARD R. PHELPS
Sunday, April 1, 1888

ℰℒ

FOLLOW-UP STORY IN THE NEW YORK WORLD
PUBLISHED MONDAY, APRIL 2, 1888:

AN UNPARALLELED SENSATION

———

WHAT STATESMEN AT ALBANY SAY OF "THE WORLD'S" EXPOSE OF PHELPS

———

[SPECIAL TO THE WORLD]

ALBANY, APRIL 2—THE WORLD's exposé of Lobby King Phelps's methods has created an unparalleled sensation here.

Nothing like it has so stirred up the Legislature since the press opened its guns upon the notorious Tweed Ring.

The members of the craft are terror-stricken, while the Assemblymen whose names appear in the list of those accused of being purchaseable threaten vengeance upon the man who has betrayed them.

All concede that it is the cleverest piece of newspaper work in the history of State affairs.

There seems every probability of an immediate and vigorous investigation.

The result is likely to be a full demonstration of the truth of THE WORLD's exposures from time to time of the corrupt methods openly practised upon the floor and in the committee-rooms.

Many members of both Houses to-day assured THE WORLD correspondent that they would employ every means within their power to drive Phelps, O'Brien and the remainder of the gang out of Albany.

These worthies, however, have powerful influence upon a large number of legislators, and the lines between Knights of Honor and the Black-Horse Brigade will be closely drawn.

Assemblyman Gallagher, whom the crafty Phelps declared could be bought, demands an immediate inquiry.

Mr. Mabie, Chairman of the Committee on Public Health, in which Phelps claims to have killed the now famous Medicine bill, also calls for an investigation.

Messrs. Ainsworth, Saxton, Curtis, and others of the more honorable members of the Assembly received Phelps's reply to THE WORLD with unconcealed derision, and all agree that concerted effort must be made to smash the bill-brokers' ring.

Nellie Bly's feat is the one topic discussed to-day and her name is on every tongue.

Phelps has not yet returned to Albany.

Some of his friends say he will not reappear in his favorite haunt until the thing blows over.

Questions of privilege, of information and exciting scenes generally are expected in the Assembly chamber this evening.

❦

FOLLOW-UP STORY IN THE NEW YORK WORLD
PUBLISHED MONDAY, APRIL 2, 1888:

LOBBYIST PHELPS'S LOST GRIP

————

HIS CAREER LIKELY TO BE ENDED BY THE EXPOSURE IN "THE WORLD"

————

Nellie Bly's interview with Edward R. Phelps, King of the Albany Lobby, published in the Sunday WORLD, is the cause of much excitement and comment among State and local politicians.

The members of the Legislature are apparently greatly concerned over the revelations, and those whose names were mentioned by Lobbyist Phelps as purchaseable are angry and threatening. Many of the friends of the King of the Lobby are surprised that he should have been so thoroughly duped by the young women who made him believe that she wanted a bill killed and would pay a round sum for his services.

There are other acquaintances of Lobbyist Phelps, however, who are not surprised at this being taken in. They say that the interview in which he told how he conducted his lobby business, reads just like him. Said one of his former friends: "Phelps has lost his grip on Albany. He is no longer trusted. This expose will end his career as a lobbyist."

Phelps's letter of explanation published in this morning's WORLD is laughed at by the knowing ones. It is said to have been written by an ex-State Senator yesterday afternoon in an uptown hotel.

There is every prospect of fun in the Assembly chamber this evening. Several members of the Committee on Cities whose names were mentioned by Phelps as men who would sell their votes, have announced that they will rise to a question of high privilege. It is expected that they will demand an investigation.

❦

STORY IN THE BUFFALO EVENING NEWS
PUBLISHED MONDAY, APRIL 2, 1888:

LATEST!
FIVE O'CLOCK.
GALLAGHER IS HOT.

————

THE "WORLD'S" NELLIE BLY STORY RAISES A SENSATION IN ALBANY.

————

SHE SAY SHE HAD A LIST OF PURCHASEABLE COMMITTEEMEN AND THEIR
PRICES.

————

GALLAGHER WAS NAMED BUT HE WASN'T ON THE COMMITTEE AT ALL—A
COMICAL BLUNDER.

————

[SPECIAL TO THE EVENING NEWS]

ALBANY, APRIL 2—There promises to be a big sensation in the Assembly tonight over the "Nellie Bly" story published in the WORLD yesterday in reference to her dealings with Lobbyist Phelps for the defeat of the patent medicine bill. At the St. James' Hotel, New York, where she represented herself to Phelps as the daughter of a Philadelphia patent medicine man and obtained Phelps' price for the defeat of the bill, and the names of six Assemblymen upon the cities committee whom Phelps said he could secure for so much money to bring in an adverse report on the measure. Mr. Gallagher of Erie he mentioned as one of the men he could control. The bill never went to the cities committee. It was sent to the public health committee, of which Gallagher is not a member, and the cities committee had nothing to do with it, and an averse report upon the bill was agreed upon by the public health committee some time before the alleged transactions took place between "Nellie Bly" and Phelps.

Your correspondent has just seen Mr. Gallagher, and he indignantly denies all connection with the matter, and says the only conversation he had about the bill was with Dr. Fenner of Chautauqua, and Dr. Pierce of Buffalo, when he told both that the measure was iniquitous when it was first introduced; that the committee would report it adversely, and even if reported favorably it would have no chance of passing the House.

Chairman Crosby of the cities committee, it is understood, will send up a resolution to-night asking for an investigation so as to exonerate his committee, and an attempt will be made to bring "Nellie Bly" before the bar of the House to find out just exactly what took place between her and Phelps regarding the bill. —G

❧

STORY FROM THE BROOKLYN DAILY EAGLE.
PUBLISHED TUESDAY, APRIL 3, 1888:

BOTH DENY IT

————

TALLMADGE AND MCLAUGHLIN DEFEND THEIR REPUTATION.

————

THEY SAY IN THE ASSEMBLY THAT THEIR RECORDS ARE OPEN TO THE FULLEST INVESTIGATION

————

[SPECIAL TO THE EAGLE]

ALBANY, N.Y., APRIL 3—Tears flowed in the House last evening in personal explanations by members of the Cities Committee whose names had black marks drawn against them by Lobbyist Edward Phelps, while bargaining with a WORLD lady investigator who wanted a bill killed by that potential person, as legislators who were purchaseable. Two Brooklyn members, Mr. Tallmadge and Mr. McLcaughlin, were of this number.

When the clerk had droned out the journal, Mr. Tallmadge rose and created a dramatic scene by emotionally repelling the published assertion of the lobbyist that he could be purchased for less than $200. This was his speech:

"Mr. Speaker—I hold in my hand a copy of the NEW YORK WORLD of yesterday. In this paper there appeared an article under the caption 'The King of the Lobby.' In that article is printed a copy of a bill that is stated to have been in the Committee on Affairs of Cities. There also appeared what purports to be an interview with a person known as a lobbyist by the name of Phelps, in which Mr. Phelps is reported to have said that he has control of this House and can pass or kill any bill that he pleases. He is also reported to have put in the hands of a representative of this paper a copy of the name of the Committee on Cites with a mark opposite certain names, mine among them, of those whom he claims to be able to purchase. He also said in that article 'We buy Gallagher, of Erie; Tallmadge, of Kings; De Witt, of Ulster; Prime, of Essex; and McLaughlin, of Kings.' Is it necessary for me to tell this assembly here that this is untrue? It is unnecessary for me to tell those who are here that the bill which purports to have been under consideration between the representative of this paper and Mr. Phelps was never in the Committee on Cities. All you know it. But while those here know it and know how silly this matter is, as published in the paper, there are to every one of us thousands who do not know the facts as we know them and who are inclined to believe what they read. I have debated in my own mind what is the proper course to pursue in this matter. It is certainly a serious matter—serious to me, serious to every one of us, serious to the State of New York. I want to say, in behalf of the Committee on Cities, and I think the chairman of that committee will bear me out, that I do not know of any bill that has come out of that committee this year that has cost a man a dollar, either in money or a promise to keep it there.

"Now, Mr. Speaker, this article, so far as I am personally concerned, is one that I hardly know how to handle. I come from a city where we have three-fourths of a million people. I have been in public life in that city a decade an there is no paper in that city that can point to one single thing in my official record that they can throw a shadow upon as corrupt or dishonest. I have made my good name and my reputation there, and when I find that good name made by public service of years and years handled in this way I feel unnerved as to what it is best to do in regard to it The people who know me I do not know. They know me by reputation. They know me by the good name I have established among them. When they read an article like this they do not know the fact that I know—that you know—in regard to it, and they are unable to account for how such a matter can be so. When, coming up in the cars, I was engaged in writing out a resolution calling for an investigation of this matter, the chairman of our committee came to me, I told him what I was about to do and he advised me not to. He thought it was best to wait and consider the matter that we might not make any mistake about it. The session of the Legislature is now at a point where business requires the utmost attention from all of its members, so that an investigation at this time seems impracticable. Something should be done. What, I am hardly prepared to say; but it seems to me that it should not go along without consideration, and I therefore desire to make this motion: That this publication be referred to the Committee on Judiciary with instructions to consider the matter and report to this House during the present week what, in their judgment, is the best course to pursue in regard to it."

The resolution was adopted.

Mr. McLaughlin's record this Winter has been excellent. He has introduced no bad bills and has voted for none. The insinuation accredited to Mr. Phelps, as far as it pertained to him found answer in this remark on a question of privilege:

"I merely wish to say that I saw this article in one of the New York papers with my name attached to it. I desire to say that in my experience in the Legislature, both in the committee and in the House, all my actions have been open and above board. I defy and invite the closest scrutiny of every act of mine in this Legislature."

Mr. Tallmadge offered a bill to alter the line of Greene avenue at Broadway; Mr. Hamilton to close Eighteenth street beyond Cropsey avenue, in New Utrecht; Mr. Bonnington to let the city purchase Dupont street at the river and build a dock for public use.

STORY IN THE STANDARD UNION.
PUBLISHED MONDAY, APRIL 2, 1888:

HOW PHELPS MAY BE PUNISHED
————

"Ed" Phelps, the notorious lobbyist, was very cleverly caught last week by a bright young woman who does a great deal of clever work for the NEW YORK WORLD, some of which she writes about over the signature of "Nellie Bly." Representing herself as the wife of a patent medicine proprietor living in Philadelphia, Miss Bly called on Phelps at his rooms in the Kenmore Hotel, Albany, and arranged with him to "kill" a bill pending before the Legislature which, if it became law, would ruin the patent medicine business. The sum to be paid was about $2,000. Of course there is nothing new in the information that Phelps is a lobbyist, who carries on the business of buying and selling corrupt members of the Legislature; but the proof secured by Miss Bly of the fact is in a specific shape and may prove of sufficient weight legally to place Phelps behind prison bars. The lobbyist agreed to buy six members of the Committee of Affairs of Cities of the Assembly, including Messrs. Tallmadge and McLaughlin, of this city, for $1,000, to kill the bill which Miss Bly represented as being opposed to her interests. Phelps put marks on a printed list of the Cities Committee opposite the names of six of the Assemblymen whom he said were purchaseable. When Miss Bly said she would take the list to her to her husband, Phelps said it would be better to put marks against all the names. Fortunately, he laid the slip to make the second series of marks on a rough surface, and in the fac-simile of the slip printed in the WORLD the difference can be detected at once. A not unusual phase of the lobbyist's work is shown by the promise of Phelps to kill the bill on receipt of about $2,000, when he know that the bill was already practically dead. That is what Phelps and his associates call accumulating "velvet," which, being interpreted, means that the share which would ordinarily go to buy the corrupt legislator finds its way into the pocket of the lobbyist when he can get paid for defeating or passing bills which have already been, or are certain to be, defeated or passed without his help. When Phelps went to the place agreed on to receive the money from Miss Bly, of course she was not there, and the fact that no money passed to bribe members of the Legislature may render deficient the legal proof necessary to send the lobbyist to State prison. But there is another method open of getting at the corruptionist. He has wantonly and criminally libeled six members of the Assembly Committee on Cities, two of whom represent local constituencies. Both Messrs. Tallmadge and McLaughlin are old members of the Assembly, whose records made at Albany have been approved again and again by the people of their respective districts. Perhaps these gentlemen could personally afford to let their records speak for themselves and to treat with silent contempt the charge of a professional corruptionist who would not hesitate to asperse the honor of any man living if he could gain a dollar by doing so; but they owe it to the people and to the cause of good government to leave no effort untried to make Phelps feel the full vengeance of the law. The fact that he wrote opposite their names signs which he said indicated that they were corrupt scoundrels, and that he gave this writing to another to show as proof that she had negotiated for their purchase, constitutes a criminal libel.

At any rate, it furnishes enough for a jury to pass on, and Messrs. Tallmadge and McLaughlin ought not to let a day go by without applying for a warrant for Phelps' arrest on a charge of criminal libel. Of course Phelps denies that he said he could buy Messrs. Tallmadge and McLaughlin and the other four gentlemen against whose names he first put marks. That is natural enough. No professional criminal makes an admission of his guilt which would send him to State prison while there is the remotest chance of wriggling out of the penalty attached to the crime which he has committed. But he is forced to admit having the interview with Miss Bly, and his well-known reputation as a corruptionist will be proof enough to the people that he said the things concerning Messrs. Tallmadge and McLaughlin which Miss Bly is prepared to make oath that he did say. At any rate, the question is one for a jury to pass on. The exposure of Phelps will doubtless be made the subject of a legislative investigation, but try as they may, honest members of the Legislature will find great difficulty in fastening legal proof of guilt on the "King of the Lobbyists." If there were not corrupt members of the Legislature there would be no reason for Phelps' existence as a lobbyist. That fact of itself demonstrates that the corruptionist will have allies in the body which undertakes to expose his wickedness and bring him to punishment. It should not, of course, be allowed to stand in the way of a legislative investigation, but it should be potent with the gentlemen aspersed in moving them to proceed personally against Phelps before a tribunal so constituted as to be out of the reach of the corruptionist's influence. It is gratifying to learn that Messrs. Tallmadge and McLaughlin propose to take just that action. They will demand a legislative investigation, but, as our news columns show, they are determined also to take the matter before the Grand Jury. In the meantime, the thanks of all lovers of good government and opponents of corruption are due to the WORLD at to "Nellie Bly," its clever and cultivated correspondent, for an exposure of the "King of the Lobbyists" in a way that bids fair to lead to his arrest and punishment.

STORY IN THE BUFFALO EVENING NEWS.
PUBLISHED TUESDAY, APRIL 3, 1888:

NELLIE BLY'S LIE
———

THE PHELPS LOBBY STORY DENOUNCED IN THE ASSEMBLY LAST NIGHT.
———

BOTH HOUSES FIX DATES FOR FINAL ADJOURNMENT—TALK ON VEDDER BILL.
———

Albany, April 3 – In the Assembly last night Mr. Tallmadge read the NEW YORK WORLD's Article in Lobbyist Phelps and said it was unnecessary for him to say that the statement that he could be bought was untrue. No bill had been reported or delayed by the Committee on Cities in consideration of money.

This was the first time in his public life of ten years that his integrity had been assailed. He had desired an investigation, but Mr. Crosby had suggested that it might be better to wait. But some action must be taken, and he moved to refer the matter of the publication to the Judiciary Committee.

Mr. Gallagher said he had also been assailed. Mr. Pierce of Buffalo had spoken to him about the patent medicine bill referred to, but he had told him he would have nothing to do with it. He had never had any dealings with Mr. Phelps.

Mr.McLaughlin said his record was open for investigation, and he hoped the Judiciary Committee would inquire into the attack on him.

Mr. Hagan had also been accused, and he hoped action would be taken to protect the reputation of members.

Mr. DeWitt said it was an infamous lie that he had ever been offered or given a bribe.

Mr. Prime said he did not know Phelps and had never been offered a bribe. He was willing to let his reputation speak for itself.

It was decided to hold sessions Tuesday evenings.

STORY FROM THE DEMOCRAT AND CHRONICLE.
PUBLISHED TUESDAY, APRIL 3, 1888:

LOBBY AND LEGISLATURE

———

"NELLY BLY" WRITES A WICKED LETTER TO THE NEW YORK "WORLD"

———

THE MEMBERS ARE INDIGNANT

———

THEY REPEL CHARGES AND INSINUATIONS WHICH ARE BASED ON MALICE
OR IGNORANCE—LEGISLATIVE WORK AND STATE CAPITAL NEWS.

———

[SPECIAL DISPATCH TO THE DEMOCRAT AND CHRONICLE]

ALBANY, APRIL 2.—The Assembly Chamber is a quiet place on a Monday. At 10:30 this morning it was occupied by the journal clerks, Anderson Lawrence and two pages, the janitor and three spectators. The latter sat in the easy chairs outside the railing and slept peacefully. These chairs are especially designed to invite people to repose and the invitation is usually accepted. Mr. Lawrence, who is the busiest man about the Capitol, was helping the pages "lay out" bills. The files are so unwieldy that it is a man's work to lift one from its place. The Monday morning crop of newly printed measures numbered sixty-two this week, and the addition to the current literature of the day will keep the conscientious members busy if they do their duty and read the lot, captions and all.

A few assemblymen who, with the fear of high water and washouts before their eyes, remained in Albany over Sunday, were gathered in the Assembly postoffice. The topic of conversation this morning was the WORLD's alleged expose of the way in which Ed. Phelps does business. "This is article had been published in any other paper it might have some weight," said a leading New York Democrat whose name was not mentioned in the story; "but," he added, "the course of that paper latterly, so far as adhering to the truth is concerned, has not been calculated to inspire confidence." That "Nelly Bly" visited Ed. Phelps at his room in the Kenmore and at his office in the Boreel Building, and that she induced that astute lobbyist "to give himself dead away," Mr. Phelps admits in his "reply" published in this morning's Tribune. The trouble with Nelly's story is that she was either led by Phelps or by ignorance or carelessness to place several reputable members in a false position as "commercial." The slip of paper containing the names of the committees on cities, with a hieroglyphic mark opposite the name of every member excepting the chairman, is an outrageous attack on the honor and honesty of gentlemen who stand high in the estimation of their constituents and of their colleague. Mr. Prime is Essex, who is marked as purchaseable according to "Nelly Bly" is regarded as one of the straightest men in the Assembly. He is serving his second term and is known to be a cautious, conservative man, who has never been counted among the "suspects" even by the most careless New York correspondent. He said to your representative this morning:

"The bill mentioned was never before the cities committee. During my two terms in the Legislature I have never been approached by any lobbyist outside the house, or inside either for that matter, with anything bordering on a proposition or a hint that I should be paid for voting for or against any measure. I may not have the property qualification which entitles me to be classed as unapproachable, but I am not compelled to resort to that method of obtaining a livelihood and I never have done so. When I decide to accept a bribe to influence my vote I shall be ready to resign my seat in the house." Mr. Prime needs no defense to those who know him, but the general public may be misled by the publication referred to, hence his consent to make the brief statement quoted.

Mr. Gallagher of Erie is serving his sixth term and with one exception ranks next to General Husted in point of service. That his vote could be purchased is not believed by any one, and even his political enemies never charged him with membership in the Black Horse Cavalry. He is at his home in Buffalo, but it is safe to predict that he will call the attention of the house to the WORLD article as a question of privilege. A newspaper ghost story, however skillfully concocted, always has a weak point which betrays its fictitious character either in whole or in part. Either Phelps, "Nelly Bly" or her assistant, made the mistake of stating that Assembly bill 191 had been before the committee on cities and that it had been transferred to the committee on public health, the members of which could be handled "easier." The bill was introduced January 28th by J. Wesley Smith and was referred to the committee on public health. February 3rd it was reported back "to be printed and recommended to the same committee."

The printer made an error in the caption which read "to be recommitted to the committee on affairs of cities." This mistake was noticed and corrected by the bill clerk and the measure has never been before the committee on cities for a moment. Whoever looked over the files fell into the error and assumed that the latter committee had the bill in charge, and the story about the members of the cities committee was evidently based on erroneous conception. The bill, which was classed as "a strike" by correspondents generally, including the representative of the WORLD, was opposed by the manufacturers of proprietary remedies and it was evident that its fate in committee was settled. Last week the measure was finally reported. The vote in committee, according to chairman Mable, was "six for an adverse report; one (Mr. Smith, the introducer of the bill) for a favorable report with an amendment that the formula should be filed with and approved by the state board of health; one not voting, and three absent." How Phelps came to tell "Miss Consaul" (sic) that he had the reference changed to suit his own purposes, if he ever said so, is a question which will probably never be solved. The point is that by this misrepresentation reputable members have been grossly maligned for the sake of making a sensational article and regardless of the facts in the case. If the WORLD representative, male or female, had wished to ascertain the truth a reference to the books would have made it plain; but the facts if stated would have spoiled the story, and that, from the WORLD standpoint, would have been the unpardonable sin which would not be forgiven. The members who are here are, without exception, indignant at the attack on their colleagues, and divide their expressions of animadversion between Phelps and the WORLD. This paper has so frequently misrepresented the members and their action that its reputation for truth, if it ever had any, is among the things of the past. Its representative is kept busy explaining mistakes and correcting "errors," but the corrections are usually devoured by the office cat before they reach the composing room. It is predicted that the attention of the Assembly will be called to the WORLD, and that "Nelly Bly" will be called on to explain.

Senator McNaughton was the only occupant of the Senate Chamber, except pages and officials, this morning. He has all his bills in good shape.

J.W.S.

❧

STORY IN THE BUFFALO TIMES.
PUBLISHED TUESDAY, APRIL 3, 1888:

SERIOUS CHARGE.

———

THE KING OF THE LOBBY GIVES A LIST OF BOODLE LEGISLATORS.

———

THE STORY OF ONE MAN.

———

ALLEGED STARTLING DISCLOSURES BY THE FAMOUS ED. PHELPS.

BUFFALO REPRESENTED

HON. EDW. GALLAGHER'S NAME IN COLD, BOLD, BLACK TYPE.

PRONOUNCED A LIE.

A CYCLONE STRIKES THE BIG BUILDING AT ALBANY.

A GREAT SENSATION.

STATESMEN SHAKING AT THE KNEE AND RED WITH RAGE DENOUNCING
METROPOLITAN NEWSPAPER.

The NEW YORK WORLD has some bright ladies within its reach whom it occasionally uses to do the fine work of the office, such as personating insane persons for the purpose of studying the inside work of the asylums; playing detective for the purpose of running down murderers and thieves, etc, etc.

One of these sports the nom de plume of "Nellie Bly" and she has been at Albany trying to find out how lobbyists do their work and how much money it takes to kill an objectionable bill by the objectors through their lobby agents. The bill selected as a decoy to win from the lobbyist the secret of his trade was the J. Wesley Smith bill relating to patent medicines and which THE TIMES has heretofore printed and enlarged upon to some considerable lengths.

The efforts of this enterprising woman were quite successful, altogether too successful for the comfort of some of the legislators, among then being the Honorable Edward Gallagher of Buffalo.

It is quite true that "Nellie Bly" has told nothing or gained nothing specific against any of the ones mentioned. She only gives the "say so" of the lobby agent who in this case was E. R. Phelps, otherwise known as "the king of the lobby." She tells the story of personating the wife of the Philadelphia patent medicine maker, how she found out and met the lobbyist; how he fell into the trap set for him, and gave her a list of assemblymen that he said he could influence by the use of money. A part of the conversation alleged to have taken place is here given:

(Editor's note: here is reprinted selected sections from Bly's first interview with Phelps. The article then continues:)

It is fair to presume that Mr. Phelps did not get the money or check then or thereafter.

This is the story told by the NEW YORK WORLD stripped of the unnecessary matter with which it was adorned. It is a painful story and reveals, if true, a shocking state of affairs in the legislature. It looks, however, as though Mr. Phelps would be called upon to answer to a charge of malicious and criminal libel.

[NOTE. Phelps, the "King of the lobby," says that he was fooling the WORLD's petticoat detective. His story will appear in this column tomorrow.—ED. TIMES]

❦

STORY IN THE BUFFALO TIMES.
PUBLISHED TUESDAY, APRIL 3, 1888:

THE NEWS IN ALBANY

GREAT EXCITEMENT BECAUSE OF THE ALLEGED PHELPS DISCLOSURES OF
MEN WHO CAN BE BRIBED

ALBANY, APRIL 3.—In the Assembly last night Mr. Tallmadge read the NEW YORK WORLD's article on Lobbyist Phelps, and said it was unnecessary for him to say that the statement that he could be bought was untrue. No bill had been reported or delayed by the Committee on Cities in consideration of money. This was the first time in his public life of ten years that his integrity had been assailed. He had desired an investigation, but Mr. Crosby had suggested that it might be better to wait. But some action must be taken, and he moved to refer the matter of the publication to the Judiciary Committee.

Mr. Gallagher said he had also been assailed. Mr. Pierce of Buffalo had spoken to him about the patent medicine bill referred to, but he had told him he would have nothing to do with it. He had never had any dealings with Mr. Phelps.

Mr. McLaughlin said his record was open for investigation, and he hoped the Judiciary Committee would inquire into the attack on him.

Mr. Hagan had also been accused, and he hoped action would be taken to protect the reputation of members.

Mr. DeWitt said it was an infamous lie that he had ever been offered or given a bribe.

In the Senate last night Mr. Mase's prisons appropriation bill was ordered to third reading and made a special order for to-day.

Mr. Vedder moved and Mr. Cantor opposed third reading of the quarantine commission bill. The motion was lost by a party vote, Republicans yes, Democrats nay, a two-thirds vote being required.

Mr. Vedder called up the liquor bill on final passage. It imposed a $100 tax on a general retail liquor business and $20 on sale of beer and wine.

Mr. Cantor said the bill discriminated against cities.

Mr. Vedder denied it.

Mr. Reilly said the local tax ought to go to the city treasury, not the State.

Mr. Sloan said the principle involved was the same as in the collateral inheritance law. Mr. Cantor reported that the tax would weigh heaviest on first-class places in New York City.

Mr. Erwin said this was an error.

The report of the Commission of Labor Statistics was received.

Mr. Husted's state printing bill was discussed. Mr. Husted said it would save

30 per cent. of the expense of state printing. As Mr. McCarthy, who desires to debate the bill, was absent, Mr. Husted moved its reference to the Ways and Means Committee for a full report.

Mr. Prime said he did not know Phelps and had never been offered a bribe. He was willing to let his reputation speak for itself.

It was decided to hold sessions Tuesday evenings.

The Field code was made a special order for Tuesday, April 10.

A resolution by Mr. Husted for adjournment sine die May 4 was opposed by Mr. Sheehan and adopted.—Adjourned.

Mr. Langhein opposed indirect taxation of this kind, really intended to restrict the liquor business. If money were needed tax personal property, which now escapes.

Mr. Cantor charged the Republicans with straddling the liquor question by choking high license at Saratoga, then making it a party measure here.

Mr. Vedder argued for the bill as a tax measure. Debate was here suspended.

The resolution for adjournment May 11 was adopted.

The bill for a $35,000 armory at Poughkeepsie was passed; also some bills of minor importance.

Adjourned.

$$\mathcal{C}\mathcal{O}$$

STORY IN THE BUFFALO EVENING NEWS.
PUBLISHED TUESDAY, APRIL 3, 1888:

"NELLIE BLY."

———

SHE TOOK A BACK SEAT IN THE ASSEMBLY CHAMBER LAST NIGHT.

———

HOW LOBBYIST PHELPS WAS TRIPPED BY A PRINTER'S MISTAKE—A LADY
REPORTER MADE FAMOUS.

———

[SPECIAL TO THE EVENING NEWS]

Albany, April 3.—Nellie Bly, the WORLD's detective reporter, is not very pretty, but she is sharp—too sharp perhaps. She received in some way an intimation that her bribery fiasco with Lobbyist Phelps would have a ventilation in the Assembly last evening; so Nellie planked down five cold dollars for her fare and came up here from New York on the "flyer." She had a back seat in the Chamber last evening among 200 prettily dressed women who come every Monday evening to study legislation or watch their own or other folks' husbands. Nellie was incog. Nobody knew her except a select few, and they knew enough to keep their mouths shut, for Nellie was terribly afraid that if known, the great big-hearted Ike Scott would dance her before the bar of the house to explain herself. So Nellie kept perfectly still while she heard the clerical-looking Tallmadge of Brooklyn get up and offer a resolution that her story be sent to the judiciary committee for them to make a report upon before the week is over as to what was to be done in the matter. This will be the hardest kind of a job for that committee.

Hagan of New York arose to a question of the privilege and said he know nothing about the patent medicine bill and exonerated himself.

Mr. Gallagher also spoke, as stated in THE NEWS yesterday, and emphatically repudiated the assertion of ever having anything to do with Lobbyist Phelps. He used some pretty strong language and everybody believed him.

McLaughlin of Brooklyn and De Witt of Ulster also repudiated any connection with Phelps. These are the men Nellie Bly said Phelps told her he owned on the Cities Committee. He gave her a list of them, which was published, and wanted $5000 from Nellie to get the Patent Medicine Bill killed in that committee. She promised to go back to Philadelphia and get the money from the patent medicine father of Phelps would only wait. He is still waiting. But his agents are all here, and they give out that Phelps is no fool. He was up to Nellie's game and he "played her," knowing full well that the patent medicine bill had been reported adversely, but he got balled up on the committee to which it had been sent. The printed bill reads that it had been sent to the Cities Committee. That was a mistake of the printer. He should have said "Public Health Committee" upon the title, and when Phelps read the names of the members of the Cities Committee to Nellie, checking off those he said he owned, and who would be against the patent medicine bill for a consideration, he was perfectly unconscious of the fact that the bill had never seen daylight in that committee room.

The game between Nellie and Phelps looks like a draw, but the female detective reporter is having lots of fun out of it, but if dragged before the Judiciary Committee she may collapse at the sight of Chairman Saxton's great big white moustache as he fires legal conundrums at her. What the Judiciary Committee will report will be hard to conjecture. They may decide to go into an investigation, but this is not probable, as the session is too near its end. —G.

HEADLINES TO THE REPRINT OF PHELPS' LETTER AND THE WORLD'S REPLY IN THE ASSOCIATED PRESS. PUBLISHED WEDNESDAY, APRIL 4, 1888:

"YOU'RE A LIAR,"

————

IS WHAT THE NEW YORK "WORLD" SAYS TO LOBBYIST PHELPS.

————

"YOU DID," "I DID NOT."

————

THE OLD SCHEMER SAYS HE WAS ONLY FOOLING NELLIE.

CRAWLING IN HIS HOLE

EDITOR PULITZER SAYS HIS FAIR WRITER IS A DANDY.

A REAL MERRY WAR.

HOW THE KING OF THE ALBANY LOBBY SUCCEEDED IN MAKING A FOOL OF HIMSELF.

STORY IN THE NEW YORK WORLD.
PUBLISHED WEDNESDAY, APRIL 4, 1888:

BRIBERY RAMPANT.

On Sunday THE WORLD exposed the character and methods of Ed Phelps, the "King of the Lobby." As a result of this exposure, Speaker Cole banished the lobby from the Assembly Chamber and revoked all passes to the floor.

This morning's WORLD contains specific charges that Lobbyist Eugene Wood offered to bribe two Senators to introduce the street-stealing Metropolitan Transit Bill. Both the Senators spurned the bribe, but the suggestion of it shows still further how the lobby works.

Legislative investigations rarely amount to much. But the District-Attorney and Grand Jury of Albany County could soon make the capital too hot for these "legislative agents."

STORY IN THE BROOKLYN DAILY EAGLE.
PUBLISHED WEDNESDAY, APRIL 4, 1888:

THE ALBANY LOBBY.

The disclosures recently made concerning the methods of Mr. Edward Phelps, who is at the head of the lobby at Albany, have been watched with interest. Yesterday Speaker Cole revoked all passes to the floor of the Assembly, and expressed a determination to do all he could to get rid of the legislative agents who haunt the corridors of the capitol. Several "statesmen," two from Kings County, on whom suspicion has been cast, are clamoring for an investigation. And this morning another shot is fired into the ranks of the lobbyists in the form of a charge of attempted bribery against Eugene Wood, who is the associate and helper of Mr. Phelps.

These facts indicate a condition of affairs at the Capital which has been long familiar to the public. Phelps and his agent have more than once bee indicted by an Albany grand jury, but the exigencies of Republican and Democratic machine politics have rendered both parties favorable to the nullification of the indictments, and the accused persons have escaped. The danger of prosecution by the authorities is so small that not the slightest heed is paid to it—the lobbyists knowing well that so long as they confine their operations to Albany County, they are as safe as though knowledge of them was locked in the brain of Jacob Sharp. It may be asked why passes to the floor are granted at all? The answer is that passes are as free as water. The clerks and pages and all persons connected with the Legislature in any capacity, keep them and distribute them as they please. What is called the privilege of the floor is no privilege. Mr. Cole is without doubt the most honest speaker the Assembly has ever had at the hands of a Republican majority, and yet singular as it may seem, he owes his election to the corrupt influences of a body than which there has not been one more dishonest in the legislative history of the State. General Husted was defeated for the Speakership because he said he knew how to make matters "cold" to the lobbyists and starve them out, and there is no question that in this instance he told the truth. Defeated as he was because he was "smart," the honor which he coveted was bestowed on a man who is more of a political moralist and infinitely less of a political tactician than the Westchester veteran. In other words, Cole was elected by a ring which hoped, by trading on his inexperience, to make the session the most profitable one that has been known at the Capital for the last twenty years. The cards were well played and the result, it is assumed, has not been disappointing to those who took the trouble to arrange the details in advance.

This loud demand for "investigation" which now fills the air is one of the humorous incidents of the situation, for it is will known that Phelps and his associates in the THIRD HOUSE are but the natural products of a tainted and vicious atmosphere. The "investigations" at Albany do not investigate; the indictments do not indict. It is idle to say that one party is to blame more than the other, for where both are equally at fault there is a common interest in strengthening the fortress of defense. Legislatures have been just as venal under Democratic control as under the sway of the opposition party. The voters as a whole and what is known as the "machine" in particular are to be held responsible. There is no trouble with the laws. Our statutes bearing upon bribery ad conspiracies and combinations against public policy are sound enough as they are, but they are not carried into effect, and they never will be while public apathy is so marked. In this county the people have certainly had sufficient experience to know that the administration of the law is in some respects a burlesque. They have seen indictments persistently pigeonholed, and they have witnessed the trial of criminals who had a political "pull" delayed so long that patience ceased to be a virtue. If it has been impossible to convict Phelps in Albany County on charges as clear and specific as words could make them, it has been none the les difficult to bring to justice equally notorious offenders on other parts of the State. The trouble is not so much with the lobbyists and men like them as with a public sentiment which does not take the trouble to discriminate at the polls, and which permits itself to be swayed by vicious combinations on the plea of "loyalty to party."

STORY IN THE HERKIMER DEMOCRAT.
PUBLISHED WEDNESDAY, APRIL 4, 1888:

HURRAH FOR NELLIE BLY!

————

Nellie Bly, who not long ago made a name among journalists by getting herself committed to the Ward's Island Insane Asylum, and afterward describing in the NEW YORK WORLD the abuses to which the inmates were subjected, is an indefatigable worker and each week places before the readers of the SUNDAY WORLD a startling expose of some phase of human crookedness. Her contribution for Sunday was of unusual interest to State legislators and to lobbyists, and especially to Edward R. Phelps, who is please to take rank as the leader of the "Third House." On the plea of desiring to kill J.W. Smith's bill in relation to patent medicines—as the story goes—she called upon Mr. Phelps at his headquarters in Albany, and secured his promise to defeat the measure, she agreeing to pay the sum necessary to purchase a majority of the Assembly Cities Committee, and a reasonable fee to the lobbyist for his work. Phelps when so far as to take a list of the Committee and check the names of those whom he said he could purchase. Before giving Nellie Bly the list he checked the other names, but did it in such a careless way as to leave the original marking distinct from the rest. A fac-simile of this list appears in the WORLD. The story concludes with an account of a second interview in New York, and Mr. Phelps vain waiting for the check which never came. The men whose names appear thus publicly branded as purchasable will doubtless take an early opportunity to interview the "King of the Lobby," who finds his boasted shrewdness no match for the wiles of a clever woman. He was denounced in open session, Monday, by the men whose named appeared checked.

STORY IN THE WORLD.
PUBLISHED THURSDAY, APRIL 5, 1888:

AN INVESTIGATION.

————

MR. CROSBY WANTS "THE WORLD'S" CHARGES LOOKED INTO.

————

HIS RESOLUTION REFERRED TO THE JUDICIARY COMMITTEE.

———

SOME OF THE ASSEMBLYMEN RAISE A HOWL, BUT THAT DID NOT MATTER—
KING EDWARD PHELPS HAS DEPARTED—HE TOOK A TRAIN FOR THE SOUTH
AND THE KENMORE MOURNS HIS LOSS—A COMMITTEE OF FIVE GIVES FULL
POWER IN MR. CROSBY'S RESOLUTION.

———

[SPECIAL TO THE WORLD.]

ALBANY, APRIL 5.—Mr. Crosby, of New York, startled the Black-Horse Brigade to-day by offering a resolution into THE WORLD's disclosure concerning the practices of Lobby King Ed Phelps and his gang.

It provided for the appointment by the Speaker of a committee of five to proceed at once to inquire into the charges made by King Edwards and file its report at the assemblage of the next Legislature.

Mr. Crosby asked that the resolution be referred to the Committee on Judiciary, which is to make a report to-morrow on THE WORLD's exposé.

—Immediately objections were fired from all quarters of the House.

Mr. Crosby then asked that the question be decided at once.

Judge Green, of Orange, sponsor for the New York and New Jersey bridge grab, entered a vigorous protest, while Crank Platt, the Poughkeepsie bridge speculator, bawled out: "I object."

Finally the resolution was referred to the Judiciary Committee.

It reads as follows:

Whereas, It is a matter of common belief and report that persons interested in legislation and known as the lobby have been accustomed for many years to obtain money upon representing that they are able to secure the passage or defeat of bills in the Legislature by corrupt or unlawful means, and

Whereas, Specific charges of this character have recently made in the public press; and

Whereas, It is important to the fair name of this State that such charges should be disproved or such practices be discontinued; therefore, be it

Resolved, That the Speaker appoint a committee of five to investigate the condition and methods of the lobby, and in such investigations said committee is authorized to ascertain as far as possible the manner in which persons interested in legislations endeavor, or have heretofore endeavored, to influence the same; and be it further

Resolved, That said commission report to this Assembly on or before Jun. 10, 1889, to the end that the Legislature may know the condition and methods of the lobby: and that efficient legislation may be had to prevent corruption and scandal, said commission is authorized to send for books, papers and persons and employ counsel and a stenographer and incur such other expenses as it may deem necessary, and said committee is authorized and directed to conduct this investigation at any place or places in the State.

King Edward has skipped town.

Last night he closed up his brokerage establishment at the Kenmore, paid his bill and took a train south.

❧

STORY FROM THE TIMES UNION.
PUBLISHED THURSDAY, APRIL 5, 1888:

PHELPS MAY BE INDICTED.
————

A SPEEDY INVESTIGATION URGED BY TALLMADGE AND OTHERS.
————

TALK ABOUT THE GRAND JURY BEFORE THE JUDICIARY COMMITTEE OF
THE ASSEMBLY
————

Albany, N.Y., April 3.—No member of the House, perhaps, feels more keenly than does Assemblyman Tallmadge the statement made by Lobbyist Phelps at the famous interview between the latter and "Nellie Bly," as published in Sunday's NEW YORK WORLD, in which the member from the Twelfth District was classed by Phelps as one of those whom he could control by the use of money. His reply has been given, both in the shape of an interview and as a question of privilege on the floor of the Assembly, when, at his request, the whole subject was referred to the Committee on Judiciary for investigation. This afternoon when the committee met, Mr. Tallmadge and an associate from Erie, Mr. Gallagher, were on hand, ready to urge the inquiry with all possible speed. The talk between the two accused members and the members of the committee was but preliminary and formal. The committee, but more especially Chairman Saxton, of Wayne, were in full sympathy with the motive which had prompted Messrs. Tallmadge and Gallagher to respond with so much promptitude to the resolution, but they did not relish the idea of having an important investigation, which would consume more time than they could devote to it during the present week—with so many important bill in their hands—thrust upon them. The Chairman so informed Mr. Tallmadge, who did most of the talking before the convention.

Nor did Mr. Saxton see how they were to proceed with a formal inquiry under the resolution adopted or without authority from the House itself to summon and examine witnesses and compel the attendance of persons and papers. Mr. Tallmadge said it was a serious matter to him, involving his personal and public reputation, and suggested that something be done which would serve as a basis for calling the attention of the Grand Jury to the subject. He certainly would object to the committee permitting the matter to rest, but had no objection to the inquiry by some other committee or a special committee if the Judiciary Committee was already too much occupied with bills.

One of the members of the committee said he thought it was the most important matter they had before them.

Mr. Tallmadge said he was glad that the gentleman thought so and hoped the other members were all of the same opinion.

Chairman Saxton recognized that it was a serious question, but had his doubts whether it would be wise on the part of the committee to take the investigation on their own shoulders.

Mr. Tallmadge said they could not go too far or be too searching for him if they undertook the task. This insinuation that he was open to corruption and bribery had gone broadcast all over the land—through the State and beyond it. It would come up against him as a public man whenever he was a candidate for the suffrage of the people hereafter. The injury done him was very great, and it was but proper and right that he seek reparation as far as possible.

A member suggested that the statement of Phelps did not charge a crime.

Chairman Saxton said it did, when it stated that these men (Tallmadge and the others) could be bought or sold. The matter was serious, and the committee would be glad to do all that it could to have justice done.

Mr. Gallagher said he indorsed all that Mr. Tallmadge had said. "Here," said the Erie member, "are eleven intelligent and able lawyers in this committee. Do what you can and make a report to the House; pursue whatever course you may see fit to adopt, but make an early report. The truth cannot be known too soon."

Mr. Tallmadge, who had meanwhile left the committee room, returned while Mr. Gallagher was still speaking and handed to Chairman Saxton a copy of the WORLD of Sunday for the perusal of such of the members of the committee as had not already read the article. The informal talk which Mr. Tallmadge's departure had temporarily interrupted was then resumed, Chairman Saxton remarking as he looked over the paper, "Well, it is not charged that you have been bought." The question of how far it would be necessary to go in order to bring the matter to the notice of the Grand Jury and the relative liability of Phelps, "Nellie Bly" and the newspaper in a criminal suit was considered. Mr. Saxton thought that as there was yet no proof either that Phelps had made the statement or that "Nellie" had written it, the WORLD was the responsible party in any suit that might be brought, for it had published what was plainly a criminal libel, no matter from what source emanating.

Mr. Tallmadge—Suppose they prove that Phelps said this?

Mr. Saxton—Even if he did that does not justify the publication. It is a libel all the same.

Mr. Tallmadge—All I ask is that you take up the matter and make your report.

Mr. Saxton said the committee would see what was best to be done, and after a brief interchange of views, which developed no new feature or point of interest, the committee proceeded to other business and gave the patentee of the ballot box which Mr. Tallmadge is endeavoring to have introduced all over the State a hearing in favor of the bill which the latter has presented upon the subject.

❧

STORY IN THE WORLD.
PUBLISHED FRIDAY, APRIL 6, 1888:

DRIVEN FROM HIS THRONE.

————

KING PHELPS OF THE LOBBY LEAVES ALBANY FOR THE SOUTH.

————

THE ATMOSPHERE WHERE "THE WORLD" CIRCULATED WAS TOO HOT FOR
HIM—ASSEMBLYMAN CROSBY CALLS FOR AN INVESTIGATION OF THE LOBBY,
BUT HIS RESOLUTIONS ARE REFERRED BECAUSE OF PROTESTS.

————

[SPECIAL TO THE WORLD.]

ALBANY, APRIL 6.—"Lobby King Phelps has abdicated," was the rumor
that floated through the corridors of the Capitol to-day. It was passed from
mouth to mouth and rapidly developed into an apparently trustworthy report.
Speaker Cole had heard it before leaving the breakfast table at the Kenmore.
He had been told by the clerks of that hostelry that the notorious bill-broker
had, to the astonishment of the management, announced that he proposed
to leave town indefinitely. The atmosphere where THE WORLD circulated
was too hot for him. He therefore would surrender his luxurious parlors and
seek, temporarily at least, pastures new and green. Where he would go he
had not yet determined. He might try Virginia and gloat over his possessions,
purchased at the price of many a legislator's character; then, again, he might
proceed to Florida and bask in the sunshine or recline beneath the shade of his
orange groves. At any rate, he proposed to go somewhere.

————

THE LOBBY KING'S DEPARTURE.

And go somewhere he did. The crafty Phelps boarded the 9.55 a.m. train for
the south, bag and baggage. His rooms have been closed the greater part of the
day. Eugene Wood, his man Friday, remained behind, but business was so bad
that he had expressed his intention of taking a trip himself pretty soon. He did
not put in an appearance at the Capitol. Indeed, he has given the seventeen-
million dollar elephant a wide berth since the publication of THE WORLD's
accusation as to his attempt to bribe at least two members of the Senate.

Various reasons are given for Phelps's departure. His --- will not talk about
it except to say that he will return soon. Some say he left to escape a ------
------ inquisition. In that case he is ------- to be miles away from the State.
Others ----- that business called him South. Those who favor an investigation
of his traffic fear they will lack a very important witness, and are denouncing
the Assembly Committee on the Judiciary for delaying action until the bird
has flown. If Phelps has as many friends in the lower house as he has claimed
it would seem that he has nothing to fear, at least at their hands. If Phelps

returns during the present session of the Legislature many will be surprised. His friends assert that he will willingly come back and face the music when wanted.

———

AN INVESTIGATION CALLED FOR.

Ernest H. Crosby created dismay among the members of the Black Horse Brigade when, during a lull in proceedings of the Assembly to-day, he offered a resolution calling for a vigorous investigation of the lobby and its methods. Mr. Crosby is the Chairman of the Committee on Cities, six of whose members Phelps claimed to own. The Judiciary Committee had frittered away nearly four days without taking action upon THE WORLD's exposure. To remove all possible doubt as to his attitude, Mr. Crosby thought it time he assumed the offensive. The resolutions he presented are as follows:

Whereas, It is a matter of common belief and report that persons interested in legislation and known as the lobby have been accustomed for many years to obtain money upon representing that they are able to secure the passage or defeat of bills in the Legislature by corrupt or unlawful means, and

Whereas, Specific charges of this character have recently made in the public press; and

Whereas, It is important to the fair name of this State that such charges should be disproved or such practices be discontinued; therefore, be it

Resolved, That the Speaker appoint a committee of five to investigate the condition and methods of the lobby, and in such investigations said committee is authorized to ascertain as far as possible the manner in which persons interested in legislations endeavor, or have heretofore endeavored, to influence the same; and be it further

Resolved, That said commission report to this Assembly on or before Jun. 10, 1889, to the end that the Legislature may know the condition and methods of the lobby: and that efficient legislation may be had to prevent corruption and scandal, said commission is authorized to send for books, papers and persons and employ counsel and a stenographer and incur such other expenses as it may deem necessary, and said committee is authorized and directed to conduct this investigation at any place or places in the State.

———

HOWLS AND PROTESTS WENT UP.

Clerk Chickering was scarcely given a chance to read the communication. A howl went up from all quarters of the chamber when the author asked that the resolution should be read at once. It emanated not only from men who have been known to be for sale but even from some of those who have heretofore, at least, served the State without suspicion or taint upon their character.

Amid the hubbub Judge George W. Greene, of Orange, and Editor John I. Platt, of Poughkeepsie, were conspicuous for offering indignant protests against the immediate consideration of the resolutions. Some members suddenly discovered that the ninth joint rule was likely to be violated, and bawled out their objections on that ground. Others clamored for an adjournment. Messrs. Greene and Platt insisted upon their objections and the Speaker sustained them. Mr. Crosby then requested that his resolutions should be referred to the Judiciary Committee. This was done. Had Johnny O'Brien and Charley Swan been upon the floor, clothed with the same authority, they would surely have been as strenuous in their opposition as were Messrs. Greene and Platt.

MR. CROSBY DID NOT DESPAIR.

Later on Mr. Crosby appeared before the Assembly Judiciary Committee and pleased that decisive action might be taken at once. Direct charges had been made and the good name of the Legislature was involved. That being the case, the most rigorous inquiry should be immediately initiated. If the charges were untrue it would do no harm to ascertain it. If, on the other hand, they were true, the people should know it. The longer the investigation was put off so long would this cloud rest upon the legislators. The committee concluded to hold another session this evening before determining what its report should be.

DISCUSSING "THE WORLD'S" EVIDENCE

The Assembly Committee on the Judiciary held an executive session to-night. The question to be decided was whether or not THE WORLD had established sufficient evidence upon which to base an investigation. Previous to the assembling of the committee, Chairman Saxton said that in all probability a report would be presented to-morrow recommending an inquiry. Whether it would be thought best to begin it immediately or after final adjournment he could not say. The committee was in session about two hours. A resolution prepared at its direction by Assemblyman Roesch was discussed.

At the last moment a member of the committee secured the ironclad oath of every member that no information as to the proceedings should be furnished previous to the presentation of the report to-morrow. It can be safely predicted, however, that the report will recommend a vigorous investigation as to THE WORLD's disclosures. When and by what committee, if any, it is to be conducted cannot be positively stated. It seems likely, however, that Mr. Crosby's proposition will be accepted. The vote upon the adoption of the report, it is anticipated, will be significant. While the Assembly seems to be disposed to prosecute an investigation, the Senators put themselves on the back row, call themselves good members and apparently are afraid to force an inquiry. It would be an injustice to include them all in this category.

THEY PRAISE "THE WORLD."

The Lieutenant-Governor and Senators Walker, Laughlin, Liason, Kellogg, McNaughton, Reilly and one or two others have already expressed to THE WORLD's correspondent their hearty approbation of the good service THE WORLD is seeking to accomplish, and also their opinion that the charge against Lobbyist Wood should be thoroughly ventilated. No movement in that direction has yet been detected, however. Some fear that the lobby has such a powerful influence with certain members of this august body that a proposition of this character would surely meet with overwhelming defeat.

Senators Ives and Langbein, to whom Wood offered bribes to introduces the Metropolitan transit steal and who spurned them, do not feel called upon to take the initiative, owing to the delicate position in which they are placed. Senator Cantor, whose integrity no one questions, is in a similar situation. There are others, however, who might not desire to have their former and present affiliations with the third House exposed.

————

MISS BLY READY TO TESTIFY

Yesterday the following letter was addressed to the Chairman of the Assembly Judiciary Committee at Albany:

New York, April 5, 1888
Hon. Charles T. Saxton, Chairman Judiciary Committee,
Dear Sir: I have waited almost a week to see what action your committee would take in regard to the statements made to me by Mr. E. R. Phelps touching a certain measure pending in the Assembly. I am ready and willing to appear before the committee and substantiate the statements printed in the NEW YORK WORLD Sunday, April 1, over my signature.
I can be addressed, care of the editor of the WORLD.

Very respectfully, Nellie Bly.

℃℈

STORY IN THE BUFFALO TIMES.
PUBLISHED THURSDAY, APRIL 6, 1888:

WELL, THEY WILL INVESTIGATE

————

WHAT THE ASSEMBLYMEN THINK ABOUT MR. CROSBY'S PROPOSITION.

————

ALBANY, APRIL 6.—The Assembly had been wrestling all the morning with THE WORLD's disclosures concerning the allegations of Lobby King Ed Phelps that he could buy any member of the Legislature.

The Judiciary Committee reported in favor of an investigation to be begun after final adjournment.

A provision was also made that the Speaker should appoint a committee of five to prosecute the inquiry.

Immediately upon its reception "Crank" Platt, the Poughkeepsie bridge grabber, arose and announced that he did not propose to advertise in the NEW YORK WORLD, although he might be an editor himself. Legislative investigations had always proved frauds. So it will prove in the present instance. He objected to appointing a roving commission with power to ascertain what would end in the wind.

Mr. Hamilton wanted the Grand Jury's attention called to Ed Phelps and his gang, and offered a resolution to that effect.

Gen. Husted declared that the lobby was not nearly so bold as in previous sessions. He offered a resolution that the whole thing be referred back to the Judiciary Committee with instructions to inquire at once as to the truth of King Edward's allegations and report to the House May 1.

Mr. Crosby indignantly accused Gen. Husted of endeavoring to take away the power of the resolution. This would certainly end in condoning the offenses of the bill brokers.

Gen. Husted retorted that he had heretofore borne the reputation of being an honest man, and he considered Mr. Crosby's reflections unwarranted.

Mr. Sheehan thought a special committee should be named to probe the thing to the very bottom. He belived (sic) the charges to be untrue, but they had been preferred and the good name of the Legislature would remain under a cloud so long as they were not refuted.

Mr. Ainsworth contented that if Nelly (sic) Bly possessed the papers alleged to have been given her by Phelps, there would be sufficient evident upon which to base an indictment.

Judge Greene denied that he had objected to a consideration of the Crosby resolutions offered yesterday.

The debate was continued for two hours and a half.

Finally it was decided by a vote of 96 to 2 (Messrs. Kimball an Magner) to authorize the Judiciary Committee to proceed at once with an investigation as to Phelps's strictures upon Assemblymen Tallmadge, Hallagher, Prime, Dewitt, Hagan and McLaughlin, and report May 1 whether, in its judgment, the inquiry as to the general methods and practices of the lobby should be continued during the recess.

An attempt was made to secure the appointment of a joint Senate and Assembly Committee in order that the charges of attempted bribery against Lobbyist Wood might be examined.

This was defeated.

It is likely that the greatest difficulty will be experienced in ascertaining the whereabouts of Ed Phelps. The lethargy of the Assembly has permitted him to get out of the State, and the impression prevails that he will give Albany a wide berth for the remainder of the season.

The inquiry will begin probably next Wednesday.

STORY FROM THE STANDARD UNION.
PUBLISHED SATURDAY, APRIL 7, 1888:

HONEST MEN ARE SOLD.

————

THE INTERESTING METHODS OF THE PROFESSIONAL LOBBY AT ALBANY.

————

OTHER WAYS OF PUSHING LEGISLATION.

————

HOW THE SUB-COMMITTEE OF THE WHOLE BECOMES A USEFUL ADJUNCT
IN PUTTING BILL THROUGH—A SAMPLE OF SMOTHERED BILLS—THE
GOVERNOR'S NEW NOMINEE

————

[SPECIAL TO THE STANDARD UNION]

Albany, April 7.—The Assembly, by its action yesterday, has opened up a very interesting subject entitled: "How do the lobby control the Legislature?" The answer is in two ways, and the Legislature knows as much about it now as it will later. The first way they control it is to buy it; the second way is to appear to buy it. A man who starts in the profession opens up his place of business with the following stock in trade: First, "cheek," or "nerve," as unfailing assurance is designated; second, a list of the members of the Legislature. A lobbyist does not consider his business one that ought to be suppressed. He considers it perfectly legitimate to "influence legislation." If he can do it by argument he is so much ahead; if he must buy, his profits are decreased—that is all.

The way an outsider wishing to influence legislation does it is to see the lobbyist. He tells the man of influence what he wants. The man of influence has an idea of the people who will support the bill, gained by a knowledge of them and their ways, and he deliberately sits down and checks them off as his property, as did Mr. Phelps on the Cities Committee list in the case which has caused the discussion, along with those whom by previous purchase he knows he can control. Thus it is that even the good men like Mr. Crosby are alleged to be bought and sold by the lobbyists along with the wicked men. Phelps, the King of the Lobbyists, is not a favorite with his brethren in the profession. They assert he is guilty of many offenses like that told by Nellie Bly. In this case, it will be remembered, he was selling to her members of the Cities Committee; whereas the bill was originally sent to the Public Health Committee and had been killed there three weeks before he saw the woman. He knew the bill was dead and yet he would have cheated her out of $3,000. That is what is called "velvet." The story is told of Phelps that he promised an Assemblyman $3,000 for his vote several years ago. The Assemblyman voted as he agreed, and, in the language of the lobbyist who told the story and who is a well-known Brooklynite, "Phelps hung him up," that is, refused to pay him. The Assemblyman was not of the kind of man to stand that sort of treatment, so he bought a pistol, went to Phelps' office in New York, locked the door behind him and put the key in his pocket. Catching Phelps by the throat and pointing the revolver at him, he said: "I want my money or I will kill you." It was an unhappy position for Phelps, who weakened and drew a check for $6,000, which he handed to the Assemblyman. It appears he had sold the Assemblyman twice—once with his consent and once without consulting him—but thinking he had been found out he paid for both times.

That's the way the lobby works.

Mr. Saxton says the committee will meet Tuesday and decide then how it will conduct the investigation.

The way bills are pushed through the Legislature is amazing. Unless one is constantly upon the watch all sorts of tricks are played. A bill that is perfectly harmless is introduced. In the committee it is amended. The sessions are held in executive session and no one knows save those interested what the amendment is. Sometimes an entirely different bill is submitted. It is reported by its original title with the information that it is reported favorably with some amendments. If the bill is pushed through without being printed there is no way of getting at its contents save by the courtesy of the clerks. They are overworked and it adds greatly to their inconvenience if their papers are disarranged, and while access may be had with some difficulty to the documents, still it is not a pleasant duty. Then there are bills buried away in committees for months that are suddenly brought forth and rushed through. A bill is sometimes in one committee and by some hocus pocus of those interested it gets into the Sub-Committee of the Whole People opposing it think it is dead when suddenly it comes to life, and the clerk announces it has been considered by the Sub-Committee of the Whole, reported favorably, and is thus put upon the order of third reading. As nine-tens of the members don't hear what is going on when reports are read, and do not realize the difference between this committee and other committees, a bill gets through. A case in point is the bill which extends the term of service to five years of the counsel, the clerks and the messengers of the Board of Supervisors and of the Board of Charities. This bill was in the Committee on Internal Affairs, and it was vigorously opposed as being against the welfare of the county government by Supervisor-at-Large Quintard and by the Republican General Committee's Executive Committee. Yesterday this measure came in from the Sub-Committee of the Whole. No one noticed it, and the bill is now upon the order of third reading in the Assembly.

The Sub-Committee of the Whole consists of sixteen members, and to it are referred bill of a minor character, the idea being that the time of the House will be saved; but, as will be seen above, it gives opportunities for pushing through measures of a doubtful character, especially in the latter part of the session, when the high pressure is being carried to the fullest extent to get bills through. April 5 is the date set for the final report of committees on bills. This year at that date there were nearly as many bills yet in committee as have been reported, and the date for adjournment gives only twenty day and twenty-five night sessions to pass over 2,000 bills. This would make it necessary to pass over eighty bills a day to get through the list. The members realize this and they are making up for lost time by having morning sessions extend to 2 P.M., holding committee meetings till 6:30 P.M. and night sessions every night until 10 P.M. This is wearisome and the strain is heavy. The result is carelessness and even worse, because members, seeing the end draw near, in their anxiety to save pet measures, enter into deals with other members to have bills forwarded, and this bad laws are enacted. There are many excellent bills smothered in committee, and concerning some of these bills it is rumored that money is used to effect the result. Among such bills is the one designed to remove the toll-gates on the Jamaica Plank Road outside of the city limits. That bill was introduced by Mr. Tallmadge the first week of the session and, though it has been pushed and demanded by the people whose property is blighted by the gates, still the bill has slept quietly and peacefully, while many bills of an iniquitous nature have come out of the same committee. And those who know—men who thoroughly understand legislative proceedings—say that money is being used.

❧

STORY IN THE WORLD.
. PUBLISHED TUESDAY, APRIL 10, 1888:

THE LOBBY KING RETURNS.

————

EDWARD R. PHELPS, THE OWNER OF THE LEGISLATURE, AGAIN IN ALBANY.

————

HE LISTENS TO THE REPORTS OF HIS MENIALS AND RUBS HIS HANDS AT THE
THOUGHT OF HIS ILL-GOTTEN GAINS—THE INVESTIGATION STILL FURTHER
DELAYED, AS THE COMMITTEE LACKS INSTRUCTIONS.

————

[SPECIAL TO THE WORLD.]

ALBANY, APRIL 10.—Edward R. Phelps, king of the lobby, swung into Albany to-night as fresh as a two-year-old colt, and took possession of his quarters at the Kenmore. He lifted a shiny new crown of brass out of his gripsack and placed it on his head and waited for his menials to bring in their reports. The first to arrive brought him cheering news. The Western Union $162,000 resolution will be reported from the Senate Judiciary Committee on the morrow.

"How about the Hudson River Bridge bill?" asked the king, anxiously.

"Ordered to a third reading," replied the menial.

"Good!" exclaimed the king. "Did our vassals do their duty?"

"All of them; but some are objecting to the low figure. They all demand that we must put up more swag to pass the bill in the face of the strong public sentiment that is being worked up against it."

"We will have it on its final passage and will be capable of taking care of all of them. Then the outlook for the session is good?"

"It is, Your Highness. You have no reason to apprehend any trouble from this Legislature. It has neither backbone, brains or courage enough to prosecute an investigation against you."

Other menials came and went. As time goes on the chances of bringing this boss of legislation to terms seem to grow less. There is no disposition to push the grave charges against him. The Republican party does not seem inclined to take up a matter that is likely to prove a boomerang. They are beginning to realize that it will not do to enter a Presidential campaign with a scandal that might deprive them of a few hundred votes. Phelps's pickets have done noble work since his temporary departure from the city. Canfield and Reilly have pitched their tents in the Assembly parlor and have there received old comfort and information from their ever faithful informers of the lower house. In this manner Phelps himself has been able to keep thoroughly informed of all that was going on—so well, in fact, that the moment all danger of his incarceration and indictment had passed he returned as undisturbed as if nothing had happened.

The session is now reaching that funnel shaped point where the bills weighted heaviest with gold will drop out soonest. Phelps knows it. Now is his harvest time. He cannot afford to leave Albany and his business to roll in the hands of hated rivals. All the swag which he will capture must come to his net within the next four weeks. All the measures that carry money with them are yet to be pushed, and Phelps has shown in the past that he is a good pusher. He is here to look after his interests and those of his clients in and out of the Legislature. He realizes that the Legislature will protect him, and that in the event of undue prosecution by a Republican Legislature he can withhold from the Republican campaign fund next fall many thousands of dollars.

The Assembly Judiciary Committee is still coquetting with the lobby. It was expected that the investigation would proceed to-morrow. At the session of the committee this afternoon, however, it was discovered that whereas the journal told the members they must, according to the Husted resolution, confine their inquiry to the cases of the six members whom Phelps boasted he could buy, the legislative record warranted them in prosecuting a thorough investigation into the practices of bill-brokers for years back. Chairman Saxton was therefore requested to report the situation back to the House and ask an interpretation of instructions. It was decided to-night to go by direction of the journal, and to-morrow, Mr. Saxton says, the committee will meet again for the purpose of perfecting plans and the issue of subpoenas. He said further that the first sitting would be held Thursday afternoon probably.

STORY FROM THE NEW YORK SUN.
PUBLISHED SUNDAY, APRIL 15, 1888:

ALBANY'S LOBBY KING

———

THE PECULIAR RELATION OF EDWARD R. PHELPS TO THE STATE CAPITAL CLAD IN MYSTERY.

———

A little man at whom no one would look at twice paced impatiently up and down the Hudson River Railroad waiting room in the Grand Central Depot the other day, and now and then went out upon the sidewalk and walked up and down there. It happened that whole those who did not know him paid him no attention, others pointed him out to their friends with mysterious whispering, and each person thus enlightened at once stood still and stared at him. For he was Edward R. Phelps, the king of the Albany lobby. If you could imagine the Rev. Dr. Talmage very much shortened, very much thinned, and with even a more wizen face than he has, you could give yourself a fair idea of the appearance of the arch lobbyist. He has the same tufted side whiskers, the same prominent nose, and same sharp, quick-moving bright eyes as the good doctor. But he is lame in one leg, and that gives him a swaying motion when he walks.

In all probability, no other man in the United State occupies so remarkable a position as Mr. Phelps. To the honest man in Albany, everything about him is mysterious, and to the others who have sold their political souls to him he is scarcely less impressive. Albany is a little place, with only two or three important streets where all business is done, and all the people meet, and with a small political circle and a still smaller social one allied to it. The consequence is that concealment and privacy are out of the question there, and gossip is as rife as if the place were a sewing circle. As you walk along the street with a Senator or an Assemblyman, you many find him suddenly missing from your side, or he will beg you to excuse him while he steps into a store. In another instant you will understand why. Mr. Phelps is coming down the street, and the politician does not want to recognize him and does not dare to snub him. Some of the old birds in Albany in the Legislature have learned that Mr. Phelps is not too particular. He never sees anybody who does not want to be seen, nor does he ask anybody to see him.

The greatest plight that a new man in Phelps's power ever finds himself in is when he discovers the king of the lobby on a railroad train. Certain trains are monopolized by the Legislature, particularly one to New York on Friday afternoon and one back again on Monday morning. Mr. Phelps sometimes travels on these trains, in which case there is a general desire on the part of certain legislators to avoid the car he has a seat in and pack the next one to suffocation. It is not only the dishonest men that dislike to give rise to gossip by making or acknowledging the acquaintance of Mr. Phelps. A great many honest men who have gone to Albany have been just as timid.

Eve more peculiar than these experiences out of doors is the mystery that surrounds him in his own quarters. For many years his rooms have been in the Kenmore Hotel, the fashionable hotel of Albany. Hundreds upon hundreds of men, lobbyists, politicians, legislators, and capitalists must have been in those rooms, but it is utterly impossible, and always has been impossible, to find anybody in Albany who will say he has been in them and know what they contain. The whereabouts of Mephistopheles when he is not at the ear and elbow of Dr. Faust is not more mysterious than the hidden appointments and proceedings within those chambers.

The consequences of this disinclination on the part of Mr. Phelps's friends to tell what they know is that the Albany atmosphere is always charged with astonishing stories about that dread interior. For instance, it is said that Mr. Phelps has the most complete encyclopedia of political biography in this State, in which he keeps a record of every social, commercial, and political act of every man in the Legislature. Another of the rumors is that the Legislature itself keeps no such record of its own proceedings as Mr. Phelps does. It is said that the entire history of every bill that has been introduced can be turned to at a second's notice in his books, so that its exact position on the calendar and its condition, and all the changes that have been taken upon it, are there set forth. This is probably true, for, both in the Senate and Assembly, the instant either House adjourns a half dozen men, who are not reporters, struggle to forestall the newspaper men by getting at the bills and clerk's books ahead of them. Some of these are Mr. Phelps's clerks, some are the clerks for other lobbyists, and some are lobbyists themselves.

Nobody says that Mr. Phelps is a good fellow in the convivial sense of that term, and there are no records of any dinners or drinking bouts or good times of any sort in his rooms. Those who go to see him are said to be very numerous and frequent caller, but they are neither very eminent nor what are called high-priced men in Albany. The leaders of the Black Horse cavalry that do the work of the lobby in the Legislature are not believed to find it necessary ever to go to Mr. Phelps's rooms. This work with him is done by his lieutenants, one of whom is the most popular man in the capital—a jolly, circumspect, wideawake young man. He makes it his business to know everybody who comes to town, and he has built up a remarkable reputation for being able to distinguish an honest man from a dishonest man every time without the shadow of a mistake. The honest men get a good deal of valuable information from him, and doubtless he does from them, but he never attempts to practise business in their presence, and no blame or suspicion attaches to any man who is seen talking with him, although in all probability he does more actual work of Mr. Phelps's kind than Mr. Phelps himself.

FULL TESTIMONY OF NELLIE BLY BEFORE STATE ASSEMBLY
WEDNESDAY AFTERNOON, APRIL 18, 1888

PINK COCHRAN, sworn, testified as follows:
Examined by MR. SAXTON:

Q. Will you please tell us what your name is?
A. My name is Cochran.
Q. Your first name?
A. Is it necessary that I should give it?
Q. Yes; I think you had better tell us.
A. My first name is Pink.
Q. Where do you reside?
A. New York, at present.
Q. Can you give us your address in New York city?
A. Yes, sir; 69 West Ninety-sixth street.
Q. What is where you reside?

A. Yes, sir.

Q. Are you married?

A. No, sir.

Q. And what is your occupation?

A. Well, some call me a journalist, and some call me a reporter — a newspaper writer.

Q. You are engaged in the journalistic business?

A. Yes, sir.

Q. And on the staff of the *New York World*?

A. Yes, sir.

Q. A reporter for that paper?

A. Yes, sir.

Q. How long have you been in that business?

A. About three years.

Q. And you write articles for that paper over a certain signature, do you not?

A. Yes, sir.

Q. And what is that signature?

A. "Nellie Bly."

Q. And you are the lady, I believe, who made an investigation in regard to our methods in lunatic asylums?

A. I did.

Q. Which was published in the *New Work World* and elsewhere?

A. Yes, sir; that was my first work on the *World*.

Q. Had you been engaged in the newspaper business before that?

A. Yes, sir.

Q. Not for the *New York World*?

A. No, sir; not in New York.

Q. How long have you lived in New York city?

A. Well, almost a year; a year next month.

Q. You were engaged upon the *World* before you came there, were you?

A. No, sir; I worked for the *Pittsburgh Dispatch*.

Q. I understood you to say you had been at work for the *World* before that?

A. No, sir; I said I had been in the newspaper business before that.

Q. I show you a copy of the *New York World*, or a portion of the *New York World* of Sunday, April first, page 19, and refer you to an article there, the principal article upon that page; did you write that article? *[Presents paper to witness]*

A. I did.

Q. And the signature to that is your *nom de plume*, is it?

A. Yes, sir.

Q. "Nellie Bly?"

A. I wrote all of it except the poetry.

Q. You were not responsible, then, for the poetry?

A. No, sir.

Q. Now, this article I see, refers by name to certain gentlemen, members of the Assembly of this State?

A. Yes, sir.

Q. It refers to Mr. Gallagher, of Erie; Mr. Tallmadge, of Kings; Mr. Prime, of Essex; Mr. De Witt, of Ulster; Mr. Hagan, of New York; and Mr. McLaughlin, of Kings; I desire to ask you whether you have any acquaintance with any of those gentlemen yourself?

A. No, sir; I never have seen any of them.

Q. You have never seen any of them to your knowledge?

A. No, sir.

Q. Did you ever have any conversation with any of those gentlemen or hear any conversation which they were holding with any other person?

A. I do not think I ever did.

Q. Then, of course, you do not know anything of your own knowledge, that is, know anything yourself with regard to the integrity of these gentlemen.

A. I did not write that I knew it.

Q. No; I understand.

A. No, sir; I do not.

Q. You do not know anything of your own knowledge?

A. No, sir.

Q. You have no knowledge, then, as to the connection of any of these gentlemen with any measure pending before this Legislature?

A. Nothing. Only what Mr. Phelps told me.

Q. You have no knowledge as to any matter contained in this article, except the statements and declarations of Mr. Phelps in regard to it?

A. That is all.

Q. Now, this article relates what purports to be an interview between yourself and Mr. Phelps?

A. Yes, sir.

Q. There was such an interview, was there?

A. Yes, sir.

Q. And that interview occurred on what day?

A. On Tuesday, I think it was.

Q. Tuesday before the issuing of this edition?

A. Yes, sir; I am not positive that it was Tuesday.

Q. I think it states in here that it was Tuesday?

A. It was in the first of the week; or Wednesday; I am not positive.

Q. Did you come here with a definite purpose in view from New York city to Albany?

A. Yes, sir.

Q. And that purpose was to interview Mr. Phelps, was it, upon the subjects practically that are stated in this communication?

A. My purpose was to find if it was really true that people could be bought by Mr. Phelps.

Q. That was the general purpose of it?

A. Yes, sir.

Q. To interview him with regard to his relations to members of the Legislature here?

A. Yes, sir.

Q. Were you sent up by the *New York World*, the managers of the *New York World*, for that purpose?

A. Well, not exactly; I asked to come, and they said they didn't think I should come, because I would make a failure of it; they said Mr. Phelps had, as far as they knew, been in the business such a long time that he could not be caught, and they advised me not to come.

Q. As a matter of fact it was with the permission of the paper that you came up here?

A. Well, they said: "Well, you can go, if you are determined."

Q. Now, the interview that you had with Mr. Phelps was at the Kenmore hotel?

A. Yes, sir.

Q. At his room in this city?

A. Yes, sir.

Q. And was anybody else present during that interview?

A. There was a man in another room, but I do not know who he was; he was at the first door I went to.

Q. During the interview?

A. Well, he was there all the time, yes, but I don't know as he could hear what we said, because I pretended to be very much afraid.

Q. Do you know whether he was within such a distance that he could hear?

A. I told Mr. Phelps I was afraid, and asked him to close the door.

Q. Do you know who that gentleman was?

A. No, sir, I don't; he was writing at a desk.

Q. Now, Mr. Phelps in that interview mentioned to you the names of these six gentlemen whom I have mentioned, did he?

A. Yes, sir.

Q. Will you, please, tell me what Mr. Phelps said in reference to those gentlemen?

A. Well, I told Mr. Phelps I had a bill.

Q. Wait a moment; I want to tell you right here that our investigation limits us to the charges that are made in this paper against these specific gentlemen, and I desire simply to ask you what Mr. Phelps said in reference to those particular gentlemen, Mr. Gallagher, Mr. Prime, Mr. De Witt, Mr. Hagan, Mr. McLaughin and Mr. Tallmadge, those six gentlemen?

A. He said he could buy them for a thousand dollars to kill the bill.

Q. Did he mention their names?

A. Yes, sir; at the same time marked the paper.

Q. Now, he said he could buy those gentlemen for a thousand dollars to kill the bill?

A. For a thousand dollars to kill the bill.

Q. The bill you refer to is what is known as the Smith Patent Medicine bill?

A. Yes, sir.

Q. And which is published in this communication?

A. Yes, sir.

Q. You say that at the time he said that, he had a piece of paper, did he?

A. A piece of paper?

Q. Well, a paper of any kind?

A. He went to a table there and picked up a sheet of paper on which was a great number of names, and the laid this paper down on the desk, and he told me, read those names off, he said as you read them there, "Gallagher of Erie," mark them.

Q. Have you that paper present?

A. Yes, sir.

Q. Will you show it to me please?

A. It has been cut since I took it away from Mr. Phelps *(witness produces paper)*; I pasted it to that because I didn't want to lose the other.

Q. The paper here which is headed "Affairs of Cities," is the paper you refer to?

A. Yes, sir.

Q. The paper attached to it was not handed to you by him at that time?

A. No, sir; that was later.

Q. You say he took this piece of paper headed "Affairs of Cities" from a table?

A. Yes, sir; not exactly a table, a little ledge between the windows.

Q. Did he bring it where you were?

A. Yes, sir.

Q. And what did he do in reference to that paper?

A. He put it down on the table so, and he said "I can buy Gallagher, Tallmadge, Prime, DeWitt, Hagan, and McLaughlin;" then he told me he could not buy the rest.

Q. Now, did he, at the time he spoke these names, make any mark upon the paper?

A. Yes, sir; with a lead pencil.

Q. With a lead pencil.

A. Yes, sir.

Q. The marks that he made, are those the ones that appear there now opposite the names?

A. Well, not exactly; they were with a lead pencil, but in order to reproduce them in the paper we had to make them blacker so they would show to be photographed, and the artist on the paper, McDougal, he covered them with ink, just as they were, but covered them in ink.

Q. Then you mean to say that the marks that are there now are the same in shape that they were then?

A. Yes, sir.

Q. But they are now covered with ink?

A. Yes, sir.

Q. And then they were in pencil?

A. Yes, sir.

Q. Did you do that yourself?

A. No, sir.

Q. The artist did that?

A. The artist did that; I gave it to the managing editor just as Mr. Phelps gave it to me, and the artist had to do that in order to reproduce it in the paper;

it would not reproduce from lead pencil.

Q. What about these marks opposite the other gentlemen's names?

A. I told him I wanted to take the list home to show my husband, because I wanted to save the list to put it in the paper, and he said, "Oh, that won't do to take it away," because "my husband" may know some of the men whose names he had marked, and he said he would scratch them all out, and then I could show him the paper; he did not want "my husband" to see it; he put it down on the table, took this paper from me, put it down on the table, and took the lead pencil again and scratched across all the other names except Mr. Crosby's, and when I looked at it again when he handed it to me, I saw that by laying it on a book that he had different marks; instead of making the straight stroke it made dots from the cover of the book.

Q. And did he make them, the second time when he put those marks on there, on a book?

A. Yes, sir; a book lying on his table.

Q. What kind of book was it?

A. I cannot say.

Q. Cloth?

A. I am not positive, but it was rough, and as he drew the pencil across it, it made dotted marks.

Q. These marks on here now opposite those names, Burns, Cromwell, Blumenthal and Sullivan are no the same as they were then?

A. Except that they have been dotted with ink to make them show more, as I told you the artist had to do.

Q. Did this same gentleman who covered the other strokes with ink do this also?

A. Yes, sir.

Q. What is his name?

A. McDougal; he is the artist for the *World*; the head office.

Q. He is there in the *World* office?

A. Yes, sir.

Q. What is his first name?

A. I don't know that.

Mr. Hastings.— Walter

Q. *[By Mr. Saxton, resuming]* Then after he had marked these other names what did he do with the paper?

A. He handed it to me and I folded it and put it in that satchel and took it down to the *World* office; but it was a longer paper then; it had lots of names on, under headings of what the committees were; you can see on the other side.

Q. Then it was a paper containing the names of all the committees of the Legislature?

A. Yes, sir?

Q. At that time?

A. At least I thought it was.

Q. When you took it away?

A. Yes, sir.

Q. And then cut it—

A. No, the artist did it.

Q. You haven't the rest of the paper with you?

A. No, sir.

Q. Do you know where that is?

A. I do not, unless it is in the *World* office.

Q. What did you do with the paper; you say you put it in your pocket there and took it down to New York?

A. I gave it to Colonel Cockerill, the managing editor of the *World*.

Q. When did you see it again?

A. I asked for it by the time my story was ready for print; I said I wanted to get this, because it was the only evidence I had, and then he gave it to me.

Q. How long was that after you had give it to him; how long did he have it?

A. That was two days; I gave it to him on Thursday—no, sir; I gave it to him Friday, and I got it Saturday; Saturday night.

Q. Has it been in your possession ever since?

A. Yes, sir; ever since.

Q. The artist did that work upon it, then while it was out of your possession?

A. Yes, sir.

Q. And you don't know about the inking of these pencil marks, excepting as you have been told, I suppose?

A. That was all; the colonel explained that to me, why it had to be done.

Q. Did you cut this portion of the paper off before you gave it to the colonel?

A. No, sir; I gave him the whole page.

Q. And did he return to you the whole page?

A. No, sir, just that much, and he cut it, or somebody in the office did, I guess.

Q. Now, in that interview did Mr. Phelps say anything more about any of those six gentlemen you have named aside from what you have said?

A. Not in that first interview.

Q. As a matter of fact, when you told him about that you wanted to show this to your husband, that was not true, was it?

A. No, sir, it was not true; told a story to catch a story.

Q. And that is the reason of your getting the paper, was to use it to corroborate your communication or your story when you had told it?

A. Yes, sir.

Q. Have you any objection to leaving this here and having it placed in evidence?

A. No, if you will keep good care of it; it is the only evidence I have.

Q. Well, we will take good care of it; we will leave it with the stenographer. *[Paper marked "Exhibit A."]* I think you said that during this interview he said nothing about those gentlemen except what you have already stated, that he could buy those six gentlemen?

A. That is all he said about them, telling me the amount; of course I was anxious to know the amount.

Q. That he could buy them for a thousand dollars?

A. Yes, sir; the six.

Q. Six of them for a thousand dollars?

A. Yes, sir.

Q. Did Mr. Phelps in that interview, when he was speaking of these six gentlemen, use the word "buy?"

A. Use the word "buy?"

Q. Yes?

A. Wait; I think I can remember his exact words.

Q. I wish you would give them if you can; his exact language?

A. I don't think I can remember his exact words; I would not try to give his exact words, but—

Q. Well, give them just as near as you can recall them now?

A. Well, in the first interview he said he could get the six men for a thousand dollars.

Q. Now, let us see if that is correct; he said he could get the six men for a thousand dollars.

A. He could get their votes.

Q. Get their votes for a thousand dollars?

A. A thousand dollars.

Q. Then, if that was the case, and that was the language he used, he did not say "buy those six votes for a thousand dollars?"

A. But he said so the second time.

Q. That is at another interview; that is not down here in that paper, is it?

A. Oh, yes; that is in that paper.

Q. This was at the first interview at the Kenmore?

A. Yes sir.

Q. When he said he could get those six votes for a thousand dollars?

A. Yes, sir.

Q. Is that the language that he used at that time?

A. Well, I am not so positive that that was the language.

Q. As near as you can now recall it?

A. Yes, sir, as near as anyone could recollect a conversation.

Q. When was the next interview that you have spoken of?

A. On Friday at his office in New York.

Q. Did he say something then about these six particular gentlemen; did he call their names to you at any time in the interview?

A. Yes, sir, of course he did.

Q. What was it he said about those six gentlemen of any one of them at that interview?

A. Why, he said it was easier to get the Committee on Public Health—easier and cheaper than it was to get that committee.

Q. He said it was easier, then, to get the Committee on Public Health than it was to get the cities committee?

A. Yes, sir.

Q. Well, is that the only way that he referred to those six gentlemen in that interview?

A. Well, I asked him why it was transferred.

Q. I ask you if that is the only way—that is all we care about here; I do not care about public health, except as it might have come in relation to those six gentlemen; was that the only way in which he referred to those six gentlemen upon the cities committee whom you have mentioned?

A. No, in another way.

Q. In another way?

A. Yes, sir.

Q. You say he referred to them in another way?

A. Well, he referred to them in connection with a lot more.

Q. Oh, no—

A. Can I divide them from the others?

Q. Did he mention their names?

A. Well, he mentioned the committee.

Q. I do not care about that; I do not care about spreading abroad any further the names of any other gentlemen whom Mr. Phelps mentioned, if he did mention any in that interview; that is not the object of this investigation, and I do not desire you to mention any other names except those of the six gentlemen mentioned in this interview?

A. Well, he did not mention them individually afterwards.

Q. Then if he did not mention these gentlemen individually in any other way except as you have state, that is as far as I care about going, and that is the fact, is it.

A. Yes, sir.

Q. Now, did you make any memorandum of this conversation with him?

A. Yes, sir; just as soon as I got away from him I did, but not in his presence.

Q. Where did you go to make the memorandum?

A. First I went down to Stanwix Hall, where I was stopping.

Q. Down to Stanwix Hall?

A. Yes, sir; the second interview I went to the *World* office.

Q. The first interview did you go immediately from his room to Stanwix Hall?

A. Yes, sir; he wanted me to go home, but I did not.

Q. Did you go to your room there?

A. Yes, sir.

Q. And there you made a memorandum, did you?

A. Yes, sir.

Q. Did you write out any portion of this article there?

A. Oh, no.

Q. Just made a memorandum?

A. Just made notes so that I could get it exactly correct.

Q. Have you got those notes with you?

A. No, I haven't.

Q. Can you tell where they are?

A. Yes, or I can tell where they were; I tore them up after I wrote my article, as I do all my notes.

Q. You did not preserve them?

A. No, sir I never do.

Q. You had the memorandum before you when you prepared the article, did you?

A. Yes, sir.

Q. Did you write down the article, the language, from the memoranda which you had?

A. Yes, sir; I tried to get it as near as possible for one to repeat a conversation.

Q. And the second interview that you had with him, you say you went to the *World* office after that interview, did you?

A. Yes, sir.

Q. And how soon after the talk?

A. Directly; I drove right to the *World* office.

Q. And did you there make memoranda of the conversation?

A. Yes, sir; I made memoranda of that conversation first, and then I wrote my entire article.

Q. On that same day?

A. Yes, sir, which was Friday.

Q. And this article, as it appears in the *World*, is the article as it was written by you, is it?

A. Yes, sir, except for the poetry.

Q. Except the poetry?

[The witness made a statement to the chairman of the committee.]

Q. I will ask you in reference to that. Was it in the first interview?

A. The second.

Q. What was it he said about that?

A. I asked him what would be done—when he wanted me to write out the check and give it to him to pay him for his work; I asked him what would be done with me if I was found—known to pay him to kill the bill, and he said "nothing;" and I said "but it is criminal; I am afraid, and my husband would not like me to be connected with anything like this;" he said, "Well, if it was found out, these men whom I pay have to protect me in order to save themselves;" so I was satisfied; I did not pay the money.

By Mr. ROESCH:

Q. I understood the witness to say that Mr. Phelps said to her that he could get those members whom he mentioned to her, as she says, for so much?

A. Yes, sir.

Q. That was your answer, was it not?

A. Yes, sir.

Q. I read here in this article that you say you wrote that he said the following, using your own language: "Mr. Crosby of New York, is a rich man, and cannot be bought, but we can buy Gallagher of Erie, Tallmadge of Kings, Prime of Essex, DeWitt of Ulster, and McLaughlin of Kings; the rest are no good." Now, which answer is the correct one?

A. Both.

Q. The one you make here or the one in the article?

A. They were both correct, because we talked it over repeatedly, and I, in order to make him talk a great deal, pretended I was very much afraid.

Q. How many conversations did you have with Mr. Phelps in the Kenmore?

A. Only one.

Q. What name did you give to Mr. Phelps when you went there?

A. Consol.

Q. Could you identify the gentleman whom you say was in Mr. Phelps' office at that time of you were to see him again?

A. Well, I am not positive that I could.

Q. Were there any marks made on that paper which has been in evidence other than those necessary to print it?

A. No, sir.

Q. Beyond what were made by Mr. Phelps himself?

A. No, sir.

Q. You say the other portion of the paper you haven't with you?

A. The other portion, no. The artist cut it in order to be able to reproduce it in the paper.

Q. Do you know what has become of the other portion of that paper?

A. I suppose it went into the waste-basket, as they thought that was the only piece that was important to save.

Q. I understood you to say that you went directly to the Stanwix and wrote out the notes of the conversation you had?

A. I did.

Q. Where did you write out the notes of the second conversation you had with him?

A. In the *World* office.

Q. What induced you there in the first place to start this investigation; I understood you to say that you were not instructed by the editorial staff?

A. No, sir; I was not; they rather opposed it because they said he was too clever to be caught.

Q. What induced you in the first instance to suggest it?

A. Several letters that we had, or rather that were sent to me at the office speaking about people being bribed; that was the first thing that started it; I commenced to study it up then, and suggested to the Colonel that I come up and find out if it were true; I did not think it was—until I got up here.

Q. This telegram from Philadelphia was fictitious, was it?

A. Fictitious? How? I sent it.

Q. You actually sent the telegram?

A. Yes, sir.

Q. But the contents of the telegram were fiction?

A. I wrote out the contents of the telegram sent him because I wanted to make him entirely easy when he came back to see me on Friday.

FULL TESTIMONY OF EDWARD PHELPS BEFORE STATE ASSEMBLY WEDNESDAY AFTERNOON, APRIL 18, 1888

EDWARD R. PHELPS, sworn, testified as follows:
Examined by MR. SAXTON:

Q. Where do you live?

A. White Plains, Westchester county.

Q. You spend your time in Albany to some extent during the sessions of the Legislature, do you not?

A. I have all but this year; this year I have not been here much.

Q. Well, you have been here a portion of the time this winter?

A. Yes, sir.

Q. How long have you been here; how much of the time?

A. Well, in the month of January I was only here at the organization; then I went south in February; I was here twice; I went to the southwest; in March I was here the forepart of the month; then I went west; returned to Albany about the twentieth of March.

Q. And have been here since then most of the time?

A. No, sir; I was here about a week or ten days—about a week, and since then I have been away.

Q. And you have been here in former years during sessions of the Legislature, have you?

A. Yes, sir.

Q. For how many years past?

A. Twenty years.

Q. What is your business?

A. Well, I am engaged in railroading; deal in stocks, grain; speculator.

Q. What is your business in Albany?

A. When I have been in Albany I have been looking after bills I have been interested in.

Q. Well, it was legislative business, was it not?

A. Yes, sir.

Q. You have been in Albany, I suppose, principally engaged upon business relating to legislation?

A. Well, yes, sometimes.

Q. Measures before the Legislature? You are commonly known as a lobbyist?

A. Yes, sir.

Q. Mr. Phelps, do you know Mr. Gallagher, of Erie county?

A. I have known him slightly for two or three years.

Q. You say you have known him slightly for two or three years?

A. Yes, sir.

Q. Have you known him outside of Albany?

A. No.—

Q. Your acquaintance with him has been principally at Albany?

A. Yes, sir.

Q. While he has been engaged in his legislative duties; do you know Mr. Tallmadge, of Kings?
A. I have a slight acquaintance with Mr. Tallmadge.
Q. How long have you known him?
A. Well, probably not over—I think I knew him when he was here the last time; I am not certain, though.
Q. You have no very intimate acquaintance, then, with Mr. Tallmadge?
A. No, sir.
Q. Nothing but a speaking acquaintance?
A. No, sir.
Q. Do you know Mr. Prime, of Essex?
A. No, sir.
Q. Not at all?
A. No, sir.
Q. Do you know Mr. DeWitt, of Ulster?
A. No, sir.
Q. Not at all?
A. No, sir.
Q. Mr. Hagan, of New York?
A. Well, I have just known him, a speaking acquaintance for several years.
Q. And Mr. McLaughlin, of Kings?
A. I knew him, I have known him when I saw him.
Q. You have no acquaintance with him?
A. No, sir.
Q. Now, did you ever have any business with any of these gentlemen, with reference to matters pending in this Legislature?
A. No, sir.
Q. Did you ever have any conversation with any of those gentlemen with regard to matters pending in the Legislature?
A. Not to my recollection.
Q. Have you, during this session, had any conversation with them?
A. No, sir.
Q. Or any one of them?
A. No, sir.
Q. With regard to measures?
A. No, sir.
Q. That were before their branch of Legislature?
A. No, sir.
Q. Have you, either by yourself or any person acting for you, had any transaction of any kind with either of these gentlemen?
A. No, sir.
Q. With regard to any matters pending here?
A. No, sir.
Q. You have not?
A. No, sir.
Q. Have you to any of these gentlemen in any way, suggested or intimated that

there was money to be had, or anything that was valuable as a consideration for any action of theirs in their official capacity?

A. No, sir.

Q. Have you done any such thing as that either directly or indirectly?

A. No, sir.

Q. Yourself or through anybody else?

A. No, sir.

Q. Has any of these gentlemen ever suggested to you or intimated to you or to any other person where it has come to your knowledge that they desired or were willing to receive anything as a reward for any official action of theirs?

A. No, sir.

Q. Do you know anything else, Mr. Phelps?

A. Well, not much.

Q. Well, I had come to the same conclusion with reference to matters that I had interrogated you upon; at any rate, do you know anything, Mr. Phelps, that would tend—do you know it I ask—that would tend to impeach the integrity or cast a doubt upon the honesty of any of those gentlemen whom I have named to you?

A. No, sir.

Q. Did you ever have any communication with any of those gentlemen, directly or indirectly—of course that is covered already by your general answers, but I will ask you the specific question—in regard to what was known as the Smith Patent Medicine bill?

A. No, sir.

Q. You knew there was such a bill?

A. I did not know it until this lady—well, till this lady called upon me.

Q. Then you did not know that there was such a measure pending here until the day that lady called upon you?

A. No, sir.

Q. Then of course you could not have known what committee that was in?

A. Not at all.

Q. Did you have the bill there?

A. I may have had the bill on the files we keep in the room.

Q. Had you ever had any business prior to that time in connection with that bill?

A. No, sir.

Q. You have had no business, then, to transact with any other person with reference to that bill?

A. No, sir.

Q. Nobody transacted any business with you in reference to that bill until that day?

A. No, sir.

Q. Then Miss Cochran is the first one who approached you on the subject of killing that bill?

A. Yes, sir.

Q. There was such an interview, or there was such an interview, I suppose, between you and this lady shortly before the first of April, was there not?

A. Yes, sir.

Q. And where did that interview occur?

A. At the Kenmore; room 99.

Q. That is the room occupied by you?

A. That is my parlor.

Q. Did this lady come to your room?

A. This lady came with a boy to 98, which is a general room where gentlemen sometimes come in and sit; there were three or four gentlemen sitting there with me; they sat smoking at the time and talking; the boy rapped and said this lady wished to see me; I was somewhat surprised, because ladies did not call on me, and I says, "in the parlor?" he says, "here."

Q. I don't care about going through with all the conversation you had with the boy; as a matter of fact, the lady was shown in, was she?

A. Yes, sir.

Q. And you say there were several gentlemen there at the time she was announced?

A. Yes, sir.

Q. Did they remain there after she came in?

A. Yes, sir.

Q. How long did they remain there?

A. After she went away.

Q. In the same room?

A. No, sir.

Q. Who were those gentlemen?

A. Well, perhaps it would not be right to name them, would it?

Q. I don't know of any reason why; they did not hear the interview; I think we had better have their names?

A. One was an ex-member of Assembly, Mr. Seaver; another was an ex-member of Assembly, Mr. Sheridan of Kings; and I am not certain who the other gentlemen were; I would not like to swear who they were, but those are two I recollect.

Q. How long do you say they remained in the room after the lady came in?

A. Well, probably ten minutes; the lady was with me about ten or fifteen minutes.

Q. Did they retire to another room?

A. No, sir; they were in an adjoining room; I have two rooms, Nos. 99 and 98.

Q. The lady did not go into this room?

A. No, sir.

Q. You received her in the other room?

A. Yes, sir.

Q. There was no one in that other room but yourself and her?

A. No, sir.

Q. You had an interview with her there?

A. Yes, sir.

Q. Was anybody present during any portion of the interview besides you two?

A. No, sir.

Q. Was the door open between the room you were occupying and the room where these other gentlemen were?

A. It was on ajar; she requested me to close it; I said, "Oh no; that is all right."

Q. Well, did you close it?

A. No, sir.

Q. And how near were you to that door when you were having this talk.

A. About five feet.

Q. And do you know where those men were in reference to the door on the other side?

A. Well, they were in the center of the room, say about five or six feet, or ten feet—probably about five feet from the door, ten feet altogether.

Q. Now, you heard the testimony of Miss Cochran as to what you said with reference to the six gentlemen whose names have been mentioned, did you not?

A. Yes, sir.

Q. Now, will you give us your version of what was said between you upon that specific subject as to those six gentlemen?

A. There was nothing in particular said about those six gentlemen; after she took out the satchel and showed me this bill of Mr. Smith, the patent medicine bill—I would like to go on and explain.

Q. I don't care about going into all that now; I want to know what was said in reference to those six gentlemen?

A. Nothing at all.

Q. Between you two?

A. Nothing at all.

Q. You say that their names were not mentioned?

A. No, sir.

Q. Then the name of Mr. Gallagher was not mentioned?

A. I went over to the mantle-piece and got a copy of the committees.

Q. Was it a similar paper to this? *[Presenting paper to witness]*

A. Yes, sir; as clean a bill as that, too, and handed it to her and told her she had better go and see the committee herself.

Q. What committee?

A. The Committee on Cities; she said it was in the Committee on Cities; I told her I thought not; to satisfy myself I went to look; she insisted it was in the Committee on Cities; I told her she had better go and see the committee herself.

Q. You showed her a list of the Committee on Cities, did you?

A. Yes, sir; and gave her the list.

Q. Before you showed her the list, did you speak the name of any of these six gentlemen to her?

A. No, sir.

Q. After you showed her the list, did you say anything about those six gentlemen to her?

A. I immediately said Mr. Crosby boarded in the house, in the hotel, and that she could see him; she said she wanted to go down on the early train; she did not want to have anything to do with these men; she wanted me to attend to this bill myself; I said I did not wish to do it; didn't wish to have anything to do with the bill; it was out of my line.

Q. You don't answer the question, which was whether you said anything to her about any of those gentlemen by name?

A. I am certain I never said anything to her about any of those gentlemen by name; she spoke about buying; I never used the term "buy," in my life.

Q. Did you mark the names of any of the members of the cities committee?

A. No, sir; no, sir.

Q. Did you in any way place a mark upon that paper which you produce here, the list of the committees; did you place a mark of any kind upon it?

A. No, sir.

Q. Did you say to her that you could get Mr. Gallagher, of Erie; Mr. Tallmadge, of Kings; Mr. Prime, of Essex; Mr. De Witt, of Ulster, Mr. Hagan, of New York; Mr. McLaughlin, of Kings?

A. No, sir.

Q. Or anything to that effect?

A. No, sir.

Q. For one thousand dollars?

A. No, sir.

Q. In that in substance?

A. No, sir.

Q. Or anything to that effect?

A. No, sir.

Q. Did you say that you could get those gentlemen whose names I have mentioned, or any of them for one thousand dollars?

A. No, sir.

Q. Or that in substance?

A. No, sir.

Q. Did you use an such expression as that, or anything similar to that with reference to those gentlemen, in that interview?

A. No, sir; there was nothing of the kind talked about.

Q. Or at the interview you had with her in New York; you had an interview with her in New York city, did you?

A. Yes, sir.

Q. Where was that?

A. That was at 115 Broadway.

Q. That is where your office is?

A. Yes, sir.

Q. Did you use any such language as that in that interview?

A. No, sir.

Q. Or anything like it?

A. No, sir.

Q. Did you mention the names of those gentlemen, or any of them, during that interview in New York city?

A. No, sir; there was no occasion to.

Q. I did not ask you that; I simply ask you if you did; you say you did not?

A. Yes, sir.

Q. Did you at any time, in any conversation you had with her, mention the names of any of these men in her presence?

A. No, sir; as I said in the first place, I spoke in the first place about Mr. Crosby; that he roomed in the house; was in the house.

Q. Any of the others besides Mr. Crosby then?

A. No, sir.

Q. Did you mention any of them by name besides Mr. Crosby?

A. No, sir.

Q. I think Miss Cochran testified that in the second interview you said it was easier to get the Public Health Committee than it was to get the Committee on Cities, or something to that effect?

A. I never made any remark; there was no occasion to make any remark.

Q. Did you say that or anything to that effect?

A. No, sir.

Q. Did you say anything about getting the Public Health Committee?

A. No, sir.

By Mr. Coon:

Q. Mr. Phelps how many days have you spent in Albany this winter?

A. It's hard work to tell, sir.

Q. You say you were here in January; about how long were you here at that time?

A. I was here at the organization; came up Sunday night; I think I staid (sic) until Monday.

Q. When did you come again?

A. I think I came again in February.

Q. About how many days did you stay here then?

A. I could not—well, perhaps ten days.

Q. Is that all you were here in February?

A. That was.

Q. In March you came again?

A. I came again in March and staid (sic) perhaps ten days; well, we will say fifteen days off and on; I went wet in the meantime; I was in Chicago the twentieth of the month, the twentieth of March.

Q. You say you were dealing in stocks and grain, etc.; are you a broker, do you call yourself a broker?

A. I am a speculator, I am sorry to say.

Q. Well, what do you mean by that?

A. I mean to say I buy 100,000 bushels of wheat, 100,000 bushels of oats and sell 100,000 bushels.

Q. Buy and sell on margins?

A. Yes, sir.

Q. Do you carry that business on here in Albany?

A. Not here, no, sir; I have done it here by telegraph.

Q. Well, during the time you have been here this winter have you conducted that business at the Kenmore, or here in Albany?

A. I merely kept watch of what I had; I was carrying a large amount of grain, carrying a large amount of stocks.

Q. That is, you were doing it on your own hook, so to speak?

A. Yes, sir.

Q. Not dealing with the public in that respect?

A. Not at all—well, you mean to say if I was dealing with—what do you mean?

Q. I mean you were not taking the business of other men.

A. No, sir.

Q. You are not here for the purpose of conducting any business in that particular line?

A. I have no business at all this winter.

Q. You said you kept files in your rooms of bills?

A. Yes, sir.

Q. And you had lists of the committees?

A. There was lists of the committees, files and all those things in my room; if a gentleman calls and wants a bill, if I can give it to him, I will do so; if he wants a list of the committees and I can give it to him I will do so.

Q. Is that your object in getting those bills?

A. Yes, sir

Q. To supply any gentlemen that might call?

A. Yes, sir.

Q. A sort of an—

A. Accommodation.

Q. Assistant to the document room here?

A. Yes, sir.

Q. And do you say you did not point out these names to this lady on this list?

A. I do say so; yes, sir.

Q. You did not point out any names?

A. No, sir.

Q. You did not point out any names?

A. No, sir.

Q. To her?

A. No, sir.

Q. Did you show her the list?

A. I did.

Q. Of names of the Public Health Committee—that is, point out the names to her at all?

A. No, sir; I have here the list like that.

Q. No more than to give her the paper containing the lists of the other committees?

A. That is all.

Q. You did not call specific attention to that committee?

A. No, sir.

Q. Was there anything said at all about the Committee on Public Health?

A. Not more than what I said myself; I thought the bill was before the Committee on Public Health.

Q. She rather insisted it was in the cities committee?

A. Yes, sir.

Q. And then was your attention directed to the members of the cities committee?

A. No, not any more so than it was on any occasion talking about them.

Q. Was there any talk between you and this lady about influencing these six gentlemen in regard to that bill?

A. No, sir.

Q. No conversation of that kind?

A. No, sir.

Q. On that subject?

A. Not at all.

Q. That you could influence those six gentlemen?

A. Not at all; it was not talked about.

Q. Was there anything said that Mr. Crosby was a wealthy man and could not be bought?

A. No, sir; that question was not—I will say here that has been stated in the *World* several times: I said, "Mr. Crosby in the House was an honorable gentlemen *(sic)*, and that she could call and see him;" I never said anything about Mr. Crosby's wealth at any time; I did not know as Mr. Crosby was wealthy any more than any other members of the committee; there may be other members of the committee as wealthy as him.

Q. You had an interview with this lady in New York.

A. Yes, sir, in the presence of another party.

Q. Was there anything said there about those six names?

A. No, sir.

Q. Those gentlemen?

A. No, sir.

Q. Or this cities committee?

A. No, sir.

Q. Did you not discuss that subject at all?

A. Not at all.

Q. Anything said there about her giving you a check for a thousand dollars, or twelve hundred, or whatever the amount mentioned in the paper is?

A. No, sir; I gave her a copy of the *Evening Journal*, and I said to her when she came in, "Madam, your bill is already reported adversely; you must have done good work in Albany, and here is a copy of the *Evening Journal*;" I never thought anything more about this bill after she went away from my room until I received her telegram about three or four o'clock in the afternoon on Thursday, and then, laughing, I showed it to several parties; and then in the evening I saw in the *Evening Journal* that they had reported the bill.

Q. Was there any arrangement made there in your office on Broadway that you should meet this lady at a hotel subsequent to that interview?

A. No, sir.

Q. No agreement of that kind?

A. No, sir.

Q. No talk of that kind?

A. The understanding was this—

Q. No, did she tell you where she was going?

A. She told me she was going to the St. James; she generally stopped at the Sturtevant, but she was stopping at the St. James.

Q. Was there any talk that you should go to the St. James also?

A. She wanted me to come to the St. James; she wanted to pay me for my trouble; I said: "There has been no trouble about this matter; I have done nothing."

Q. There was a little talk, then, about paying you something?

A. Yes, sir.

Q. Was any amount talked about?

A. Yes; she talked about a thousand dollars; I said no; I did not wish anything; she said she wanted to give me something; I said: "Give me two hundred and fifty dollar," I said.

Q. Why did you suggest to her to give you two hundred and fifty dollars?

A. She was so persistent to give me something.

Q. You did not claim that you had done her any particular service at that time, did you?

A. No, sir.

Q. Was anything more said in that conversation?

A. No, sir.

Q. Did you sat to her, or anything of the kind, that you had not done her any particular service?

A. Yes, sir.

Q. That you had not secured any votes for her?

A. I did not say anything; did not talk about the votes.

Q. Well, had not exerted any influence for her?

A. Exerted any influence—I mere said I had done nothing towards the bill; the bill was reported adversely, and I understood it was reported adversely when she was in Albany.

Q. And that you had done nothing at all about it?

A. And that I had done nothing at all about it.

Q. But you were willing to receive this $250 as a little souvenir of the occasion?

A. Yes, sir.

Q. Did you subsequently go to the St. James?

A. I subsequently went to the St. James at the suggestion of my son, and went to all three hotels; this lady had told me that she stopped at the hotel above the St. James, corner of Twenty-ninth street; I cannot think of the name now.

Q. Gilsey?

A. Gilsey; stopped at the Gilsey, and then at the St. James, and then at the Sturtevant, and I thought there was some mystery about this lady, and my son called me to one side—

Q. We do not care about your son; you did go up there?

A. Did not go in the hotel.

Q. You went up to it to inquire for her?

A. No, sir.

Q. What was your object in going up there?

A. Well, it was on my way home.

Q. Was that all?

A. Yes, sir.

Q. Did you not stop there?

A. No, sir.

Q. Simply passed there?

A. Stopped there; my son went in the hotel to see if she was there.

Q. To see if the lady was there?

A. Yes, sir; went in the Gilsey House; went in the St. James too.

Q. And he reported to you, I suppose, that she was not?

A. That she was not; he also reported to me then who she was; *[turning to Miss Cochran]* he knew you very well by the marks you have on the side of your face.

Q. The only object in going there was to get the two hundred and fifty dollars?

A. My object in going there was to see what the woman was.

Q. Was it to get two hundred and fifty dollars?

A. No, sir.

By Mr. MAGNER:

Q. You say you have been up here twenty years?

A. Yes, sir.

Q. Attending the sessions of the Legislature during that time?

A. I was sometimes.

Q. During all that time have you furnished bills for persons who inquired for them?

A. Who wanted them.

Q. And in an accommodating spirit?

A. Yes, sir.

Q. Never charge anything for them?

A. No, sir.

Q. Did you neglect your own business during this time?

A. My own business.

Q. Your own business in New York; this grain business?

A. No, sir.

Q. You do not carry it on up here?

A. You can buy all the grain you want here by telegraph.

Q. You were further away from the market?

A. Probably a minute.

Q. Do you not inconvenience yourself by being up here?

A. Not at all.

Q. Were you employed by any person up here?
A. Not at all.
Q. Were you in the habit of furnishing such information as Miss Bly called for
   without any charge?
A. Yes, sir.
Q. Have you done it heretofore for charge?
A. No, sir.
Q. Never received any consideration for doing it?
A. Sometime I have and sometimes I haven't.
Q. Have you ever this year?
A. No, sir.
Q. From whom have you received consideration heretofore?
A. I don't recollect.

MR. COON—I am frank to say if the Legislature did not limit us to a particular
line of though, we could make a much more interesting inquiry, probably.

MR. MAGNER—I am of the opinion that they instructed us to make further
inquiry.

MR. SAXTON—No; it is in regard to the charges made, published in the *New
York World [reads]*, previous to May 1, 1888; that is all of this resolution, and
that is all we have to do.

By MR. MANGER:
Q. I understand, then, Mr. Phelps, you say your business is that of lobbyist?
A. Well, you may call it that way.
Q. What do you understand by that?
A. I don't know.
Q. In whose presence was this conversation in New York between you and
   Miss Bly?
A. My son.
Q. What is his name?
A. John E. Phelps.
Q. Is he here?
A. No, sir, not in the room.

By MR. SAXTON:
Q. I will show you, Mr. Phelps, this piece of paper that was marked "Exhibit
   A," and I will ask you if you made any marks upon that piece of paper of a
   similar piece of paper on that day in pencil similar to those that are upon
   that? *[Presents "Exhibit A" to witness]*
A. No, sir.
Q. Then you did not make those marks?
A. No, sir.
Q. Did you make any marks upon any piece of paper similar to those?
A. No, sir.
Q. In pencil?

A. No, sir.

Q. You say you keep these lists in your room?

A. Yes, sir.

Q. What is the reason; why do you keep these committee lists in there?

A. Well, for accommodation.

Q. For accommodation; to accommodate whom?

A. Well, any friend that may come in and want to know something about any matter, who might ask me to give them a list.

Q. A list of the committees?

A. Yes, sir.

Q. And for no other purpose?

A. No, sir.

Q. You kept those for no other purpose?

A. No, sir.

Q. Except to accommodate your friends who may desire a list?

A. Yes, sir.

Q. This list you handed to her, I understand, as the same as that? *[Presents paper to witness]*

A. Yes, sir.

Q. That is, it was a copy of this list?

A. Yes, sir.

Q. And not marked?

A. No, sir.

Q. Now, I understand you to say that at the first interview you told her to go and see Mr. Crosby in reference to that bill?

A. Yes, sir.

Q. Well, if you told her to see Mr. Crosby and deal with him in reference to that bill, why did you have your other interview with her?

A. What other interview?

Q. The second interview.

A. Because she insisted that I should look after this bill; insisted that I should inquire into the bill and see where it was.

Q. After you had told her to go and see Mr. Crosby?

A. Yes, sir.

Q. And then did you consent to do that?

A. I told her I would do so, but never thought of it after she went away.

Q. You told her you would do so, and did you make an appointment at that time to see her at a future time?

A. I told her to call at my office in New York; she wanted me to call at the hotel.

Q. Did you make an appointment with her as to time?

A. Yes, sir; I told her on Friday; I told her I would make it Friday morning.

Q. And it was in pursuance of that appointment that you made with her then that you had the second interview?

A. Yes, sir.

Q. I show you a paper, and ask you if that is your signature upon that paper? *[Presenting paper to witness]*

A. Yes, sir; I wrote my name and address on it.

Q. The signature and address on there is in your handwriting?

A. Yes, sir.

Q. You wrote it on there in that way?

A. Yes, sir.

Q. In your room?

A. Yes, sir.

Q. While she was present?

A. Yes, sir.

Q. And this paper is a copy of the bill referred to; the bill of Mr. Smith in regard to patent medicine; is it not?

A. Yes, sir.

Q. Did you hand that bill to her?

A. No, sir; she handed it to me.

Q. How did this bill which I show you first come into your possession?

A. She took it out of a little bag she had and handed it to me.

Q. Was it in the shape it is now in?

A. Yes, sir.

Q. Cut off; the margin cut off?

A. Yes, sir.

Q. Well, what did she say when she handed the bill to you?

A. Well, she handed the bill to me and said she wanted that bill killed, it would ruin her business.

Q. And when was it that you wrote your name upon that bill?

A. She asked me far a card; I told her I had no cards to give her; she wanted me to come to the hotel, to meet her at the hotel; I said I didn't want to, if she wanted to see me she could come to the office.

Q. You have not told me yet when you wrote your name upon it?

A. Right at the time of the conversation.

Q. Was that just before she went away?

A. Yes, sir.

Q. Was that the last thing you did before she went away?

A. Yes, sir, I think so.

Q. What did you do with this after you had written your name upon it?

A. She carried it away with her.

Q. You handed it to her, did you?

A. Yes, sir; it belonged to her, it was her property.

[Paper referred to was marked by the stenographer "Exhibit B.—Edward R. Phelps."]

Full Testimony of Eugene Woods Before State Assembly

Eugene D. Woods, sworn, testified as follows:
Examined by Mr. Saxton:

Q. Where do you live?

A. Albany.

Q. This is your permanent residence, then?

A. Yes, sir.

Q. How long have you lived here?

A. All my life.

Q. What is your business?

A. Well, I have studied law.

Q. Were you ever admitted to the bar?

A. No, sir.

Q. That does not hardly answer the question, Mr. Wood, as to what your business is, that you have studied law.

A. Well, I have been in the horse racing business.

Q. Selling pools?

A. No, sir.

Q. Buying pools?

A. No, sir.

Q. What way?

A. Owner of race horses.

Q. Have you any other business?

A. Well, nothing that I know of.

Q. Have you any business connected with the Legislature?

A. No, sir.

Q. Have you any business relations with Edward R. Phelps, whom I suppose you know do you not?

A. Yes, sir.

Q. Have you any business relations with him?

A. None at all.

Q. You are not an agent of his in any way?

A. No, sir.

Q. Do you assist him in the managing or conducting of any business connected with the Legislature?

A. No, sir.

Q. Well, are you yourself engaged then, independently or otherwise, in any business connected with the Legislature?

A. No, sir.

Q. Or have you been?

A. Oh, I have held places here for years.

Q. I know, but I mean aside from official positions; have you held any unofficial relations with the Legislature or any members of it?

A. No, sir.

Q. Are you acquainted with Mr. Gallagher of Erie?

A. Yes, sir.

Q. How long have you known him?

A. When he first came here as a member, fifteen or sixteen years ago.

Q. Were you then in the House?

A. I was a messenger in either House; I forgot, I have been in both Houses.

Q. How long were you in the employ of the Legislature?

A. Well, I don't know; I first was a page boy, along in 1867, I think; 1866 or 1867.

Q. And what other positions have you held in the Legislature?

A. Page boy and messenger, clerk of committee, and private secretary to different Senators.

Q. How long since you have been connected with the Legislature in an official capacity?

A. I cannot just now remember that; five or six years.

Q. You say you knew Mr. Gallagher when he was a member of the House, and you held some official position here?

A. Yes, sir.

Q. Did you ever have any business relations with Mr. Gallagher in reference to pending measures, measures pending before the Legislature?

A. No, sir.

Q. Never had any business whatever with him with relation to such measures?

A. No, sir.

Q. Directly or indirectly?

A. No, sir; I do not remember of having any business at all with him, except knowing him.

Q. Well, do you say, then, that you never did have any business with Mr. Gallagher of any kind?

A. Yes, sir.

Q. Did you ever have any financial transaction with him?

A. No, sir.

Q. Did you ever talk about any financial transaction with him?

A. No, sir.

Q. Any financial matter of any kind with him?

A. No, sir.

Q. Now, do you know Mr. Prime, of Essex?

A. Well, not certain; I don't know him personally.

Q. Do you know Mr. DeWitt, of Ulster?

A. No, sir.

Q. Do you know Mr. Tallmadge of Kings?

A. I know him by sight.

Q. Have you any acquaintance with him?

A. No, sir.

Q. Do you know Mr. Hagan, of New York?

A. Yes, sir.

Q. How long have you known him?

A. I should judge ten years—when he first came here.

Q. He was a member of the House a number of years ago, was he not?

A. Yes, sir.

Q. Do you know him intimately?

A. Personally.

Q. You do know him intimately?

A. No, not intimately; I have met him in different places, in New York and around.

Q. And do you know Mr. McLaughlin, of Kings?

A. Yes, sir.

Q. How well do you know him?

A. I don't know him very well.

Q. Not very intimately, then?

A. No, sir.

Q. In reference to those five gentlemen whom I have named, I will ask you the general question whether you ever had any business transactions with any of those gentlemen?

A. No, sir.

Q. No business transactions with any of them?

A. No, sir.

Q. Did you ever have any transactions of any kind with them?

A. No, sir.

Q. Did you ever have any conversation with any of these gentlemen; I will include, also, now, Mr. Gallagher; any conversation whatever in regard to matters pending before the Legislature?

A. No, sir.

Q. You never had any conversation with them upon that subject, you say?

A. No, sir.

Q. Did you know; did it ever come within your knowledge, any transaction between anybody else and any of those gentlemen with regard to measures pending in the Legislature?

A. No, sir.

Q. Do you know anything about this Smith Patent Medicine bill?

A. Except that I read about it.

Q. All you know about it is what you read about it?

A. Yes, sir.

Q. Did you have any business connected with that bill?

A. No, sir.

Q. Did you do any business with any person in any way, shape or manner, or have any conversation with any other person with relation to that patent medicine bill?

A. No, sir.

Q. I will confine that to the period before the issuing of that paper on the first day of April; did you know anything about such a bill here?

A. Only what I read in the paper; newspaper criticisms in regard to it.

Q. You never had any conversation with anybody, then, about that bill?

A. Never.

Q. Do you know of any money being used in any way, either to further that bill or to kill it, as it is commonly called, during this session of the Legislature?

A. No, sir.

Q. Did you ever approach any of those six gentlemen who have been named over to you here by me upon any matter connected with legislation?

A. No, sir.

Q. Did you ever say anything to them, or head anything said to them by any other person, upon any subject connected with legislation?

A. Well, I might have heard a great deal about legislation; heard others talking.

Q. I confine it to those gentlemen; did you every *(sic)* say anything yourself, or overhear anything that was said to them by any other person in the subject of legislation?

A. No, sir.

Q. Those six men?

A. No, sir.

Q. Or any one of them?

A. No, sir.

By Mr. Magner

Q. Are you what why call a lobbyist, Mr. Wood?

A. I don't know what that is.

By Mr. Saxton *(resuming)*:

Q. I guess you don't mean that, Mr. Wood; you do not know what a lobbyist is, do you?

A. No; I have never heard it defined.

Q. You have an idea yourself what a lobbyist is, do you not?

A. I have heard what a lobbyist is.

Q. It is a fact, I suppose, and it is a fact within your knowledge, that it is commonly understood that a lobbyist is a person outside of the Legislature who seeks in some way or another to influence legislation; is not that your idea of a lobbyist?

A. Well, that is what I have heard.

Q. Have you not got a well-defined idea of that in your own mind?

A. No, I haven't.

Q. Then your mind is a blank upon that subject, as to what constitutes a lobbyist?

A. Well, I have seen a great many lawyers, you could not call those lobbyists.

Q. Well, of course, that depends upon your idea of what constitutes a lobbyist; I suppose a lawyer is not a lobbyist unless he has something to do with legislation outside of the Legislature?

A. He trys *(sic)* to influence legislation.

Q. That is your idea of a lobbyist, that he is a person who tries to influence legislation from the outside?

A. Yes, sir.

Q. Then you have an idea of what a lobbyist is?

A. I have an idea.

By Mr. MAGNER:
Q. From that idea, are you such a person; are you such a one?
A. No, sir.

Mr. VAN GORDER—He has only studied law; he is not a lawyer.
A. No, I am not admitted yet.

The evidence here closed, whereupon the committee went into executive session.

STORY IN THE NEW YORK WORLD.
PUBLISHED THURSDAY, APRIL 19, 1888:

THE LOBBY KING ARRAIGNED.

————

NELLIE BLY REPEATS IN DETAIL HER STORY ABOUT LOBBYIST PHELPS.

————

STEP BY STEP SHE SHOWS HOW SHE TRAPPED HIM AND EXPOSED HIM.

————

HER APPEARANCE BEFORE THE HOUSE JUDICIARY COMMITTEE IS THE
SENSATION OF THE DAY—THE COMMITTEE ADMITS ITS LIMITED POWERS,
BUT INTERROGATES HER CLOSELY AS TO THE EXPOSE IN "THE WORLD,"
AND SHE ANSWERS CLEARLY AND DIRECTLY—PHELPS GOES ON THE STAND
AND MAKES A SUCCESSION OF DENIALS AND ADMISSIONS—HE SAYS HE
NEVER MENTIONED THAT HE COULD BUY ANY LEGISLATORS, AND THAT
THE NAMES OF THE SIX INTERESTED MEN OF THE CITIES' COMMITTEE
WERE NOT REFERRED TO—HE CALLS HIMSELF A SPECULATOR AND A
BILL FURNISHER—HOW HE EXPLAINS THINGS—LOBBYIST WOOD IS ALSO
EXAMINED, BUT DENIES EVERYTHING—THE TESTIMONY IN FULL.

————

[SPECIAL TO THE WORLD]

ALBANY, APRIL 18.—The sensation of the day in Albany was the appearance before the House Judiciary Committee of Miss Nellie Bly, the bright young correspondent of THE WORLD who so neatly entrapped the shrewd old lobbyist, Edward R. Phelps, into betraying the secrets of his profession. For the past two weeks the greatest curiosity has existed in Albany to see her. Many country papers declared that Nellie Bly was a myth and that the stories were prepared in the WORLD office. But Nellie Bly was there, and so was a vast crowd, including scores of Albany women.

The entire committee was also there. Many Senators and Assemblymen were drawn there out of curiosity. Gen. James William Husted, who mutilated the resolution to such an extent as practically to destroy its value, was also there, chuckling at the impotency of the committee's effort in sifting the lobby business to the bottom.

When Chairman Saxton announced that the committee could confine itself only to that part of Nellie Bly's story that related to Phelps's boast that he could buy Messrs. Gallagher of Erie, Tallmadge of Kings, Prime of Essex, DeWitt of Ulster, Hagan of New York and McLaughlin of Kings, the weakness and worthlessness of the resolution were fully apparent.

NELLIE BLY APPEARS.

The committee waited until 4 o'clock for Mr. Phelps to appear. He did not, and Nellie Bly, who had been sitting in the room of Col. McEwan, acting Adjutant-General, took the stand. She fully sustained every detail in the interview she had with Phelps and which was published in THE WORLD on April 1. Her answers were clear, direct, straightforward and uttered with a naïveté that captivated the spectators.

After she finished there was not the slightest doubt in the minds of all honest men of the accuracy of her statements and the truth. A sensation was produced, however, when Edward Phelps, pale and trembling with excitement, rose from a chair at the foot of the table, where he had come without being noticed, and, pointing his finger at the witness, who was perfectly cool and self-possessed, asked:

"Did I say buy—did I say buy?"

The witness answered the question. He resumed his seat and then began to prompt Mr. Roesch, of New York, a member of the committee, who proceeded to ask the witness a number of questions, plainly to embarrass her. But the witness foiled every movement of this sort, and left Mr. Roesch at very much the same disadvantage as she had left Mr. Phelps.

PHELPS ON THE STAND.

Then Phelps was called. He approached the table and Miss Bly with a broad grin. He frankly admitted that he was a lobbyist. He was first questioned by Chairman Saxton. He said he was a speculator and bought and sold grain. He practically admitted all of Miss Bly's story, except as to the mentioning of name. He never said he could buy any men.

"Oh, what a whopper!" whispered Miss Bly, who sat directly behind him.

There were many other things that Mr. Phelps denied, but the auditors looked askance. Some of his answers were so innocent that several times the audience broke forth into laughter. But when Mr. Coon, of Oswego, one of the keenest criminal lawyers in the State, took hold of Phelps, all his innocence and bluster departed and his admissions were very damaging. The Chairman, Saxton, took a final turn and made the poor old man wilt in contradiction.

PHELPS CALLS HER CLEVER.

As the close of his testimony Phelps stopped before Nellie Bly, reached down and took her hand. "You are a clever girl," he said, "a very clever girl."

"But Mr. Phelps," said Miss Bly, "you are very clever, except you made a great mistake in not acknowledging the truth of the entire interview. In that way I might have believed and other people would have believed that you were trying to fool me. But when you denied one-half of the story and admitted the other half you made a great mistake."

"You are a good one," exclaimed the old lobbyist. "You are a good one." This incident edified the audience exceedingly.

Mr. Whipple, a member of the committee from Cattaraugus, said to Miss Bly: "I wish every witness before us were as enlightened and as explicit as you are." Mr. Coon, of Oswego, and other members said they regretted that the scope of the committee was limited, because he was certain valuable testimony would have been elicited.

(Editor's note: there follows a reprint of selected parts of the transcript, omitting only Bly's real name and several redundant questions)

Story in the Buffalo Times.
Published Thursday, April 19, 1888:

NELLIE BLY TESTIFIES

———

AND SO DOES "ED." PHELPS, THE LOBBYIST—NOTHING IMPORTANT REVEALED

ALBANY, APRIL 19.—The assembly committee on judiciary yesterday continued its inquiry into the NEW YORK WORD's *(sic)* allegations of bribery.

"Nellie Bly" was sworn. She testified that her name was Pink Cockrane. She retold her story of interviewing Phelps as already published.

Edwards Phelps swore that he was a resident of White Plains, but spent most of the winters at Albany. He was commonly known as a lobbyist. He spent his time here in looking after bills in which he was interested.

When Nellie Bly called on him and talked about the patent medicine bill it was the first he knew about that bill. He told her he would have nothing to do with it. He marked up names and never said it was easier to buy one committee than another, etc. He declined her offer of $1,000 to kill the bill, saying he has done nothing, but as she insisted, he finally agreed to take $250.

He was not employed by any one in Albany but kept files of bill, etc, in his room for the convenience of his friends. He knew Messrs. Gallagher, McLaughlin, Talmadge and Hogan slightly. Didn't know Prime or Dewitt. Had no talk with any of these members this winter. Did not try to influence their votes. Ex-Assemblymen Seaver of Genesee and Sheridan og Kings were in the room when Nellie Bly called.

Eugene D. Wood testified that the *(sic)* did not know what a lobbyist was. His evidence tended to show that he was equally ignorant of everything.

❦

STORY FROM THE DEMOCRAT AND CHRONICLE.
PUBLISHED SATURDAY, APRIL 21, 1888:

"I AM A LOBBYIST."

———

"I am a lobbyist!" He himself, Mr. Ed. Phelps, hath said it and it is greatly to the credit of his smartness that he has managed to keep out of the penitentiary. He did not scruple to confess the disreputable nature of the business in which he was engaged, to the assembly investigating committee and, judging by the character of the evidence taken by that body, his estimate of himself was fully confirmed. Nothing has been adduced to show that the legislators whom Phelps named as corruptible had ever done anything to merit the disgraceful imputation, but enough was proved, if indeed additional proof were necessary, that Phelps is an unmitigated rascal. Not only is he a rascal but he apparently glories in the infamous record he has made and regrets only the exposure which has interfered with "business."

So far as Phelps is concerned, the public has probably heard the last of his as a professional lobbyist. He has been so indelibly branded that his efficiency in his peculiar field is permanently destroyed, but he is only one and his removal will not check the pernicious lobbying evil. When men have something valuable to sell there are always to be found men willing to buy and so long as men are elected to public office, whose integrity is purchaseable, they will not seek in vain for a market. Phelps is bad enough for all practical purposes but those with whom he dealt are equally bad. His detection and punishment may check the buying and selling temporarily but the cure of the evil is to be found deeper than the exposure of the lobbyists.

❦

STORY IN THE NEW YORK WORLD.
PUBLISHED THURSDAY, MAY 10, 1888:

"THIRD HOUSE" LEGISLATION

It is the lobby that is now legislating at Albany.

Our correspondent's account of the shameless and unrepressed activity of the boodle dispensers at the Capitol makes one blush for the honor of the Empire State.

This saturnalia of corruption was invited when the Assembly made a farce of the Phelps investigation and the Senate refused to sustain THE WORLD's war upon the lobby while this session lasts.

The people of the State of New York must expect to be robbed, swindled and misgoverned until they take greater pains in the selections of their legislative servants.

CONCLUSION OF THE STATE ASSEMBLY

Even conceding that Phelps made the declarations attributed to him, the committee are decidedly of the opinion that the unsworn statement of a self-confessed lobbyist, made for the manifest purpose of inducing a supposed customer to believe that he could aid her in an unlawful undertaking for which he expected to be paid, ought not to bear a feather's weight against the character of any reputable person. The stock in trade of a lobbyist consists of making a person believe that he can influence legislation by buying up legislators. He trades upon the wickedness of the few and the gullibility of the many. A professional lobbyist is a plague spot upon the body politic. His calling is the most nefarious that can well be imagined. His object is to promote bad legislation and to defeat good legislation, thus striking at the vital interests of every citizen who lives under the authority of our laws. This object he accomplishes or seeks to accomplish by means of fraud of corruption. Thus he becomes a center from which emanate the worst influences; a putrid mass from which go forth those germs of disease most fatal to a State.

It certainly is commendable for a paper to call public attention to such a source of contagion, to the end that some remedy may be applied. But we do not think that any paper is justified merely as a matter of journalistic enterprise in spreading before the whole nation charges against the integrity of esteemed public servants, who are honored and trusted by the people among whom they have long dwelt, which rest upon so slender a foundation as do the charges against the gentlemen named above.

The committee, therefore, do not hesitate to say that there is no evidence whatever even tending to impeach the character of any legislator named in the WORLD article. We go further than that and say that the testimony of witnesses and the circumstances surrounding the transaction prove beyond the possibility of a doubt that the statements or what purported to be the statements of Phelps concerning the legislators mentioned, as published by the WORLD newspaper, are absolutely false in every particular.

The resolution under which the committee are acting did not require any recommendation or advice at our hands. Therefore, none is offered.

ABOUT NELLIE BLY

Nellie Bly was born Elizabeth Cochran. Her father, a man of considerable wealth, served for many years as judge of Armstrong County, Pennsylvania. He lived on a large estate called Cochran's Mills, which took its name from him. There Elizabeth "Pink" Cochrane was born.

Being in reduced circumstances after her father's death, her mother remarried, only to divorce Jack Ford a few years later. The family then moved to Pittsburg, where a twenty-year-old Pink read a column in the *Pittsburg Dispatch* entitled "What Girls Are Good For." Enraged at the sexist and classist tone, she wrote a furious letter to the editor. Impressed, the editor engaged her to do special work for the newspaper as a reporter, writing under the name "Nellie Bly." Her first series of stories, "Our Workshop Girls," brought life and sympathy to working women in Pittsburgh.

A year later she went as a correspondent to Mexico, where she remained six months, sending back weekly articles. After her return she longed for broader fields, and so moved to New York. The story of her attempt to make a place for herself, or to find an opening, was a long one of disappointment, until at last she gained the attention of the *New York World*.

Her first achievement for them was the exposure of the Blackwell's Island Insane Asylum, in which she spent ten days, and two days in the Bellevue Insane Asylum. The story created a great sensation, making "Nellie Bly" a household name.

After three years of doing work as a "stunt girl" at the *World*, Bly conceived the idea of making a trip around the world in less time than had been done by Phileas Fogg, the fictitious hero of Jules Verne's famous novel. In fact, she made it in 72 days. On her return in January 1890 she was greeted by ovations all the way from San Francisco to New York.

She then paused her reporting career to write novels, but returned to the World three years later. In 1895 she married millionaire industrialist Robert Seaman, and a couple years later retired from journalism to take an interest in his factories.

She returned to journalism almost twenty years later, reporting on World War I from behind the Austrian lines. Upon returning to New York, she spent the last years of her life doing both reporting and charity work, finding homes for orphans. She died in 1922.

ABOUT THE AUTHOR

David Blixt is an author and actor living in Chicago. An Artistic Associate of the Michigan Shakespeare Festival, where he serves as the resident Fight Director, he is also co-founder of A Crew Of Patches Theatre Company, a Shakespearean repertory based in Chicago. He has acted and done fight work for the Goodman Theatre, Chicago Shakespeare Theatre, Steppenwolf, the Shakespeare Theatre of Washington DC, and First Folio Shakespeare, among many others.

As a writer, his STAR-CROSS'D series of novels place the characters of Shakespeare's Italian plays in their historical setting, drawing in figures such as Dante, Giotto, and Petrarch to create an epic of warfare, ingrigue, and romance. In HER MAJESTY'S WILL, Shakespeare himself becomes a character as Blixt explores Shakespeare's "Lost Years," teaming the young Will with the dark and devious Kit Marlowe to hilarious effect. In the COLOSSUS series, Blixt brings first century Rome and Judea to life as he relates the fall of Jerusalem, the building of the Colosseum, and the coming of Christianity to Rome. And in his bestselling NELLIE BLY series, he explores the amazing life and adventures of America's premier undercover reporter.

David continues to write, act, and travel. He has ridden camels around the pyramids at Giza, been thrown out of the Vatican Museum and been blessed by John-Paul II, scaled the Roman ramp at Masada, crashed a hot-air balloon, leapt from cliffs on small Greek islands, dined with Counts and criminals, climbed to the top of Mount Sinai, and sat in the Prince's chair in Verona's palace. But David is happiest at his desk, weaving tales of brilliant people in dire and dramatic straits. Living with his wife and two children, David describes himself as "actor, author, father, husband - in reverse order."

WWW.DAVIDBLIXT.COM

BOOKS BY NELLIE BLY

TEN DAYS IN A MAD-HOUSE
SIX MONTHS IN MEXICO
NELLIE BLY'S BOOK: AROUND THE WORLD IN 72 DAYS
THE MYSTERY OF CENTRAL PARK

BOOKS BY DAVID BLIXT

NELLIE BLY
WHAT GIRLS ARE GOOD FOR
CHARITY GIRL
A VERY CLEVER GIRL

THE STAR-CROSS'D SERIES
THE MASTER OF VERONA
VOICE OF THE FALCONER
FORTUNE'S FOOL
THE PRINCE'S DOOM
VARNISH'D FACES: STAR-CROSS'D SHORT STORIES

WILL & KIT
HER MAJESTY'S WILL

THE COLOSSUS SERIES
COLOSSUS: STONE & STEEL
COLOSSUS: THE FOUR EMPERORS

NON-FICTION

ORIGIN OF THE FEUD BY DAVID BLIXT
TOMORROW & TOMORROW BY DAVID AND JANICE L BLIXT
FIGHTING WORDS: A COMBAT GLOSSARY EDITED BY DAVID BLIXT

PLAYSCRIPTS

ACTION MOVIE - THE PLAY BY JOE FOUST AND RICHARD RAGSDALE
ALL CHILDISH THINGS BY JOSEPH ZETTELMAIER
CAMPFIRE BY JOSEPH ZETTELMAIER
THE COUNT OF MONTE CRISTO ADAPTED BY CHRISTOPHER M WALSH
DEAD MAN'S SHOES BY JOSEPH ZETTELMAIER
THE DECADE DANCE BY JOSEPH ZETTELMAIER
DR. SEWARD'S DRACULA BY JOSEPH ZETTELMAIER
EBENEZER: A CHRISTMAS PLAY BY JOSEPH ZETTELMAIER
EVE OF IDES - A PLAY BY DAVID BLIXT
THE GRAVEDIGGER: A FRANKENSTEIN PLAY BY JOSEPH ZETTELMAIER
HER MAJESTY'S WILL ADAPTED BY ROBERT KAUZLARIC
IT CAME FROM MARS BY JOSEPH ZETTELMAIER
THE MAN WHO WAS THURSDAY BY BILAL DARDAI
THE MAN-BEAST BY JOSEPH ZETTELMAIER
THE MOONSTONE ADAPTED BY ROBERT KAUZLARIC
NORTHERN AGGRESSION BY JOSEPH ZETTELMAIER
ONCE A PONZI TIME BY JOE FOUST
THE RENAISSANCE MAN BY JOSEPH ZETTELMAIER
THE SCULLERY MAID BY JOSEPH ZETTELMAIER
SEASON ON THE LINE BY SHAWN PFAUTSCH
STAGE FRIGHT: A HORROR ANTHOLOGY BY JOSEPH ZETTELMAIER
A TALE OF TWO CITIES ADAPTED BY CHRISTOPHER M WALSH
WILLIAMSTON ANTHOLOGY: VOLUME 1
WILLIAMSTON ANTHOLOGY: VOLUME 2

WWW.SORDELETINK.COM

Manufactured by Amazon.ca
Bolton, ON

29860267R00140